MURDER IN PARIS

A THIRD-CULTURE KID MYSTERY

MURDER IN PARIS

D-L NELSON

FIVE STAR
A part of Gale, Cengage Learning

GALE
CENGAGE Learning·

Detroit • New York • San Francisco • New Haven, Conn • Waterville, Maine • London

GALE
CENGAGE Learning

LIBRARY OF CONGRESS CATALOGING-IN-PUBLICATION DATA

Nelson, D. L., 1942–
    Murder in Paris : a third-culture kid mystery / D-L Nelson. —
First Edition.
    pages cm
    ISBN 978-1-4328-2693-2 (hardcover) — ISBN 1-4328-2693-X
(hardcover)
    1. Women authors—Fiction. 2. North Shore (Mass. : Coast)—
Fiction. I. Title.
PS3614.E4455M87 2013
813'.6—dc23   013005475

Find us on Facebook– https://www.facebook.com/FiveStarCengage
Visit our website– http://www.gale.cengage.com/fivestar/
Contact Five Star™ Publishing at FiveStar@cengage.com

Printed in Mexico
3 4 5 6 7 17 16 15 14 13

To Julia with deep appreciation for your friendship especially during the last year.

CHAPTER 1

"You *forbid* it?" Annie Young stared down her fiancé, Roger Perret. The couple was seated at his long oak kitchen table in the French coastal village of Argelès-sur-mer.

"I forbid it." He sat at an angle to her, turning the knife he had just used to peel an apple: blade to handle, handle to blade, blade to handle. Each time he turned it, it clicked against the green tile table.

Annie stood up so fast her chair turned over bringing it crashing to the red tile floor. The skin on the back of her legs where they had stuck to the green leather hurt with the suddenness of the movement, but she chose to ignore it. Still, anything more than shorts and a T-shirt would have been too warm to wear. Despite the July heat, the thick walls kept the house cool in comparison to outside and definitely cooler than the temperature of the couple.

"I've a chance to work on a dig in Paris where they've found enough of a fourteenth-century inn to get an impression about it, and *you* forbid me to go?" Annie righted the chair. "I don't believe it." With all their ups and downs, if he didn't realize how important her passion for historical research was, he didn't know anything about her.

"I've gotten used to you going off on this or that *paid* writing assignment. *Mon Dieu.* I never know if you'll be in Zurich, Amsterdam or . . . or . . . someone invites us somewhere, I can only tell them if Annie is still here, blah, blah, blah. I've gotten used to this: that's your work . . . but this is a *freebie.*"

Any other time she would have been amused by his use of the word freebie with his French accent. The couple went back and forth between English, French and Franglais. She thought they had worked through the major problems of the earlier stages of their relationship, before she had finally agreed to an engagement. She knew he still hated that she earned her living working part-time as a tech writer taking short-term contracts all over Europe.

She wished he could be proud that she was multilingual—English, Dutch, French and German. She wished he could be proud that she earned top money working less than six months a year. The rest of the time she spent indulging her passion: historical research, the same research that he didn't want her to do now.

"It doesn't matter that I'm not getting paid. This is the chance of a lifetime."

"The only reason you were asked is because Luca is your ex-boyfriend. You're not an archeologist."

It was true, she wasn't. But she had taken a course in it, and her translation and research skills on what was found would be valuable to the project. And it was a short-term project. Roger touched on the truth when he said that Luca sought her out because he knew her. Luca was as passionate about his work as she was about her love of history.

When Luca was excited about something, he talked faster and faster.

During his call inviting her to come to Paris for three weeks, the time allotted by the city for the dig, she'd had to keep asking him to slow down so she could understand his Italian-accented French. But she had caught his excitement at the chance to excavate the remains of a building hidden for centuries in Paris's Latin Quarter before a modern building would make it disappear—perhaps forever.

"Luca and I dated six months when he was on an exchange from the University of Rome to the University of Geneva. That was over ten years ago."

"But you've kept in touch with him all this time."

"He's a friend."

"He's Italian."

Annie didn't know how to answer that. Roger was not normally jealous.

Roger's daughter Gaëlle pushed her way through the multicolored ribbons hanging from the kitchen door to keep out insects. She was wearing a bikini and drying herself with a towel. Her shoulder-length hair, which had been pulled into a French braid, was wet. "What's up? I could hear you yelling all the way out to the pool."

Annie looked at the teenager with the love that ran deep between them even if she wasn't the girl's mother. She loved this house that Roger and Gaëlle had lucked out in buying when they moved from Paris several years before.

Fate should never have brought Roger and Annie together considering how different their backgrounds were. He had been a high-ranking detective with the renowned Direction Régionale de Police Judiciaire de Paris, until his wife was killed by a criminal he'd sent to jail. Within days of his release, the man had shot Roger's wife.

Annie admired how as a single father, he took the assignment of police chief of Argelès-sur-mer in the south of France, so he could be more available for his daughter. It was his devotion to his daughter that had caught her attention. And she loved the house with its several acres of land, a pool, cherry orchard and pine grove—a place which would have been unaffordable for him had not the sellers, in the middle of a nasty divorce, been desperate to sell.

The house and land were in total contrast to Annie's studio in the attic of a four-hundred-year-old building in the center of the village on a street that an SUV would not have fit through. She had found that by what she called a lucky accident while on holiday. That *coup de foudre* had become her nest, allowing her to live frugally and minimally, but it wasn't the economics that caused her to fall in love with the place.

It was the mammies sitting in the chairs outside their front doors exchanging gossip while snapping beans. It was being able to walk to the end of the street and buy some wild asparagus that Pierre had picked that morning on a walk in the nearby woods and sold to the green grocer . . . or having to have a cup of tea while the owner of the *boucherie* made her fresh mayonnaise.

Her falling in love with the police chief was nowhere as fast as her love affair with the village.

Annie and Roger turned to look at the teenager. "She wants to go to Paris."

"I've a chance to do the documentation on a dig. It's in Paris. A fourteenth-century building. They think it was an inn. In the Latin Quarter," Annie said.

"*Génial*," Gaëlle said.

"Not *génial* at all. The least she can do is stay here between assignments," Roger said.

"Papa, you know how Annie loves anything historical."

"Stay out of it." Roger turned to Annie. "You can't go."

Annie hesitated for a moment. Their existence as a couple had come so far and weathered so much mostly related to her time away and the normal problems of a commuting relationship. They used Skype and weekend visits in both directions learning about new places where Annie had contracts.

She looked at the diamond ring. The silence hung in the room. Slowly, because her fingers were slightly swollen from the heat, she worked it off and placed it among the dirty dishes from the dinner that had been interrupted by Luca's telephone call inviting her to join the team for the rest of July.

"We have to work fast," he'd said. "The dig is holding up construction of a new building until the Département des Antiquités can examine what has been under the paved-over site. That half of Paris is on holiday makes it a perfect time to work."

"How many people are working on it?" she'd asked.

"Six," he'd told her, adding that because there was a surplus of students eager to get real-dig experience onto their résumés in a profession with far more applicants than posts, they had a better choice of applicants.

Annie had asked Luca why he didn't use one of the students rather than her. "Your languages," he'd replied. "And you're over thirty and even if you don't have dig experience, you have maturity."

Annie wished age, language and maturity made up for lack of academic credentials all the time. There were companies that rejected her because she only had a master's degree, one that had nothing to do with computers. Her refusal to get her doctorate, her refusal to get tied down in any one organization would have been a career stopper if she were searching for a title or a career track in some fields.

Instead, she wanted a life with the freedom to do as she wanted when she wanted. She compromised when necessary such as lowering her financial desires. Her studio was hers. She refused to buy a car. Her wardrobe needs were minimal.

No price could be put on her freedom which was why she slipped the engagement ring off her finger and put it next to Roger's empty wineglass.

The next morning Annie woke in her own bed. For a minute she didn't remember the fight: then it came back to her—she and Roger were finished. Through sleep-laden eyes she surveyed her studio, which had once held grain for the farmers who had lived below. Probably they even had kept sheep or goats on the ground floor. She'd come across some old photos of the street at the village museum and a sheep had stuck its head out the door of the house two doors down.

The original stone of one wall reminded her of those around the house in Sudbury, Massachusetts, the kind of stone wall that Robert Frost wrote about in his poems. She'd lived in the same house in the same town until she was eight before her father found a job in Nijmegen, Holland, followed by one in Stuttgart, Germany, and then a move to Geneva, Switzerland.

Although Annie had adapted each time, learning the language and making friends, she had never felt at home: then she'd accidentally walked down the rue Vermeille when she was taking a weekend off from an assignment in Toulouse. She'd spied the *pour vendre* sign in the fourth-floor window. Had she not been looking up at the cascades of wisteria, she never would have known to call the real-estate agent. She'd made an offer within an hour.

Now she had a base that was truly hers. She made friends with not just the mammies, but also the owners of the restaurants, her neighbors who were native Catalonians, who claimed to be neither Spanish nor French but part of the ancient culture that had lived in the area from the time of Charlemagne and maybe before.

The area also had retirees from Northern France. And, like Geneva, where she had gone to high school and university, there were both summer and year-round people from Ireland, England, Germany, Austria, Switzerland, Holland, Denmark, Sweden and Norway. Many were artists in search of the Southern French light for their paintings.

Annie had found her niche and this studio was her nest.

★ ★ ★ ★ ★

Her nest was anything but neat as she tried to decide what to take with her. Paris could be stifling in July: she would be in the city where heat would radiate from the pavement. In a dig, there would be dust, so none of her good clothes were needed— well, maybe one outfit.

Her friend Rima had offered her flat as a place to stay. Rima was another university friend, who divided her time between Paris and Damascus. Annie even had her own set of keys, for she stayed with her friend whenever she had an assignment in the French capital.

Her mini laptop was already in its case and Annie was stuffing clean underwear into her suitcase when there was a knock on the door. "It's me," Gaëlle said.

"It's unlocked," Annie said.

It was necessary to walk up a flight of stairs from the entry to the living space, which made the area seem more spacious. Gaëlle rushed up the stairs. She was carrying a white box. "I brought *opéras.*" She set them on the wooden table in front of the fireplace, and turned to the kitchen area and filled the kettle.

Annie placed the small rectangular chocolate cakes on two boards which she used in place of plates for treats and sandwiches. Gaëlle reached for the bag of loose green tea and measured it into a pot. Annie resisted telling the girl that she should put hot water in the pot first to heat it before making the tea. Gaëlle knew, thus Annie assumed the teenager was upset. She and the girl had established a relationship long before that was neither friend nor mother but a bit of both.

"I hate it that Papa and you broke up." Gaëlle let the sentence again hang in the air.

As much as she was tempted to defend her decision, Annie said nothing.

"I know he can be positively prehistoric in his attitude

sometimes."

"Maybe not prehistoric, just hysteric," Annie said, which made Gaëlle smile. "However, whatever happens between him and me, doesn't affect us."

"Yes it does, because you won't come to the house and we won't do things that the three of us used to do together." Before Annie could say anything the girl went on, "But we're still friends, no matter what. I just get tired of you two being off again, on again."

Annie nodded. She got tired of it too, but even if she loved Roger, maybe the way they wanted to live their lives was too different. This was not to be discussed with the teenager. Instead she placed forks next to the chocolate *opéras*. Her train wasn't until twenty-one hours that night. Spending time with the girl would keep her mind off the breakup.

CHAPTER 2

Saverdun, France, September 1289

Four-year-old Jacques Fournier ran as fast as his pudgy legs would carry him after the three older boys. At five, six and seven it was as if they could fly and he was earthbound, an ant to their butterflies. He sucked in air with deep, rasping gasps.

Sunday morning between Mass and lunch was the only time during the week that the children had no chores. Except for Jacques, the boys were learning their fathers' trades. Henri would be a baker, Jean a tailor and Louis a weaver. Not that their work was worth much at this point. Mostly they cleaned up after their elders, who swatted them when they moved too slowly. Jacques had escaped apprenticeship in his father's cloth business, partially because he was the youngest and partially because he'd been promised to the priesthood at birth by his father, who'd made a deal with God in return for sparing his wife. As often as Jacques had heard the story, he didn't understand the connection.

Jean's and Henri's houses flanked the Fourniers'. Louis's was down the street. His parents wove most of the cloth that Jacques's father sold. All had shops which were on the ground level with the families living above.

The boys deserted the town to clamor up the hill. Pine trees perched haphazardly between boulders. The September air was summer-like during the day, although the sun went down earlier and earlier leaving the bedroom cooler and making it necessary to add blankets on the bed.

Jacques wished his companions would stay in the village. He hated the forest with its shadows, snakes and creatures that howled in the night. He wouldn't admit that. The boys already called him *Gros Jacques:* Fat Jack. They laughed at him. While watching for serpents ahead, he missed a stick in the path, tripped and skinned his knee. He wanted to cry, but he didn't want the boys to mock him.

The game was Crusades. The boys were saving the Holy Land from the infidel who had sharp pointed teeth like wolves. The infidels cooked and ate Christians. Wolves just ate people raw. Infidels defecated on the spot where Christ was born. The boys knew it was true because the priest said so.

By lunchtime, if Jacques's stomach hadn't felt so empty, he would have crawled into a ball and closed his eyes. Instead he limped home behind his playmates, who swished their swords. At his front door he straightened his shoulders so his mother wouldn't notice how miserable he felt. He walked around the orderly stacked piles of wool and cloth in his father's workroom and climbed the stairs.

The smell of onions greeted him. He knew his mother would have mixed them with broth and grain. He could already taste it as he spied the big bowl in the center of the table. He could already see himself dipping his spoon in the bowl. Sometimes his father would pretend that the spoons were swords and they would have a mock battle.

His father, Benoît Fournier, sat on a bench pulled up to the table as he worked his abacus. He marked sums on a slate, once a roof tile. When something wasn't to his liking, he would erase the offending number and start over.

His mother, Antoinette, stood in front of the fireplace where a pot was suspended over the fire on a long metal pole. Her eyes took in her son's dirty clothes and bloodied knee. "Were you fighting? Good priests don't fight: you know that."

"I know, *Maman.*" Jacques knew all about what good and bad priests did. He heard it every day.

"Never mind. Go sit down."

As she put the meal on the table, someone called from the street, "Anyone home?"

His mother went to the narrow window. Its frame had oiled paper to keep flies out in the summer but let light filter in. During the winter, they hung blankets in triple thickness to defeat the cold seeping in through the outside wooden shutters, although it left the house in a darkness that candles could not dispel. She climbed on a stool to look out. "Arnaud." Her voice was joyful. She ran down the stairs two at a time to let her brother in.

Arnaud Novelli's monk's robe was dusty. "I was on my way to Toulouse. I couldn't pass my favorite sister's house without stopping."

Benoît clapped his brother-in-law on the back. "And now she can brag to the neighbors how the Abbot of Fontfroide came to lunch."

"Is there enough for all of us?" Arnaud asked.

"Always for you," she said.

He peeked in the pot. "Enough for me and half my monks." He took the ladle she'd been using to stir the mixture and tasted it.

Antoinette plucked the ladle from her brother's hand. She took the pot to the middle of the table and poured the contents into the bowl already there. Everyone had a dented spoon. Jacques needed to kneel on the bench to reach the food, even though his spoon had the longest handle. The cut on his knee throbbed when it touched the wood. His mother, watching him wince, picked him up and put him on her lap.

"He's too big to be held," Benoît said. "Jacques, leave some for the rest of us." His voice was softer than his words.

Jacques, who'd been keeping his hand moving nonstop between the food and his mouth, tried to slow down, but it was good, and he was so hungry.

"He's grown in the last year," Arnaud said.

Antoinette patted her brother's hand. "It's God's will you came today. I need your advice."

The monk raised an eyebrow.

"Jacques knows his letters. He can spell words in Languedoc, but I can't teach him Latin or Greek." She put her son of the floor. "Get the cloth, Jacques."

The boy ran to his room and returned with a gray piece of wool that had twenty-six letters embroidered in green yarn. He handed it to his mother who pointed at one.

"G," Jacques said. Then he responded to each point with, "A, K, L, M."

"Spell this." She touched the table.

"T-A-B-L-E."

"My poor son can't get out of bed without spelling good morning," Benoît said. "I think he can serve the church as a cloth merchant. He doesn't . . ."

"He was promised to God at birth, and to God he'll be given," his wife said.

Jacques looked at his parents. Would this often-repeated conversation end with another argument forced through his mother's and father's almost-closed lips? Although they didn't raise their voices, Jacques could recognize the anger concealed behind their attempts to act like the conversation was normal.

"Benoît, I was there when you promised God. You said, if Antoinette lived through the birth, you would give the baby to the church."

"I still would like him to carry on with the business."

"I understand," Arnaud said, "but you could have other sons."

"Since my wife barely survived Jacques's birth, I won't risk her life again."

Antoinette picked up the pot and put it back on the hook over the dying fire. "What do I do about his education?"

"The priest in the village would give him lessons," Benoît said.

"He spends too much time helping poor widows," Antoinette said.

"Isn't it nice to help them?" Jacques asked.

"Not all night," his mother said.

CHAPTER 3

"Mahaba."

The man weighing Annie Young's bananas, melon, apricots and salad looked up startled. He was wearing the long gown and pillbox-type hat common for Arab merchants in the Parisian suburb of Puteaux. *"Mahaba."*

He looked up from his scale and frowned, then smiled. "You're Madame Rima's friend, the one who stayed with her last year."

Annie nodded.

"Welcome. When did you get back?" Then he looked at her suit and laptop cases.

"About an hour ago. I came straight from the station." She wasn't about to tell him about her sleepless night on the train to Paris unable to settle in her bunk. Roger, although she would have loved to delete him, was too well stored in her database. She'd arrived at Gare d'Austerlitz, crossed the bridge to Gare du Lyon and grabbed a *petit déjeuner* at Le Train Bleu, with its turn-of-the-century wall paintings, before heading over to Rima's.

By the time she'd finished, the RER to La Défense was packed. As for the 144 bus to Rima's place it was almost empty with everyone going into the city, not out, at that hour.

"You know Miss Rima is in Damascus?"

Annie nodded. Her friend had e-mailed her that there were some of her Syrian dishes in the freezer and to make herself at home and eat what was there. Although her friend was a professor of Arabic studies at the Sorbonne, she operated her apartment as a hostel for anyone coming through. "She may be back halfway through my stay: it depends on her sorting out some stuff there."

The man put the bananas, apricots and melon into a green plastic sack. Normally Annie carried her own bag for her purchases, but she was not about to go up to Rima's flat to retrieve one of her friend's bags and then come out again. She just wanted to get settled.

Rima's building was on the next block. It was six stories and of triangle-shape to match the fork in the road where it occupied the split.

Annie knew the code. The front hallway had been changed since Annie was there last: dirty green paint was now a light cream. The aging floor tiles, which probably had been put down well before World War I, had been replaced by a light parquet wood. She called the creaky-cranky elevator, as she and Rima had named it. *That* had not been upgraded as Annie discovered, although the inside had been freshened with the same cream paint as the walls. Despite her skinniness she had to straddle her normal-sized suitcase to fit in. An obese person would not have been able to close the doors.

Rima's flat was as she remembered it: small with the rooms arranged in a circle with the exception of the kitchen. It was possible to walk into the bathroom from the living room, the bedroom from the bathroom and the living room from the bedroom and then back into the bathroom. The kitchen sat pod-like off the living room. The flat had four floor-to-ceiling windows, two in the bedroom and two in the living room, looking out over Parisian rooftops.

Annie rolled her suitcase into the bedroom. The bed was unmade. Rima must have had an early-morning flight because she usually left her flat pristine.

Annie's eyes felt heavy. Before unpacking and setting herself up, she would just lie down for a few minutes.

"Who the hell are you and what are you doing in my bed?" The male voice woke Annie with a start. She was not Goldilocks.

"Luca?"

"Annie? If I could have seen those red curls, I would have known it was you, but you had a pillow over your head."

Luca was as drop-dead beautiful as she remembered him: his eyes were rainy-day gray with lashes that most women keep in a box and glue on. His dark wavy hair curled over his collar. He had his shirt collar open revealing a cross embedded in curly chest hair. "What are you doing here?"

He sat on the corner of the bed. "I'm staying here."

Annie groggily looked at her watch. She must have slept a good three hours. She began putting it all together: the fight, the train trip, the project. "Rima didn't tell me you'd be here when she said I could stay."

"She doesn't know. I knew Rima wouldn't mind."

"Why aren't you with your wife?"

"Crystal threw me out."

Annie sat up in bed. "What did you do now?"

"She found out about one of my quickies." He gave her the same look that had melted her when they had dated at university. "Well, she found out about three of them. I mean, they were different women. Nothing serious."

Annie laughed. "I'm not surprised she threw you out."

Luca looked hurt. "Anyway, Rima had given Noor a key and I convinced Noor that Rima wouldn't mind me staying here, until I can convince Crystal that it was a misunderstanding."

Annie knew Crystal from a few meetings: a stereotypical French woman in looks and style, but in terms of marital infidelity, not one to be understanding. At a dinner one night when Annie had been in Paris last year, Crystal had said that she wanted an honest and one-man-one-woman relationship. She hadn't said it outright to Annie, but when the subject of infidelity came up in general conversation she made her attitude clear. At the time, Annie questioned if such goals were possible with Luca, although she had remained quiet.

"She's very possessive, too much so. As much as I want my marriage to work, I need air."

Annie raised an eyebrow.

"I do."

Annie tilted her head.

"I do." When she still didn't respond, Luca used the same tricks when they were dating—he changed the subject. "Do you want to see the dig?"

CHAPTER 4

Annie emerged from the Saint-Michel Metro stop and looked for Luca. He had said he had errands and left the flat ahead of her, adding that he would wait for her at the fountain before leading her to the excavation. Other people stood around the plaza where a sword-wielding angel stepped on a demon. Water that looked refreshing in the early-morning heat spewed out of a gargoyle-type monster's mouth.

She observed two men in business suits with briefcases. One paced back and forth, looking at his watch every few minutes. Then a young woman approached him and tapped him on the back. Their kiss was X-rated.

Someone grabbed Annie. Instinctively she tightened her grip on her backpack straps.

"It's me."

"Luca, you scared me."

Out of the corner of her eye, a young woman in jeans strode toward the second businessman. She was at least twenty years younger and threw her arms around him.

"Liaisons," Luca said indicating the two couples walking off: one held hands, the other had their arms wrapped around each other's waists. "Quickie before they go to their offices."

She didn't disagree. He took her backpack and headed into the Latin Quarter. "We're near the Cluny Musée." When she smiled, he asked, "What?"

"At one point I had been museumed out," she said.

"I can't believe that."

"It's true. I was here on assignment, and I wandered into the Cluny Musée where I came to the room with the unicorn tapestries. I sat down. I've no idea how long I was there. Hours, probably, just staring, just wondering what the people's lives were like who set up the looms, how they worked the colors. Who did the design? I've never been museumed out since."

He smiled as he took her hand. "Our excavation is just down the street. Across from the Sorbonne. And we must be extra efficient."

"Why?"

"When the old building, a restaurant, was destroyed, a small company bought the land. They went through all kinds of hoops, but finally came up with a design that won't contrast too much with the rest of the Latin Quarter. Because the plans were limited to two stories, they thought they could make two basements: one for more storage and one to get more tables thus more meal covers."

"Sounds like a good idea."

"Except when they dug down they realized that there was something there. I'm surprised that they notified the Département des Antiquités. A lot of corporations plow on through and hope no one discovered what they did."

Because Annie had jumped at the chance to be on the project and if Roger hadn't been so obnoxious with his macho "I forbid you," she would have asked all those details before leaving for Paris. Then when Luca had surprised her in bed, he rushed out again almost as soon as he arrived.

"Not only that, the owner calls every day trying to get us to finish in advance of the end of the permit. If he had more political pull we'd be out by now."

They walked by all the restaurants flanking both sides of the street in medieval buildings. Staff was putting fish, lemons, meat and vegetables on ice in their windows, creating works of art both gastronomic and enticing for those who would be seeking lunch in a couple of hours. A few men were drinking coffee on the small tables arranged outside. One had a glass of wine.

Luca had Annie by one elbow and was propelling her faster than she wanted to go. Although she had spent much time in Paris, she'd found it hard not to stop to visually soak up each small thing she saw.

"The Département des Antiquités put a six-week hold for us to get out everything we can before it gets buried under cement. We're halfway there, but as I said, if the owner can find a way to get us out sooner, he will."

Annie was confused, not by the project but how Luca had ended up in charge. The last time she'd talked to Luca, about seven months before, he was working at the University of Paris.

As if he understood, he told her. "I left the university when I saw a job offer with the Département. I'd published enough so they hired me. I'm in a place in the food chain to get interesting work, but not so high I need political support for the top spots."

"Your being Italian didn't bother them?"

"Remember my mother was French and we're in the European Union. It's harder for you as an American."

She knew. To work in Europe she ended up needing to set up a small French company. "And your wife is French."

"Who loves being in Paris, so she was content with wherever I worked as long we stayed here."

"So it's good that the Département des Antiquités is not the highest profile French government bureau where you need political clout."

"I have a little. Crystal's uncle is in the administration. Not in a very high post. He didn't make the decision, but—and it's a big but—he got my CV looked at. No one else had a favorite. *Voilà*, we're here."

Annie didn't need to be told. A fence had been erected around a hole in the ground that went down about one and a half stories. It was about the size of an average Cape Cod house in length. Annie was terrible in trying to guess measures in either square feet or square meters.

The area had been divided with ropes into three-foot squares. To one side a small building, more like a tool shed, had been set up with wires attached to what she guessed was a generator. She could see through the open door that there was enough space for floor-to-ceiling shelves and a table with a computer.

"We're a low-budget dig," he said. "You're on board because I'm hoping you can write up our finds fast enough to buy us an extension, never mind do any research we need on what we've found. Now let me introduce you to the group."

"And your chances of getting all this?"

"Snowball in hell, but that doesn't mean we shouldn't go for it. Hey, team."

Six pairs of eyes looked up from where they were squatting in their individual square. They were all dressed in dirty jeans and T-shirts.

"Wave when I call your name."

"Laure Renaud."

Annie guessed the waving woman with her long hair plaited in a dark-brown French braid was no more than twenty-two.

"Philippe Gauthier."

He was the oldest of the group, maybe in his forties and with a bald head.

"Jacqueline Robert."

"I'm coming up for coffee." Jacqueline was pencil thin and her hair was shaved almost to the scalp. Sweat was pouring down her face.

"Amelie LaFollette."

"Don't get between Jacqueline and her coffee," Amelie said.

She held up a ceramic pot with half the edge chipped away. "Look what I found."

"Fantastic," Luca said. Amelie climbed up the ladder leading to the edge of the dig. The way she saddled up to be close to Luca to hand him a small dented metal pot made Annie wonder if the two were more than coworkers—until Luca appeared more interested in the pot than Amelie.

"Marino Wagnier."

Marino's hair was several weeks in need of a trim and his beard at least thirty-six hours away from the last shave. He waved to Annie, brushing his long blond hair out of his eyes. She thought he would make a good model for the cover of a romance novel. "Another Italian, from the north," Luca whispered in Annie's ear.

"That's not an Italian name," she whispered back.

"Mother's Italian, father is French," he whispered. "Alexander Badie."

Alexander had been sifting dirt as the introductions were made. Annie guessed he was in his thirties and was beginning to lose his hair on the top of his head, giving him a small monk's tonsure. But he could be younger too. She was terrible at guessing ages, but then again people of the same age could look many years apart.

"This is Annie, team. When you find something, catalog it and then give it to her for a write-up."

Annie wondered what she would write up since she knew nothing about nothing. She must ask Luca what were the best sources for identification of items.

Luca saw her confusion.

"We are fairly sure this place goes back to somewhere between the twelve and fourteen hundreds. We're finding lots of cooking and eating items. There's a big fireplace, which you can't see from here. It's under where we're standing. You have to walk around to the other side. That makes us suspect it was some kind of inn or relay station."

"So what do I write?"

"The quadrant where it was found, the position it was found in (there's a graph), a description which would include measurements, materials, what it was used for, supposition or not and anything else that seems relevant." He took her into the small shed. The walls were covered with small cubicles some of which had items and slips of paper. "All those slips need to be put into the computer. And of course, when you have time, try and get some history on anything you think you can get history on."

"Language?" Annie asked.

"French and English. German if you have time, which you won't. We will want to do papers on it and publish them in more than one country."

"Which the Département des Antiquités will hate," Amelie said as she almost caressed Luca's hand as she took the pot back.

The small shed where Annie was now installed was stiflingly hot. The two tiny sliding windows on opposite walls did nothing to capture the feeble breeze. Luca had told her that the electricity was a problem. The generator produced enough for a fan or for the computer—not both. Without the computer Annie couldn't work.

Because the project had started almost three weeks before Annie arrived, there was a backlog of things for Annie to describe and translate. The team's notes were made on forms for the required information, but also had room for remarks. Based on the initials of the finder, Annie found herself going out to ask what this or that word was . . . with the exception of Philippe, whose printing looked like type in a book. Unfortunately, some of the items didn't look like anything to her. A chip of glass, a piece of metal that could have been a knife, a spoon handle or who knows what. She itemized that list to ask the team about during lunch. With the race against the clock, Luca told her, the most important thing was to recover everything possible and at least get it marked up. Detailed documentation and research could come later.

Exactly at thirteen hundred the team broke for lunch. They walked by several Latin Quarter restaurants. Waiters stood outside trying to entice customers by calling out why their salmon or couscous was the best, but the team stopped at Le Chien Noir, where no waiter was declaiming on the merits of their offerings.

A man with a Salvador Dali mustache came out and gave them all double-cheek kisses and shook Annie's hand before moving a reserved sign from a table set up for eight under the awning. He didn't take any orders, but plunked a bottle of red wine down and then brought a big salad and rolls.

"We eat here every day," Amelie said. She was sitting next to Luca who had his body turned slightly away from her. "We always get the *menu du jour.*"

"And what treasures did you dig up today?" The waiter poured the wine. Annie and Philippe put their hands over the top of their glasses. Annie wasn't against wine. It was just too hot for it, she thought. A beer or just cold water from the carafe on the table would be more refreshing.

"You ask that every day, Jérôme," Luca said. "Every day I tell you knowledge of the past is the treasure."

The waiter rolled his eyes. "If you found gold, you wouldn't tell me."

"We suspect that the inn was certainly not the medieval equivalent of George V or the Ritz. I wouldn't even say it was up to a bad B&B standard," Philippe said.

"Remember in those days, you didn't rent a room but maybe

30

part of a bed, if you were lucky. Or even a corner of a floor," Marino said.

"And besides sharing with people, you might share with rats and fleas, isn't that right Luca?" Amelie said.

"I should sneak over there after midnight and see what treasures I can find," Jérôme said.

"Don't forget then to disable all the security cameras," Luca said.

CHAPTER 5

"You set the table, I'll nuke dinner." Annie was rummaging in Rima's freezer for something to thaw for dinner. She found a lentil-and-rice dish, some falafel balls. Rima had said use whatever she found, and Annie knew she would leave the *frigo* stocked with her own recipes when she left. This had been a tradition with the two women since they had lived across the hall from one another. No one ever came home from a trip without finding at least two meals and basics waiting for them.

Luca appeared in the doorway, a towel around his waist. Steam floated after him fog-like. "Let me slip on shorts and a T-shirt."

"How did the shower feel?" Annie could hardly wait to take one herself. The flat was hot and the one fan did little to dispel the heat even though they had left the shutters closed during the day to keep out the sun.

When she looked from the kitchen into the apartment across the street she saw a woman in a sundress and her husband clothed only in shorts putting food on a miniscule table on a tiny balcony. Annie was still sticky from the day spent on the site, but she figured if she waited to shower until after they ate then she could just drop into bed and read herself to sleep . . . or more likely pretend to read for a few minutes until the book fell from her hand.

She went back to the *frigo* to see if she could find enough greens to add a salad. She wouldn't even begin to try to make

Rima's *tabuli*. Her friend had shown her many times how to chop the parsley, the tomatoes and the onions, but Annie's attempts never came out like her friend's. She found some romaine lettuce (she could cut off the bad parts) and a cucumber, and she used a vegetable peeler to create slivers of a carrot. It would have to do.

The strains of Beethoven's "Ode to Joy" sounded. "Has to be your phone, Luca. Mine croaks like a bullfrog."

Luca rummaged through his backpack until he located his cell phone. *"Oui, hallo?"*

His voice dropped and he moved to the farthest part of the flat—the bedroom in front of the second window—and shut the two doors.

Annie flipped on the radio to hear Johnny Hallyday sing *"Requiem pour un fou"* with Lara Fabian. It was followed by Patrick Bruel and Garou singing about different facets of love. The microwave beeped. Since Luca was still on the telephone, Annie went into the living room and moved the table out from the wall, arranged two straight-back chairs, and set the table.

The doorbell rang. An attractive woman dressed in a jeans skirt and blouse tied at the waist stood there. Her hair was swept back in a ponytail, and sweat glistened on her forehead. "You're not Rima." Her accent was East Coast American.

"I'm not. I'm a friend who is staying here for a few weeks. Rima is in Damascus. I'm not sure when she'll be home."

"I just got back. I wondered if she wanted to go to a movie at La Défense, but I guess not." She stuck out her hand. "I'm Dorothy Richardson. I live down the hall: we—Rima and me—sometimes do stuff together." She pointed to the door at the opposite end of the corridor.

"Annie Young. Sometime I would love to go to a movie, especially if the cinema is air-conditioned. Not tonight though." She saw Dorothy's eyes open wide as she gazed over Annie's shoulder. When Annie turned, she saw Luca standing there, the towel still wrapped around most of his waist. A good amount of thigh showed. He clicked off the phone and turned around.

"I didn't mean to disturb you," Dorothy said.

"I think I saw you once a few weeks ago by the mailbox. I was visiting Rima with my . . . for dinner," Luca said. "Have you eaten? Annie, is there enough for three?"

Annie watched Dorothy try and keep her eyes above Luca's lower body. "Perhaps some other time." She backed away toward the elevator.

"Pretty woman," Luca said.

"Do you ever stop flirting?"

"Flirting adds garlic, oregano, mushrooms to the pasta of life."

"Good God, Luca." Annie started putting food on the table.

Once seated, he moved the different items around his plate, back and forth, sideways. Periodically he put something in his mouth.

"Don't you like it?"

"I'm not very hungry."

"Anything wrong?"

Luca put down his fork. "The phone call. Crystal. She says I can't see the boys. I don't deserve to."

"Are you saying she thinks you don't deserve to, or are you saying it?" Annie realized that Luca's towel had fallen on the floor. There was nothing there she hadn't seen when they'd been lovers during their undergraduate time. Seen and felt.

"She says it. Annie, I've been a good papa. Not always a good husband, but a great father. I play ball with them, I take them places—sometimes we don't go anywhere, I just read to them. Or we play computer games. Or watch a TV show together."

Annie saw the pain in his face. "Can I ask what went wrong?

34

Besides the women. I can ask, but if you don't want to answer
. . ."

"We're old friends. You can ask. Crystal is jealous. I mean
jealous. When we first married she thought I fucked every
woman on the faculty. That's why we really moved from Rome
to Paris."

"Were you? Fucking at least some of the women?"

He looked hurt. "No. I really wanted my marriage to work.
Crystal is beautiful. She's intelligent except when it comes to
me. As soon as Noëllo arrived, she gave up all work. Then when
Pablo arrived she gave up almost everything but the boys and
yelling at me for affairs I didn't have. She didn't like Italy. So I
got the job here. So it's been all combinations."

"And nothing helped?"

"She went back to work at Crédit Agricole part-time after the
kids were in the *crèche*. Sometimes she would come by my office
when I thought she would be at work as if she hoped to catch
me at something. If there was a woman in it, even if the woman
was staff or student, Crystal would be convinced I was sleeping
with her. If we went to a party and I so much as spoke to a
woman she would demand to know if I was meeting her on
the—how do you say?—the side."

He took a bite of the falafel. "I'm Italian. I'm a man. Of
course I like beautiful women. But I was faithful for a long
time. Then she shut me off."

He moved more food around his plate. "I finally figured since
I'm being blamed for the crime, I might just as well be guilty of
it, so I did have an affair or two."

"Or two?"

His eyes twinkled. "I didn't count. They were never serious.
A man has to rid himself of the tensions, and Crystal had locked
me out of the bedroom for almost a year."

Annie suspected that Crystal's story would be very different from Luca's. She tried to remember the few times she'd been with the woman. She'd gone to their city-hall wedding followed by their church service and loved the almost-vamp-tight white wedding dress. She remembered her huge brown eyes and the flowered headdress.

The last time she was in Paris, they'd invited her to dinner and Luca had encouraged her to set a date. Roger was with her. "Foursomes are better," Luca said at the time. "More balance." They had never managed to find a time that worked.

Now she wondered if he wanted to make sure she didn't seem like a woman-on-the-loose by pointing out that Annie was with someone. Another time they'd run into each other in the computer section at FNAC. Crystal had put her arm through her husband's as if she would hold him down, if he were inclined to run away, and told Annie, no, they didn't have time for a cup of coffee. At the time, Annie sloughed off Crystal's brusqueness, attributing it to being saddled with two small boys under six or to the pleasure of having her husband to herself for a day or both.

"What's going to happen?"

"She wants a divorce. I can't live that way anymore, but I don't want a divorce, maybe a separation for a while until she realizes that life is better with me than without me."

Annie wasn't sure that Crystal would realize that. She could imagine the number of nights he might have come home late with Crystal imagining him in bed with a woman. Jealous people think the object of their jealousy is having a better time than the person is probably having.

"But I want to see my boys no matter what happens. I've an appointment with a lawyer next Wednesday."

"I have to congratulate you on finding a lawyer in Paris in July," Annie said.

"Now do you want to talk about Roger? Fair's fair."

"There's not much to say."

"Annie?"

"No really. Since we were first together, our biggest problem is that I keep going away to work."

"I would think it would be more that he has a teenage daughter."

"I adore Gaëlle. I've been a buffer between stern father and normal kid. Roger doesn't understand blue-spiked hair or ten-colored fingernails."

"So you've become her mother."

"Not really, more like an older friend, big sister, et cetera. She listens to me because I listen to her." Annie wondered if she should call Gaëlle. She could do it without asking her to take sides. "The poor kid lost her mother when she was ten. Murdered, by someone Roger had arrested. The man got out of jail and got his revenge by shooting Florence Perret. She was thirty-six at the time, and from what both Roger and Gaëlle say, a great mom."

"You never told me how he ended up in Argelès?"

"He was an upper-level detective here in Paris at the time his wife was killed. He wanted to get away, wanted to raise Gaëlle in a small town, where hopefully he'd have more free time for her. When the vacancy in Argelès opened up, he fought for it and got it."

"And you got involved how?" Luca smirked.

For a few minutes Annie said very little. Recounting the history of her relationship with Roger made her feel sad, but as much as she loved him, she didn't want to give in to his tying her down. She'd seen too many of her friends sacrifice what was really important to them for their men: men who eventually left them or turned out to have some dark secret. Men who didn't back them up when they needed backing up. At least by being alone, she didn't have to compromise. She pushed the last of her salad around her plate.

Luca didn't press her. "I'm sorry, Annie. I can't eat any more. It's not your cooking."

"I didn't cook. I nuked Rima's cooking in the microwave."

"I'll clean up. You take your shower."

The cool water of the shower washing away the dirt of the dig and the sweat of the day felt wonderful. Annie shampooed her hair. Maybe that was a mistake because it would go to a mass of curly red snarls. If she blew it dry, it would fizz. She was too tired to stay up much longer. Maybe she could wrestle it into a braid tomorrow. No better to do it tonight, although it would never dry. Might keep her head cool though.

Annie had taken the bed. Luca had turned the couch into a bed. By the time she said good night he was lying down reading. He had a sheet over his private parts. She wore underpants and a T-shirt.

Although she had planned to read, her eyes closed after the first paragraph. Even though it was 21:34, the sun was still out but Annie had never needed dark to sleep.

In the middle of the night she felt Luca slip in next to her. "We could," he whispered in her ear. "We've done it before and we're both cast aside by our others."

In her half-asleep state, Annie thought she had done the casting aside. "Not tonight dear, I've a headache."

He laughed, but didn't leave her bed, just rolled over so there was space between them in the hot room.

CHAPTER 6

Saverdun, France, December 1289

Jacques Fournier counted the white heads on his tutor's pimples. Ten were ready to pop and four were hard pink knobs. Although the cleric's hair was tonsured, the little that remained was greasy. The boy had learned on the first day to stay away from his tutor's fetid breath.

They worked from early morning to lunch in Jacques's room then until dark after eating. His father had set up a table and bench for lessons. The tutor lived in the *grenier*. Jacques wished there was still grain in the attic so there was no room for his teacher. Although it was an unworthy thought of a future priest, had the tutor been smothered, he would not have mourned. He wouldn't even say a prayer for his soul.

"Repeat, repeat," the tutor yelled.

Jacques took a chance and said the first Latin phrase that popped into his mind. A swat against his ears told him he was wrong. He would be lucky if he didn't end up deaf.

Two books, one large parchment with a wooden cover and one that was a rolled parchment, were in Latin. A third smaller coverless one was in Greek. Jacques suspected within those books there were beautiful and fascinating words, although his tutor would never help him find them. When the man wasn't yelling, he was complaining about the temperature, the food and the boredom of being trapped with a fat creature unable to learn.

His tutor walked around the room waving his arms. "You're stupid, stupid!"

"Jacques, I need you to come with me," Benoît called from the workroom below.

Jacques's spirits soared as he ran downstairs. For a terrible second he thought the tutor might object, but he acted differently with his father than he did with him. His compliments smeared themselves over his parents. Jacques felt that the changes in the tutor's treatment of himself and his parents were a lesson: he just wasn't sure what that lesson was.

Last night over dinner his father kept changing his opinion every few seconds. The tutor always agreed with each new position. His father had ignored his mother's warning look, but had winked at Jacques.

Outside the sky was blue and cloudless. The air stung their cheeks. The darkest night of the year was tomorrow.

As they walked by the butcher, Jacques looked in the other direction. A boar had hung there since the hunters brought it down from the mountain. Each day there was less of it. Jacques felt sorry for it but imagined how good the roasted meat would taste in his mouth. He would know Christmas day after Mass when his mother would cook a portion. She was already using honey to make sweets for the feast and their house smelled so good that he felt hungry all the time.

Jacques walked next to his father, his chubby hand holding onto the two fingers his father had held out to him. The dirt road was no longer dusty but hard packed from the cold. A window above opened, and father and son ducked as a chamber pot spewed liquid and solids onto where they'd stood a moment before.

"I hope I missed you, Monsieur Fournier." The woman's

speech was unclear. Jacques had noticed people with no teeth spoke as if they had stuffed their mouths with food. And they kept adjusting their lips.

"You did miss us, Madame. I've come to watch the dyeing."

The woman disappeared only to appear a few seconds later to open the door and to lead them to the backyard. Wooden staves pressed into the ground surrounded the yard. A scrawny cow munched hay in a corner. Steam came from the cow's nose and matched the steam from a new cow pat behind her. Chickens pecked the ground, although Jacques could see nothing edible, even imagining it from the chicken's point of view.

Three pots with bright blue water simmered on top of metal racks over the fire holes. There was one man stirring each pot. Each greeted Monsieur Fournier with a nod. After drying his hands, the woman's husband clasped Benoît Fournier's arm and patted Jacques on the head. Everyone's forearms were colored gray from a lifetime of sticking their arms into pots of woad, madder and other pigments.

"We were about to put the cloth in," the woman said.

"I'd like to check the intensity. Remember I want this cloth to be the bluest in the area."

"We remember. Because we've been using so much woad, it will affect the price."

"Of course, but not a great deal," Benoît Fournier said. "And you won't do it for anyone else."

Jacques knew his father would take the cloth north to sell. His mother suggested finding a color no other cloth merchant offered. Where business was concerned, they were a team. Jacques wished they worked as well about him. His mother was not satisfied with the tutor, and his father refused to search for a new one, saying that since she had selected him, she had to live with him. It's me who has to live with him, Jacques thought, but he didn't know how to change the situation.

Too soon Jacques's precious moments of freedom were over. Entering his tutor's room, he found him asleep on the bed. His snores irritated Jacques's ears. He hated repetitive sounds. Should he wake the tutor? If he didn't, would it be worse? Before he could decide, the tutor gave a final snort and woke.

Within five minutes the tutor was yelling again. When Jacques didn't answer fast enough, the tutor raised the stick that he used to point to different words on the page and hit him on the hand.

"Stop it!"

Both looked around. Antoinette stood in the doorway. "You will teach my son without hitting."

No one mentioned the incident. Jacques was not hit again. He loved what the tutor taught him, but not in the boring way he was taught it. He learned another lesson. A person with authority could stop someone with lesser authority.

CHAPTER 7

"Coffee, I need coffee," Luca said as they passed a café on the way to the dig. It was not yet seven. He'd rolled out of bed without making any other attempt to seduce Annie, saying that they should get an early start and eat breakfast in the Latin Quarter.

They took two seats outside a café next to the Gibert Jeune bookstore, which would not open until 9:30, and watched the trickle of early-morning workers rush by. The waiter brought two espressos and two croissants, one slightly burnt, the way Annie liked it.

"I still think we should make love." Luca dipped the tip of his croissant into the tiny cup.

"Not subtle."

"It will help us forget—Roger, Crystal."

"How come we came to work so early?"

"Annie, you're changing the subject." He swallowed his espresso in a single gulp.

"Of course I am."

"That's what I've always loved about you, Annie. You never played games, you were never coy. I never had to guess when you were pissed off at me."

A man sat down next to them and pulled out his copy of *Le Figaro*.

"I'm not ready to jump into bed with another man."

"But sweetheart, I'm not just any man. We've already made love."

"Years ago." She giggled.

"What?"

"I couldn't recognize your penis in a lineup, it's been so long."

"You mean you didn't peek when I got up this morning? Or when my towel dropped?"

"Nope. Now, why did you want to get here so early?"

Luca let out a long sigh. "You're breaking my heart that you decided to miss such a wonderful sight, but I will go on with my duty as an archeologist despite it all."

"Your eyes are brown because there's a surplus of excrement in your body."

Luca dipped and bit another mouthful of croissant as soon as the waiter brought him another espresso. "I'm worried about Philippe. He stayed late one night, supposedly to finish up sifting part of his quadrant, but the next morning nothing was done. And he often shows up early, too early."

Annie had tried to talk to Philippe yesterday when he had brought in what might have been a table leg. He was the oldest on the dig, somewhere in his forties, or maybe even his early fifties. Mostly people on digs were younger. Also unlike the others, not including Luca, he wasn't a volunteer but was being paid by the Départment des Antiquités.

"What's his story?"

"He was a professor at one time. Well on his way to being a leading archeologist. Then he quit his job and disappeared. This is the first time anyone has seen him for years."

Annie thought it was strange that he would have been hired with that background.

Luca read the expression on her face correctly and explained, "This is France. His brother-in-law is one of the deputy directors. I imagine the sister begged her husband to take him on, but that is just a guess. His work is really good. He works fast, but he's careful. A real professional, who can recognize any shard as something, and he never complains about the heat like the kids do."

Annie finished her croissant and took a last swallow of the espresso and wondered if the rush was like that of cocaine. Drugs had never been her thing. Come to think of it, coffee had never been her thing. Luca had hurried her out of the house so fast, she didn't have time for her preferred bowl of tea, sipped leisurely while she planned her day. "We'd better get going."

As they approached the dig, the street was almost deserted. They climbed down the ladder. Philippe was standing there, his hands on his hips. He looked a bit shaky.

"Are you okay?" Annie asked.

He shrugged. "I can't get into the shed."

"I've got the key," Luca said. He went to disable the alarm. "That's strange it isn't on," he said as he opened the door. Amelie was sitting in the chair sideways to the table serving as a desk. "What are you doing in here?" Luca started to say. Then it was clear Amelie would never answer any more questions.

"Be careful where you walk," Luca said to the two police detectives. "This is a dig."

One detective was a woman in her forties, obviously the more senior of the two. Despite the sun beating down and the lack of shade, she looked cool and chic in a beige linen pantsuit. The badge she had shown said her name was Marie-Claude Du Pont from the Direction Régionale de Police Judiciaire de Paris. Annie knew it was called DRPJ or 36 because it operated at 36, quai des Orfèvres: Roger had told her that when she hadn't understood when he'd said something about being at 36. At first she thought it was something he had done during his thirty-sixth year.

"It's a crime scene first," Marie-Claude said.

"Did you touch anything in the shed?" the other detective asked. He was probably in his early thirties. Huge wet spots marked his shirt under his arms and he smelled both of soap and sweat. He had not shown them a badge, which didn't matter to Annie. She didn't know what a 36 badge looked like. Within twenty minutes they had responded to Luca's call in an unmarked police car although a blue light flashed on the roof and a siren screamed "do-ee, do-ee, do-ee."

"Only the security code box and the door knob. The code wasn't on." He pointed to the cameras that they focused on the site after everyone left. "They weren't on either."

"Is that usual?" Marie-Claude asked.

"The last one to leave sets it—the security camera, that is. I thought Philippe would be the last to leave, so I asked him."

"Amelie was still here when I left," Philippe said. "I reminded her about them. My watch said it was 21:21. We joked how I tend to leave at 19:19, 20:20, et cetera."

"Why was she staying so late?" Marie-Claude asked.

"She said a friend was meeting her here and they were going to a late movie. I've no idea who."

Marie-Claude recorded all this in her notebook. "So you didn't touch the body, Monsieur Martinelli?"

"I only went a couple of steps into the shed. When I saw the blood and her eyes, I knew she was dead. I backed out and called the police on my cell phone." Luca pulled the phone out of his pocket and handed it to her. She checked his calls and handed it back.

The medical examiner arrived, or three of them did, without sirens or blue flashing lights. They wore white suits and carried large cases. A stretcher was pulled out of the back of their van.

One of the men climbed down the ladder into the dig. The others handed the equipment down to him.

Another *flic* was rolling yellow tape, attaching it to poles around the sidewalk above until the site was blocked off. People on their way to work tried to stop, but two *flics* arrived in a second police car at the request of Du Pont. Both were in uniform, one was tall, one average in height. They urged people not to stay and gawk at what was going on below.

Jacqueline and Laure arrived together and the taller *flic* told them to move along.

"But we work here," Jacqueline said. "They do too." She referred to Marino and Alexander, who had just appeared within seconds of the women.

The shorter *flic* called down into the pit, "Marie-Claude, employees."

The detective had been standing near the door of the work shed *cum* office. Flies were buzzing around and because of the heat, a smell beyond the feces, blood and urine that had escaped Amelie's body made them want to gag. On detective shows, they never could show how bad the stink was from a rotting corpse.

Jacqueline, Laure, Alexander and Marino climbed down the ladder, looking puzzled. Luca went up to them shielding them from the sight of Amelie in the shed. "Amelie was shot. She's dead."

"*Mon Dieu,*" the two women said together. Laure crossed herself.

Marino tried to look around Luca to see Amelie's body but said nothing.

One by one, they gave the detective their identification cards.

Annie watched it all as if it were a television detective show. Although she didn't really know Amelie, she hadn't particularly liked her, but dislike would have been too strong a word. That

47

type of flirty female had never appealed to her, but she would also admit that part of her feelings was because she was no good at it—still poor Amelie.

Yesterday, Annie had observed how Amelie had stopped several times to reapply lipstick and brush her hair back into a twist which set off her long neck, and now she lay dead, the contents of her body spilled onto her clothes and fly-covered. The contrast made Annie want to cry in general sadness for a life that ended too soon.

"How long did you know the victim?"

Annie turned toward the voice. Marie-Claude must be starting her investigation.

"Only a few hours. I arrived yesterday."

"From where?"

"Argelès-sur-mer."

"Nice down there, I've gone to the region several years for vacation. Not as snobby as the Riviera."

Annie nodded.

"What brought you to the dig?"

"Luca and I are old friends. We were both students together for a short time at uni. In Geneva. He thought I would enjoy helping out."

"Helping out?"

"I've a passion for history, and I'm between jobs."

"July in France: not the best time to look for work. Your accent is Swiss, but your name is English."

The last thing Annie wanted to do was go into her Third-Culture Kid status, which had left Annie feeling for years that she never had belonged anywhere. Unless someone was a TCK or at least an international used to being bounced from assignment to assignment in different countries, few people understood, thinking it was glamorous. Annie supposed it was true on one level, until you needed to get electricity connected in a language you didn't speak. "Although I'm American, I grew up in Geneva." It was somewhat true. She had mostly grown up in Geneva through her high school and university years with the exception of one year at the University of Massachusetts. There she'd discovered she couldn't go back to the States and find things the same way they were when she was eight.

It wasn't the school's fault that the other students had never heard of the PowWow or UB2 boy bands that Annie loved. Although she knew about American and English pop groups, her new classmates had no ideas about the intercontinental groups. She'd been annoyed that some students thought she lived like Heidi, taking care of goats and drinking milk from a bowl. Well, her family had adapted the French habit of drinking their morning tea from bowls, but that was as close as they came to anything resembling life in the Alps as depicted in the children's book.

"How did you happen to come here?"

"Because I knew Luca when he was an exchange student at the University of Geneva, we stayed in touch more or less and when he asked if I would like to do the documentation and some research for the project, I jumped at the chance."

Annie supplied Marie-Claude with Rima's address before the detective moved onto Jacqueline.

Jacqueline said she was an archeological student: this project would be the subject of her thesis. She was a student in Montpellier. So were Laure and Amelie. Yes, she knew Amelie, they had shared a flat last year, the three of them. Amelie kept to herself even if they were in the same program. They had offered to let Amelie room with her and Laure here in Paris, but Amelie said she wanted to be alone because she and her boyfriend would want privacy. No, she didn't know who the boyfriend was. Laure said she thought the boyfriend might be married, only because Amelie was so secretive about him.

Theirs was a field where jobs would be scarce, but they all hoped that this dig would be a step up for them increasing their chances to find work with the Département des Antiquités to look at sites before buildings covered them over or museums. Jacqueline hoped to teach the subject, even if university posts were rare. Amelie was specializing in the Iron Age, but Jacqueline was more interested in the Middle Ages. It was Amelie who found out about the project and they all had applied.

Marie-Claude wrote in a large notebook, as fast as the girls spoke. The lines were a tight quadrille. Annie who was standing beside her noted that her printing was small and as neat as type in a book, but she still was able to take down the gist of what each girl said with amazing accuracy. When Marie-Claude realized that Annie was watching, she moved so Annie could no longer see what the detective was writing.

Marino had been sitting on the ground off to one side. As the women were talking, he was tracing lines in the dirt with a small twig that must have come off the one tree that hung over the pit.

Marie-Claude went and sat beside him.

"And you're an archeological student too?"

"Not really. I'm doing business studies at the L'Ecole de Commerce in Toulouse. My father believes students should work in the summer, even though most of my friends don't." Marino, who was already sunburned, turned a bit redder. "My father also knows the head of the Département des Antiquités. They play racquetball together. Being here is more to keep me off the street this summer." He looked at Marie-Claude.

"And you." Marie-Claude turned to Alexander.

"A history student. I go to Toulouse University. My aunt's neighbor is a secretary at the Département des Antiquités and mentioned it to me. I telephoned and *voilà*, here I am."

"How does a history student qualify?" Marie-Claude asked.

"I probably didn't qualify at all. My specialty is modern history."

"We were running out of time to find people," Luca said. "There may be tons of people who want the job, but the word didn't get out fast enough." He had stood next to Marie-Claude as she questioned each person. "I thought at least Alexander would appreciate the history of the site. He was quick to learn the technical stuff he needed."

"And I'll admit, I thought it would be a lot more interesting than it is. We spend hours digging in dirt like kids."

Luca opened his mouth to say something, than closed it. Marie-Claude looked at him.

"People think archeology is full of exciting discoveries. It is tedious work and every now and then something exciting is found. But more likely on a dig like this, almost nothing will turn up."

Marie-Claude nodded before turning back toward Alexander. "And where did you go after work last night and what time?"

"Just for your information, Detective Du Pont, my girlfriend came to the site last night maybe about 18:35 or 18:45. I'm not sure. I went to her house so I could shower, then we went out to dinner. Afterwards we went home."

"You live together?" Marie-Claude asked.

"To her apartment. I'm staying with my aunt for the summer and she wouldn't have appreciated me . . ."

"Bringing a young woman home?"

Alexander blushed. "She's a devout Catholic, isn't even sure about sex after marriage, et cetera. She almost became a nun, so I spend ninety-five percent of my time at my girlfriend's place."

"And what does your aunt think of that?"

"It's a 'not under my roof' situation. Or 'what I don't know won't hurt me.' My aunt, despite her religiousness, also knows that her way does not match today's mores. And she adores me, so we kinda have this agreement that is working out just fine."

"I saw them leave together," Luca said. Marie-Claude almost collided with him as she turned to Philippe who had found a bit of shade under the overhang of the shed.

"I'm the other paid employee besides Luca," he said. "I've done digs, mostly in Syria and Jordan. It's my job to make sure that we work as fast as we can without compromising what we find. I stand in for Luca, who sometimes gets caught up in reports."

"But with our time constraints, we all get our hands dirty," Luca said.

"Time constraints?"

"Unless we turn up Christ's tomb, the dig ends and the new building will start construction in three weeks."

"So you really don't think this is an important dig?" Marie-Claude asked.

"All digs have some importance. Preserving the past is important," Luca said. "But this was probably an inn some six hundred years ago. It doesn't pay property taxes. The new building will."

"Patrimony versus property taxes," Marie-Claude said.

"Something like that." Luca used what he called his killer smile on her.

Annie noticed that Marie-Claude smiled back but her eyes remained serious. Nice try, Luca, she thought.

Marie-Claude told one of the *flics*, who had just arrived and climbed down the ladder, to get everyone's name, address, cell and landlines if they had them. She told everyone to leave the dig but to stay in Paris.

"When can we start back to work?" Luca said.

"We'll release the site when the investigation is complete."

As she climbed up the ladder to the street, Annie looked back to see Amelie's body being zipped into a bag. The photographer was putting away his camera.

CHAPTER 8

Philippe's hand shook as he poured water over the filigreed spoon with a sugar cube in the middle into the clear absinthe underneath. The drink turned cloudy. It was his third of the sixty-eight-percent alcoholic drink, but he had not achieved the click that would exchange fear for well-being. He knew he should have called his sponsor to meet him before he stopped at the café not far from Notre Dame. Tomorrow. Now he wanted to become totally wasted. Had his old dealer not been sent to prison, he would be rolling up a ten-euro note and inhaling a line of white powder.

A year—well, eleven months, two weeks and three days—he had been straight. He had no intention of going back to sleeping under bridges. He preferred his small room, his paycheck at the end of the month. Strings had been pulled—strings as only a French civil servant can pull them—to get him this post.

If his back hurt at the end of a day rooting around in soil, it was better than standing before a class of students. Too bad there wasn't more work for archeologists: a few teaching posts, a few grants for digs. The modern world was too focused on the future to give any thought about the old.

Had he ruined his one chance? With Amelie dead, maybe he hadn't. He thought of all the others on the team: it had been enjoyable being part of a team again. Had he been the last to leave the dig last night, he would have set the security alarms and cameras on the site. Luca had been very clear on that being of major importance, but he would have done it anyway. He knew how important it was to secure a dig. Too many people imagined that a dig would produce something valuable enough to steal.

He had fiddled around while the others were leaving, saying he wanted to make sure everything was in place. Jacqueline and Laure both had had dates and were anxious to shower the dust of the day off. Marino was already gone. He always was the first one to disappear. Alexander left at normal quitting time, saying nothing about his plans for the evening, although the young woman waiting at the top of the ladder was an indication. Luca and the new woman were off to dinner someplace that Luca insisted Annie try despite her claims of not being hungry. She kept suggesting that they just go back to the flat where they were both staying. Philippe hung around waiting for Amelie to leave, but she just sat and sat in the shed. Finally, he'd given up.

That was the point he went back to his quadrant. Keeping his back to the open door of the shed where Amelie was sitting and, taking a spoon out of his back pocket, he dug up the gold bracelet he had found earlier in the day and reburied. He suspected that the gold twisted like a rigid rope with a knob on each end was pure, something between fourteen and twenty-four carats. He was sure he could sell it as gold alone and give himself enough money to buy a new mattress.

He knew he should hand it in, but he wanted that mattress. At the same time, he was curious about the bracelet and was tempted to keep it. This starting over had so many uncomfortable moments. Maybe a night's sleep would help him get through some of them and a drink would help him sleep.

"Now that's interesting."

He'd looked up to see that bitch Amelie watching him from the door of the shed.

CHAPTER 9

Saverdun, France, October 1294

Jacques Fournier's replacement tutor was the new priest at the church. Père Marty met his mother's standards. The hated Père Vital and his pimples had disappeared one night along with two gold coins that were not locked into the kitchen trunk covered with three fleeces. No one had seen the priest since.

Although it was too bad his family had lost money, Jacques considered the price small for the chance to work with a new teacher.

Père Marty never yelled, never hit. Instead he asked questions, listened to the answers, probed deeper into why Jacques had reached this or that conclusion. Then they would debate. Sometimes Jacques could hardly wait to present his next statement, but Père Marty would hold up his hands with the palms out. "Listen. Think. Then speak," he would say. "Draw the logic." Later he reduced the phrase to DTL. Jacques fell asleep each night planning the next day's arguments.

Père Marty added geometry to the lessons. The clear rules had their own beauty and Jacques began to see shapes in the circle of his mother's face, the rectangle of the table, the proportion of treetops to earth. As much as he loved anything to do with mathematics, nothing would ever replace the glory and precision of Latin whether it was the Bible or the works retained from the Romans. Even reading the Bible in Christ's own tongue, Aramaic, as thrilling as that was, didn't match his love of Latin.

"You eat books," Père Marty would complain with a smile when Jacques once again dipped into the stash of books the priest had brought with him.

One June morning the priest came to the house to say Mass for Jacques's mother. This was the third time that week. The chest at the foot of the bed had been converted into an altar. Nine-year-old Jacques sat with his book on his lap next to his mother's bed, but he couldn't concentrate on his lessons.

She slept on her back, her hand on her rounded stomach as she made small putt-putt noises. A slate lay on the floor. He knew he should rewrite the sentences over and over until he found the best way to say what he wanted in Latin. The ability to choose and change always made him shiver because not only did it give him power, but when his tutor read them, he would smile, laugh, frown or react in just the way Jacques hoped he would. Instead of working he kept looking at his mother.

Last week she had barely had the strength to walk across the room because of her constant vomiting. Her once-shiny black hair was dull, unkempt, although Jacques had tried to pull a comb through it. Even his actions tired her.

When his father found her dressed and swaying as she tried to cross the room, he asked, "Where on the crown of Jesus, do you think you're going?"

"Mass."

"You can't," father and son said in unison.

"I must."

"We'll bring the church to you," his father said. And he had. The local priest said Mass at the foot of the bed three times a week.

Jacques wished his father were here now instead of investigating yet another mill to buy. For the last three years he'd planned to purchase a new mill to try a new dyeing process that so far existed only in his head. There were plenty of mills owned by different monasteries for grinding grain, but none had ever been used for textiles.

"The monks don't want my money, they want my soul," he complained to his wife.

Jacques looked at his mother. She'd never had been so pale. "Our Father, who art in heaven, please spare my mother. Please spare my new baby brother or sister, but if there's a choice, let us keep her."

Antoinette hated staying in bed despite the number of times the midwife told her how lucky she was to have the choice. Less-wealthy women kept working and if the babe was lost, it was lost. She must save her strength for the birth three months away.

She turned on her side. Jacques brought the candle closer to her face and saw she was smiling in her sleep. He tiptoed from the room.

Downstairs the clerk sorted new fleece taken in that morning. The man stank of wine. Jacques debated saying something. He hoped that his father would be back that night. The man was swaying and mumbling. On the table was a pouch that had not been there before.

"What's that?" Jacques asked.

"Wha . . . ?" the clerk's eyes were red. He wiped his hand across his mouth stained purple in the corners.

Jacques was certain if he searched the room he would find a wine-filled goatskin or, more likely, an empty goatskin that the clerk would have recently emptied of wine. "The pouch."

"A man stopped. It's for your father." The clerk went back to his work.

"Go home," Jacques said. He hated being near drunks. They mumbled, stank and slurred their words. The clerk grabbed his cloak and stumbled out the door.

Jacques took the pouch upstairs and placed it on the trunk and began preparing dinner to his mother's specifications. He liked the physicality of cooking after all the hours spent sitting at his study bench. His knife sliced through the onions rapidly, bringing tears to his eyes.

"Jacques?" His mother's voice drifted from the bedroom.

The boy dropped the cloth he was using to wipe the table clean and went into her room. "Sleep well?"

She patted the bed next to her. "Very well. I feel good enough to make dinner."

"If Papa comes and catches you, he'll be furious with both of us. Besides, I've already started it."

A long, low whistle came from downstairs followed by footsteps. Benoît Fournier burst into the room. "I've done it. I've found my mill. Jacques, you'll come with me tomorrow. Madame Azais will stay with your mother."

The Fourniers, father and son, rented two horses from the stable at the end of the village. Neither animal was built for speed, but plodded along the forest paths. Although Benoît rode well, Jacques did not. The pounding of the saddle reminded his rear of the few spankings he'd received. "How much further?"

"Not much."

The ride seemed to go on forever, but he didn't want to ask his father how long again. In the late afternoon as they emerged from the forest Jacques saw a gray stone wall, higher than his horse's head. A red tile roof and church steeple were the only other two things visible over the wall.

Benoît slid off his horse and grabbed the rope attached to a bell to the left of the wooden gate. Rather than make a clear ring, it gave a thud similar to the horses' hoofs on the dirt path. A few minutes later a monk led them past two other monks, both of whom tottered as they hit at the weeds, which in return seemed to defy them by not separating from their roots.

Inside a little house, they were shown a single stool. Benoît sat. Jacques stood, not just out of respect, but because he did not want his sore rear to touch anything.

A fourth monk, who seemed older to Jacques than all the other monks together, shuffled behind a blackened table and eased himself onto a bench. Parchments were scattered around the table along with a quill pen and an inkwell.

"I would like to show my son the mill," Benoît said.

The monk nodded through heavily lidded eyes. "You know the way." He was asleep before they left the room, his head nesting in his arms on the table.

As they entered the building that housed the wheel, a rat scuttled out of sight. Surely, there could not be any grain still left here, Jacques thought as he looked through the holes in the roof. The mill was dilapidated, but the wheel could be turned. Benoît pointed to each scoop. "Look how much water it holds." He took Jacques's hand and shoved it into the water. It reminded the boy of the time he dipped his hand in the river just as the ice chunks were thawing.

"The water must be coming from an underground spring," Benoît said. "We'll hang the cloth here. The water will pour through it. Think how much more cloth we can handle. And the cold water will set the colors."

Back inside the house, they waited for the abbot to wake. When he did, Benoît said he would ask the Authiés, the local *notaires,* to draw up the contract.

Only five monks sat at the refractory table eating bread and turnips as the youngest monk, who would qualify as a great-grandfather had he not lived a celibate life, read about Saint Thomas. As hungry as Jacques was, as much as it hurt to sit on the stool, he felt peaceful, although he couldn't help thinking that if he were abbot, he would make sure the cobwebs over the windows were removed.

"What will happen to the monks?" Jacques asked his father as he was being jostled home.

"They're going to another monastery." His father had to turn around so Jacques could hear him.

They rode further. Although the sun set late at this time of year, Jacques didn't want to be caught in the forest at night. "What happens to the rest of the monastery buildings?"

"I'm hoping the dyers will move there."

"Move?" Everyone Jacques knew had lived in Saverdun forever and ever and before them their parents and grandparents. Shepherds moved around, but they were different. And during fair time merchants from all over came to sell their wares from strange-sounding places. However, the craftsmen, the baker, weaver, shoemaker, pot maker were always there.

At a clap of thunder, Jacques's horse reared. His father turned his own mount and grabbed the reins to calm the beast. "We'll be drenched by the time we get home."

He was right. By the time they arrived at the stable their clothes were stuck to their skin as if they had been put on directly from the washing tub.

Jacques was just grateful to be home before dark. His imagination created wild animals: bears, boars, wolves—all of whom wanted him for dinner. His fat would be ripped from his bones. When he was little his parents would pretend to eat him up, putting their mouths on his chest and tummy and blowing. Animals wouldn't pretend.

After leaving the horses, they ran through the rain, heads down until they reached home. "Get into warm clothes." His father reached for the candle and tinder left by the door.

The house was quiet. The neighbor, who was supposed to stay with his mother, must have gone home. However, when they entered the kitchen, the woman slept sitting on a bench, her arms cushioning her head on the table. She woke. "Thank God. You're home. Your wife's been crying, but she won't tell me why." The neighbor picked up a pouch. "You know Antoinette, when she gets an idea into her head she won't let it out."

Jacques and Benoît nodded.

"It has to do with this pouch."

"It came yesterday, I forgot to tell you," Jacques said.

"The letter inside was what got to her. She kept saying, 'I didn't think it would be this soon.' "

When Jacques and his father entered the bedroom, they saw a sleeping Antoinette, her face swollen and red, a parchment in her hand. Without disturbing her, Benoît extricated the document from her hands and tiptoed out.

Jacques stood still. He didn't dare peep over his father's shoulder. It must be terrible news, but he was afraid to ask.

"It's from your uncle Arnaud. He'll be here in a few days to take you to Boulbonne."

"Boulbonne?"

"To the monastery there."

"Not Fontfroide?"

"He feels you'll be better as a postulant where he isn't an abbot. You'll study, work, maybe lose some of that baby fat." He poked the boy in the stomach.

Jacques didn't even know where Boulbonne was, but then he didn't know where Fontfroide was either. "But *Maman* always said she wanted this."

Benoît put his arms around his son. "Women don't always make sense, son. As a priest you'll never learn how truly arbitrary they are."

Jacques had never heard his father say one word against his mother, although what he had just confided wasn't against her particularly, but against all womankind. "Do you think she had changed her mind—you know—about me being a priest?"

"I doubt it. I'm guessing she knows how much she'll miss you."

CHAPTER 10

Jacqueline and Laure did not really care that many people thought of them as lesbians, even though they weren't if the definition was women who had sexual relations. If it were women who loved one another without the physical act of sex, then the definition would fit.

They'd met when they were doing their undergraduate work in Montpellier. Laure had answered an ad for a roommate that Jacqueline had put in *L'Independent*. They recognized each other from the classes they shared.

The friendship had grown along with their professional interests until one could start a sentence and the other finished it.

One criterion for a boyfriend was a man who would accept the friendship. Few met the challenge. Jacqueline and Laure knew enough anthropology to realize that some men establish territory by cutting their women off from their support system. André had been different. He had lasted with Laure for two years, but they'd broken up because he had a grant to study in the United States, and she didn't want to interrupt her studies.

They had taken in other roommates from time to time and always included them in their activities. Amelie had been the last one, but Amelie was not like Danielle, Florence, George, or Christophe who went along with house rules, adding or modifying where necessary.

Amelie did not believe she should do her share of the

household chores and was usually late with her share of the rent and utility bills. Jacqueline had caught her looking into her laptop. Amelie used the excuse that her laptop's battery was dead and she just needed to check her e-mail. At the time Jacqueline did not ask why Amelie had not recharged it with the cord nor why she was into Hotmail, which Jacqueline used instead of Yahoo which Amelie used: instead, she password-protected everything thereafter.

Amelie was not planning to room with them when classes started in the fall, which neither Jacqueline nor Laure regretted. Sometimes they found Amelie amusing and just when they were ready to strangle her, she would bring home a bottle of special wine to share, bake her special *gâteau au chocolat* or suggest an outing that they all enjoyed. Despite being a lazy scholar, Amelie was a natural learner. She seemed to absorb books without reading them, retained notes by just looking at them after the lecture and tested well.

Jacqueline and Laure had learned about the dig from Amelie, and they were surprised that she shared the information with them, even giving them the e-mail address where they could apply. They never expected her to do anything to increase her competition. When all three were accepted, it was Amelie who suggested they celebrate together.

In retrospect, Jacqueline and Laure agreed the only thing predictable about Amelie was her unpredictability.

The two women were silent on the Métro to Marais where they rented a *chambre de bonne* in an old mansion. The two women stayed out of the cramped space as much as possible. Located just under the eaves there was barely enough room for the touching twin beds. Its only window was a small circle much like a ship's porthole. It did little to stop the stifling heat despite their purchase of the fan. Still it was cheap and the girls could afford it from their allowances once their parents were convinced that the dig was an opportunity and not just a way to idle away the summer.

Rather than go home to their room, which they had nick-named the oven, they stopped at one of the cafés located under the ancient stone arches housing bookstores, art galleries and boutiques featuring clothes made by the owners, surrounding the Place des Vosges with its grassy center. Whatever breeze there was, did manage to make its way to their table.

The lunch crowd had returned to work. Although the girls had not eaten since breakfast, they knew their chance to find a restaurant willing to serve them anything was minimal. They both ordered peach ice tea.

"Should we have told the detective that Amelie was having an affair with Luca?" Jacqueline asked.

"We don't know that," Laure said.

"The woman was in heat whenever he was around." Jacqueline signaled for the waiter and asked if he had any chips. He brought them a small dish. "Salt replacement."

"Sure, sure," Laure said. "And what's your excuse in winter when you're not sweating?"

Jacqueline just shrugged. "Don't need one. Maybe they slept together once. I don't think Luca was all that interested in her. He went out of his way not to be alone with her. Didn't you notice whenever she went into the shed to talk to him and shut the door, he opened it?"

"I thought it was to throw us offtrack that they were having an affair."

"Do you think Luca could have killed her?"

Jacqueline shook her head. "He's so gentle. Remember the mouse."

Laure frowned. "No."

"Maybe you had left because it was late in the afternoon. There was a mouse scuttling through the dig. He trapped it, climbed up the ladder and walked over to the river to let it go."

"Maybe he is kinder to mice than mistresses he wants out of his life," Laure said. "Still I think we should talk to the detective."

"She'll probably want to know why we didn't say anything this morning."

Chapter 11

Marie-Claude Du Pont jolted herself awake as the Métro pulled into Gare du Lyon. Her days began too early and ended too late. In fact her life had too many toos. She was *too* tired of the work that had once thrilled her. Her sons, although she adored them, demanded *too* much of the time that she couldn't find to give them. She was *too* fed up with sorting out the problems of her team, most of whom were on holiday. Although she missed their work it was good not to listen to François talk about his neurotic wife, Anna's constantly unsuccessful search for a man or Jean-Paul's teenage son refusing to take out the garbage or do anything but loll around the house.

Not that she had her personal life under control. Raphaël was being a difficult teenager, and she'd just dropped three-year-old Daniel off at the *crèche*. She should have known better than to believe her soon-to-be second ex-husband when he said a baby would help their faltering marriage and that he would be a full partner. She had been *too* trusting or maybe it wasn't *too* trusting but *too* entranced by the handsome man hiding in a boy's mind—at least as far as responsibility was concerned. However, after years of being alone, having a partner seemed like such a good idea. Rather it had been a good idea in theory—it was the reality that had been the problem.

Life would be easier now had she not had Daniel, but then again, all he had to do was to turn that smile on and tilt his head and her tiredness would melt along with her heart. He was an easy child, even missing the terrible twos and moving into his third year with a sense of joy. Sometime in the future when he was a teenager and hulking around the house or coming in late like Raphaël, sulking over cleaning his room she would try and remember Daniel as he was today—running off to join his *copains* when she dropped him at the *crèche*. He would show the same eagerness when she picked him up at night throwing himself into her arms.

She pushed through the crowds rushing to and from the trains out into the street and headed toward the morgue next to the Seine. Today she could smell the water in the heat.

God, she hated autopsies, especially on the young. They did serve one purpose: she wanted to make sure whoever killed them met their reward. She handled mainly murders. She was just one of the over two thousand two hundred other people to solve the fifteen thousand crimes that take place in Paris every year, truly a Sisyphus situation. Instead of endlessly rolling rocks uphill to have them roll down again, after one criminal was put away a new one appeared. She didn't want to think of all the crimes they never cracked.

She sat down behind the glass in the observers' deck waiting for the pathologist, Dr. Alain Martinez. She'd begged him to move up the autopsy, which he finally agreed to, saying it was only to get her off his back. Three days had passed since the murder and there was little that they had learned from the murder scene. The door had been locked. All the team had keys. None were missing, except for Amelie's and Marie-Claude did not need to be a great detective to figure out whoever killed Amelie had used her key to lock the body in the shed.

In questioning the team, she tended not to disbelieve what any of them had said, more by instinct, which had helped much more than it hindered her during her career. None of their stories offered any suspicious variations.

What was worse—no hard evidence existed.

. Footprints?

There were hundreds in the dust, none clear enough to take a plaster cast.

Fingerprints?

Only those of the team, which meant that one of them could be guilty—or more likely the murderer had on gloves or never touched anything. Even the ladder was clean of unidentified prints.

Motive?

No one seemed to hate Amelie enough to want to kill her. No one seemed to like her all that much either, but passion would have been needed to fire the gun. Or would it?

Had someone found something in the dig that they wanted to hide? Amelie could have come across a team member pocketing something, but then again, all of them said that the dig had not produced anything exceptional. Nor did Luca expect anything of value—other than historical value—to come out of the project.

She hated it, just outright hated it, when there were no real leads. Tomorrow she would order the site released so the team could get on with its work if the autopsy report did not give her a reason to send her own crew back in.

The chance of them missing something the first time was unlikely. They were as professional as those on the different CSI teams on the American series shown on French television. In the beginning she thought those programs artificial, especially in how quickly they came to the right conclusions. And their state-of-the-art equipment made her drip with envy.

Then she realized that there were a few things she could learn from the show. Finally, she'd given up watching for time and tiredness reasons. Better to read Daniel a story, or to climb into her bed with a book where she would fall asleep reading with her glasses and light still on.

Forget her personal life. She slipped on a surgical mask into which she had put a drop of wintergreen to hide the smell of death.

The pathologist entered the room and looked up and acknowledged her presence with a nod. He had once complimented her at not turning green or fainting no matter how bad the condition of the person was. That he referred to the defunct as a person was a sign of the respect toward the victims that he was about to rend asunder.

As the table was rolled in with all that was left of the victim, he adjusted the microphone hanging from the ceiling to record his words.

"Amelie LaFollette, twenty-three, student brought in on July fifth."

He discovered her last meal had been salmon, probably eaten at lunch. Her lungs were those of a nonsmoker. A bullet, which he examined closely, had gone through her heart. "It's from a Glock, a model that was introduced in 2010," he said looking up at Marie-Claude.

Last month she had taken a review course on all kinds of guns. That she could never take anything for granted, that she had learned all there was to learn, was disproven the next day when she was given a murder case where a forty-two-year-old man had been killed by a crossbow. They couldn't get fingerprints from the arrow, but they did get DNA.

Marie-Claude still had not located Amelie's parents. The two other women on the dig said the mother lived in the eleventh arrondissement. There were three LaFollette families in that district. Two were no relation to the murdered girl.

At the third location, a building with one apartment per floor, the neighbor who lived below said, yes, she had seen Amelie with an older woman. The mother had moved there a few months ago, and she had not yet had a chance to get to know her other than to pass greetings in the hallway. One neighbor described Madame LaFollette as a woman somewhere in her forties maybe, hard to tell these days. They had shared an elevator with the neighbor and a younger woman whom Madame LaFollette introduced as Amelie, her daughter.

That was what was wrong with today's world, the neighbor lamented. No one has time to make friends. No, the neighbor had said, she'd never seen a man who might be a father or husband, and as far as she knew the woman had gone off on holiday. She didn't think Amelie lived there. She was probably a student someplace, but she had stayed overnight sometimes. She had been there for one of the May holiday weekends, Ascension or Pentecost, she couldn't remember which.

There were no noises coming from the apartment. The insulation was thin in this cheaply constructed building, a rip-off that they charged so much rent, the woman said. Maybe she'd passed the woman getting into a taxi along with a suitcase, but she had her own problems to think of and couldn't say for sure.

After thanking the woman, Marie-Claude walked down the three flights of stairs, feeling she'd found the family but hating that the chore of telling them remained ahead. Focus, pay attention to Alain, she told herself.

"She was approximately five weeks pregnant," the pathologist said into the microphone.

Marie-Claude had been slouching. She sat up straight.

Chapter 12

Boulbonne, France, 1301

Green beans hung icicle-like from vines tied to wooden poles. Jacques Fournier passed among the rows reaching out to examine each bean, rejecting some while dropping others into a brown twig basket. Its pointed end caught on his white robe. He twisted the fabric to free it. His hands were as dusty as were his sandaled feet. Rain had been elusive, wilting the leaves and drying the soil.

He held a bean to his nose, inhaling its odor. Its heat matched that of his skin, darkened by the sun. He bit it, listening to the snap between his teeth and tasting its freshness. The sun beat down, making him glad that Cistercians did not wear black. Black would be a killer in the near-noon sun.

His arms, not visible under his robe, had clearly defined muscles from the fieldwork expected of all apostles. During his first few months when he fell onto his cot, almost too tired to say his final prayers, he'd suffered great pain. He wasn't sure how pushing a hoe through the earth or shoveling hay made him more holy. His reward for his labor was time to study the words of the great religious minds in Greek, Aramaic, Hebrew and Latin. He wanted to do nothing else, but he was not given a choice in any event.

Days had become weeks, weeks months, the months years. The routine of prayer-work-study had become as natural as breathing—more so if possible. And the pounds of his childhood disappeared into the routine.

The number of beans in the basket grew. Jacques watched his fellow brothers weed the *courgettes*, still thin, some yellow, some green, all too unripe to eat. Another week and they would be on trenchers of bread, another example of the sparse meals in the refractory. It wasn't that the monastery was poor, but sacrifice and moderation were called for in all things.

Beyond the monastery walls a hill was covered with grapes that the monks would turn into wine. What they could not drink would be sold or traded. At this time of year the grapes were like hard little peas without their shell.

A snail, no bigger than his thumbnail, and a slug crawled along a bean leaf as if running a reverse race to see which one could move more slowly. Fournier put his basket down to watch. Something slithered over his foot.

His breath caught in his throat. Temptress of Eve! Evil! A hoe rested against the end of the tented leaves. He grabbed and slammed it down again and again, hacking until each piece of what had been the snake was smaller than the snail. He threw the hoe as far as he could, not wanting to touch anything that had touched the snake. Sweat poured down his brow as he walked back to the dark cool of the monastery's shelter.

At the door he gave his eyes a chance to accustom themselves to the light fighting its way through a sliver of a window. He made out the bench to the right of the door under a crucifix. It bothered him to see Christ suffer—to see the torture. He knew the Latin root for torture and crucifix were the same, but Christ taught love, not pain.

The thick slabs of the stone wall became visible. Brother José shuffled into view. The old man signaled for Jacques to wait as he made his way down the corridor. When he reached Jacques he said, "The abbot wishes to see you."

Jacques didn't understand the words. It was nothing new. When Brother José read the lessons during meals he rolled the r's of his native Catalonia blurring the sounds. Since conversation was discouraged, Jacques could not ask why he had not chosen a monastery closer to home. He said a quick prayer for allowing his mind to wander from holy thoughts. "Pardon me?"

"The abbot wants to see you." The old man took the basket and shuffled toward the kitchen.

Jacques headed in the opposite direction toward the abbot's office. Had he done something wrong? As he ran through the list of possible infractions, he could come up with nothing.

He paused at the abbot's door, made of wood as thick as the length of his hand. He swallowed his pride at the shine because polishing the door was his chore. He rapped hard.

"Come in, come in." The abbot often repeated himself.

His abbot sat behind the table he used as a desk. A small bowl held ink, and several quills were nearby along with the knife that brought them to a sharp point. The abbot had once been a scribe in the monastery and his penmanship remained a work of art. A bound book was open. Jacques knew it contained monastery accounts: the produce sold, the cost for the new roof after a windstorm sent tiles skittering to the ground.

The abbot wasn't working on his books. He sat with his fingers forming a steeple, the longest fingers Jacques had ever seen. The abbot's hands were always clean, with well-trimmed nails, for he alone avoided fieldwork.

The office had one of the largest windows in the abbey. It was open. Sunlight formed a path shining on the abbot like heaven, like the painting of Christ rising into heaven.

Since the abbot was smiling, Jacques let out a long breath. He had not disobeyed a rule. Why he worried, he didn't understand, for he had not broken a rule since he had arrived eight years before.

"Jacques, you're no longer a podgy boy, but a man."

Jacques turned. He had not seen the other man in the room. The voice sound familiar, but before he could examine the face, the man grabbed and hugged him. Only when he took Jacques by the shoulders and held him at arm's length, did he recognize the voice.

"You're surprised to see your uncle Arnaud, eh?" the abbot said.

"Mother? Father? Maria?" Jacques asked.

Arnaud let out a long laugh. "Your family is perfectly well. They're looking forward to seeing you."

Was his family coming here? He let his uncle guide him to a stool. They made a triangle: three men in white robes.

"I'm here to help you decide your future," Uncle Arnaud said. He got up and sat on the edge of the abbot's table, his leg dangling over the corner as he looked down on his nephew. His foot was clean. Jacques tucked his dirty feet under his robe.

"All your life we've told you that you must be a priest. The Church needs men of the highest abilities and motives. We've enough wastrels."

"Far too many," the abbot said.

"What do you want, Jacques—to go home and work with your father or take your next vows?"

When Jacques started to speak, his uncle held up his hand. "Don't tell me now. Think on it."

Jacques felt a surge of love for the man, although he hadn't seen him in years. "I can answer now. I know it's my mother's wish to have me in the Church. Had I not wanted to join the Church, I would have sided with my father when he said I could serve God as an honest cloth merchant." He faltered for words. He was no longer used to talking. "I can't express the peace I feel in these halls. When we sing, I want to cry. I . . . I . . ."

"I told you he'd say that," the abbot said. "I always know

which of my young men will stay."

"But he won't stay here. I want him to come to Fontfroide with me to take his vows."

"You're stealing him from me?" The abbot's smile told Jacques it was all right.

"And you stole Brother Andrea from me not too long ago," Uncle Arnaud said. Then turning to Jacques he added, "I'm going to Toulouse and will pass through Saverdun. You'll come with me to see your parents before we go back to Fontfroide."

Jacques found it strange to be outside the walls where he had not ventured in eight years. The world seemed to be divided between the countryside baked by the summer sun and towns filled with chatter. He heard more human voices in one morning than he had heard in months. "It's so noisy," he said to his uncle after they had stopped at a church to eat. The priest, who had greeted Arnaud with a smile, rushed to feed them bread, cheese and a concoction of mashed vegetables.

His uncle stopped with his food-filled hand halfway to his mouth. "You need to get out of the monastery more often. I know what you're going to say about contemplation, The Rule and all that, but you need to fight temptation, real temptation. God doesn't love those who hide as much as he loves those who've fought the devil and won."

Jacques and Uncle Arnaud led their horses into Saverdun. One limped slightly from a pebble in its hoof. Uncle Arnaud told the man, who ran the stable, to remove it. Jacques remembered the man from his childhood as a real grouch, but the man did not recognize Jacques.

The lack of recognition neither bothered Jacques nor pleased him. A top could not have swerved more than Jacques's head as he recognized the baker's, the fullers', the church where he made his first communion. The houses had shrunk, the trees had grown and some things seemed out of place. He hadn't remembered a fountain for humans and horses to drink, across from the butcher's. His mother often sent him for water, but the fountain had been nearer the baker's. Or had it?

When they turned onto the road leading to his parents' house, his pace quickened. As he stood in front of his childhood home, a client emerged. Jacques saw his father, who almost looked the same except there was less hair on his head. His father saw him at the same time and upset a table as he rushed to the door. "Antoinette, come quickly. Jacques is here."

Antoinette Fournier rushed down the stairs and threw herself at her son. When they separated he saw her tear-wet face had lines near her eyes and there was more gray than black in her hair.

Standing behind her was a small girl. Jacques knelt before the sister he had never seen, and for a moment regretted that the brother born after he'd left had died in birth. "You must be my sister."

"I'm Maria. I'm five." She held up all five fingers of her right hand.

He spent a week at home while his uncle went to Toulouse. No king had a better welcome. His sister followed him everywhere and paid him such rapt attention that he worried about her soul. Only God should be loved as much she loved him.

His mother kept asking if everything were all right because he was so quiet. "You used to be such a chatterbox."

"We don't speak much at the monastery," he said. "I must be out of the habit."

When he climbed into bed at night, he was exhausted, not just from the stream of childhood playmates, now grown and married with babes of their own, but from all the talking and laughter. He tried slipping into the church, but his sister followed him. He understood why it was necessary to divorce himself from worldly things to deal with the holy.

He no longer belonged to Saverdun or his family, which he remembered loving. He belonged to God. He was happy when his uncle returned and they began their trek to Fontfroide.

CHAPTER 13

Alexander Badie unlocked the door to his aunt's house. What a bummer the summer had turned out to be. First his father had insisted that this summer would not be spent hiking through the mountains with his friends. It would be spent doing something useful.

Useful.

Useful was one of his father's words. Everything had to be useful.

Productive.

Productive was another one of his father's words right up there with profitable. No . . . profitable came first.

Alexander knew what a disappointment he was to his father. He had failed, deliberately, although he never told his father that, to get into one of the Grandes Ecoles, thus having to settle for L'Ecole de Commerce in Toulouse, which he had dropped out of after four weeks. Not that it was a bad school, he just didn't want to go into business. He then changed to the University of Toulouse to study history, but a year into the program, he was unhappy, which he hadn't dare tell his father. It wasn't that it wasn't interesting. It was just he could picture himself teaching or rummaging around old documents the rest of his life.

His father wanted his son to be *DG—directeur générale—*material. Alexander knew he didn't want to do that.

Ever since he was little he'd dreamed of working with plants and trees, not on a farm, but in forests. That was not an option he had been given by his father. Business. Business. Business. Those were his choices and he'd said no to it all. His father had said that if Alexander did not go back to business school, he would have to support himself, so Alexander had reapplied to L'Ecole de Commerce. He was upset that they had accepted him back.

At the dig he saw how much Luca, Jacqueline and Laure loved what they were doing. He wanted to share the same enthusiasm for what he devoted his life to.

So he started researching what until this summer he had thought was impossible. His girlfriend helped and found the Dynamiques Forestières dans l'espace Rural, National University of Agronomy in Toulouse where he could study forestry. He wondered why he had wasted so much time, not going there in the first place despite his father's pressure. And if it meant he had to work to support himself, so be it.

The opportunity of the dig had come up, thanks to Marino, his former classmate, and Alexander had grabbed it. At least he wouldn't be cooped up in an office all summer like last summer, disliked as the boss's son by people who were afraid to speak openly in front of him.

Maybe the summer hadn't been as wasted as he thought. He was heading in a new direction that he might not have found through totally unrelated conversations.

"Alexander, is that you?" his aunt called out from the library where she was curled up on the sofa reading. He entered the room with its floor-to-ceiling bookcases. It always stayed cool in summer and warm in winter. It was here that his family had come for Christmas when he and his brother were little.

His father did not particularly like his sister-in-law. She was now a professor of religion. Professors didn't live in the "real world" according to his father. But Alexander had always loved his aunt Lillian. She let them build tent cities when his parents were off to this or that event.

"You're home early."

"Is there any more about that poor murdered girl?" she asked.

He shook his head. He had not brought any of the team home, although he knew his aunt would make them welcome, because he liked to keep his private life separate, not that he did all that much at night except see his girlfriend. Sometimes they took a walk along the Seine, which wasn't that far from his aunt's house in Neuilly. And there was a park where a couple of times a week there would be concerts. He didn't like cities, period, and any chance to see grass and plants helped make the summer go faster.

"How terrible to die so young and in such a way," she said. She got up and poured him a glass of wine without his asking. "How are you feeling?"

One thing he loved about his aunt, she seldom said he should feel this way or that. Instead, she asked what he thought, felt, cared about and then didn't pass judgment on what he answered. He wanted to climb into her lap as he did when he was little after his father had yelled at him. However, he was now at least two heads taller than his aunt, and outweighed her by seventy-five pounds. Crushing her would be the likely outcome, not comfort.

"Shocked. This is the first person my age that I knew died."

"When that happened to me, I was eighteen and although my grandparents had died, I never thought anyone my age would. Oh, I knew it intellectually, but I hadn't internalized it. Then one of my friends was killed in a car crash. And of course, if Laeticia could die, then I could too." She swirled the wine in her glass.

"You always get it right, Aunt Lillian." He took a sip of his wine.

"Not always."

"Which one was she? I met them all at the same time." Lillian had stopped by the dig bringing a picnic lunch for everyone saying it was her excuse to check out where her nephew disappeared every day.

"Amelie, the one who wore her hair in a twist."

"The one who wouldn't go out with you?"

"How did you know?"

"ESP?" Her eyes twinkled.

"More likely you heard me asking her on the phone."

"I walked in when you said, 'Maybe some other time, Amelie,' but I knew by your tone, you didn't believe it."

And it was a good thing that she hadn't, because his real girlfriend had come up from Toulouse, and although Aurora was not jealous, she wouldn't have liked him dating someone else, no matter how casually.

He put down his empty wineglass. "I think I'll go to my room."

Alexander occupied the second bedroom in the small house, but he wanted to shower off the dust from the dig before flopping on the bed to try and forget the day. The cool water washed away the dirt, but none of his emotions. Relationships were complicated, he decided, wishing that everyone would be more supportive of what he wanted for himself and in return he would support what they wanted. The closest thing he had found like that was his aunt Lillian.

Wrapping a towel around his waist in case his aunt was lurking in the hall, he dashed back to his room. She may have diapered him, but that didn't mean he should expose himself now.

The more he had learned about Amelie, the more he was glad that she didn't go out with him the second night he was on the dig or any other night. It didn't take him long to see she was after Luca, and he suspected they had slept together just by her body language. Sometimes she would flirt with him and the first couple of times it had given him hope. Then he realized that she only did it when Luca was watching, as if to make him jealous. Then he'd met up with Aurora, whom he had gone with for three years, and getting back together with her had felt right. Okay, another reason that maybe the summer wasn't a total bummer.

The word *bitch* would probably define Amelie, but that didn't mean that she should be murdered.

He didn't want to go back to the dig. He didn't want to go back to business school in the fall. And most of all he didn't want to confront his father on what he was planning to do with his future.

CHAPTER 14

"For God's sake Luca, stop pacing. Rima will have an indentation in her floor when she gets back if you keep this up." Annie was lying on the couch trying to watch the news on TF1. She was wearing shorts and a T-shirt. A thundershower had broken the *canicule*. They did not need the fan this evening: it still was warm, just not heat-wave hot.

"We need to get back to the dig."

"Pacing won't help make the police release the site any faster."

"I know. I just hate not being able to make any progress."

"Don't you care that they find Amelie's killer?"

He ran his hands through his hair. "Of course I care. But us not being on the dig won't bring her back."

For a minute Annie thought Luca was callous at best. The idea he might have killed Amelie flashed through her mind, but then she eliminated it and chided herself. From their time together, short though it may have been, she knew he was too gentle to kill. "Do you want to go out someplace to take your mind off this? A movie? Café? Walk along the Seine, where you have a path to wear down?"

Annie's phone croaked. Since Luca was near her purse, he reached in and handed it to her. "Maybe someday you'll put in a normal tone."

She made a face. *"Hallo?"*

"C'est moi, Gaëlle."

Annie used the remote to lower the TV volume. "Hi, sweetie.

What can I do for you?"

"Still mad at Papa?"

"If I answer that you'll feel like you're in the middle."

"No, I won't. What I want is to come and spend the July Fourteenth weekend with you in Paris. Can I?"

Annie would like nothing better, but she didn't want to cross Roger's wishes. "What does your father say?"

"He says it is up to you."

Annie did not want to talk with Roger, but she had to make sure Gaëlle wasn't doing one of those Papa-says-it's-okay-if-you-say-it's-okay-Annie-Annie-says-it's-okay-if-you-say-it's-okay-Papa moves. They had only caught her doing it a couple of times, but Gaëlle might be counting on their fight to play one off against the other. Not that Annie would blame her. In the teenager's place she would have tried it herself. "Is your father there?"

"Hello Annie." Roger's voice was cold. "This wasn't my idea."

"It's okay with me: I'd love to see Gaëlle."

"I'll put her back on the phone. Take care of yourself, Annie," Roger said.

Gaëlle spoke breathlessly. "*Merci, merci, merci.* I've already checked the schedule and I can be there on the eleventh at about 15:47. Gare du Lyon?"

"Did you already buy your ticket?"

"*Oui.*"

Annie laughed that the girl knew her well enough to know that she would say yes, although tickets were refundable.

When she got off the phone, she turned to Luca. "My non-future stepdaughter will be with us from the eleventh for a few days."

"And if we get back on the dig, does that mean you'll take the time off?"

"We can't work on the fourteenth anyway. I bet Gaëlle would

love to be part of the dig, so you might think of her as extra hands."

He looked around the tiny flat. "Where will she sleep?"

"Rima has an inflatable mattress somewhere. I hope your lungs are in good shape. She doesn't have a pump."

"I blew up a lot of balloons for the boys' birthdays, but a mattress?"

"We can take turns and it fits in the kitchen or on the floor of my room."

Luca groaned. "I'm jealous. I tried to see if Crystal would let me have the boys for the holiday weekend."

"And . . ."

"She's taken them to her mother's in Toulouse, then shipping them off to holiday camp for the rest of the summer."

Annie used the remote to shut off the news. "So let's talk about you. Did you sleep with Amelie?"

"A little bit."

"Luca!"

"It was her idea. And it was after Crystal threw me out." He reached for his shirt. "Maybe we should go out for a beer. Or I'll treat you to a kir royale."

Annie changed into a long peasant skirt and blouse belonging to Rima, which she must remember to wash and iron. She knew her friend wouldn't mind. When they lived in opposite flats back in Geneva, they often exchanged clothes, food, books and anything else that wasn't tacked down.

A sidewalk café, not too far from the flat, was set up in front of the city hall and flanked by green lawns, fountains and a kid's playground. Pop music was piped out of the stand serving as a bar, but it was too soft to make out the lyrics and the singer.

After the waitress had brought their drinks Annie asked, "Do you want a divorce?"

He picked up his glass and held it until Annie touched her kir royale to his. "*Santé.* You didn't answer my question?"

"We tried counseling."

"And . . ."

He shrugged. "I don't love her. Too many years of her constant jealousy and temper tantrums over my imagined affairs are enough to kill any marriage."

"Luca . . . you cheated on her."

"*Not* in the beginning. Well, the very beginning."

Annie didn't want to ask how long the "very beginning" was. A week? A month? Six months?

He took a long drink of his beer. "Why do you insist on talking about it?"

"Because you're my friend and I want to help."

At that moment a woman stepped up onto a small bandstand that Annie hadn't noticed. A man sat down at a white upright piano. The woman wore a red dress with a deliberately uneven hem. There was no doubt about the curves underneath. Her black, black hair was cut in a Dutch-boy style. *"Bienvenue pour une soirée de la musique de Jacques Brel et George Brassens."* The pianist struck up the first chords of *"Quand on a que l'amour."*

When she finished Annie said, "That's appropriate . . . if you only have love."

Luca took another drink of his beer.

The singer went into *"Ne me quittes pas."*

Luca broke into laughter. "Don't say it." When Annie cocked her head, he added, "Songs are not prophetic. Unless . . . unless they are telling me that you and I should get together."

"Luca, cut it out."

"No, think about it. You and Roger have broken up. Crystal and I are finished. We have similar interests. We were good together years ago."

Annie almost said, "Until you cheated on me." Instead, she

said, "I suppose you don't believe that when you break up with someone you need time to recover."

"There's also the school of thought that when you fall off a horse, you get back on." He leaned across the table and kissed her. She returned the kiss.

"Let's go home." As he paid the bill, Gaëlle flashed into her mind. When the girl came, Luca would not be in her bed. Maybe not even tonight.

As they walked back, Luca had his arm over her shoulder. Annie realized that she had not slept with anyone but Roger for four years. Even when they had separated before, she had resisted offers. This time, however, she felt that she and Roger were truly finished and she needed to move on. Luca was definitely not her future, but for tonight he would be her present.

CHAPTER 15

Fontfroide, France, 1305

Jacques Fournier twisted in his sleep. The rough wool blanket, which made his skin itch but kept the chill away, had slipped to the floor. Rather than reach for it, he curled into a ball with his knees over one side of his bed and his rear protruding over the other. He did not stay still but thrashed through his reoccurring nightmare, an arm shooting out or a foot kicking the air.

The nightmares had started when he was sixteen, the day his uncle had arrived at Boulbonne. Every few nights he woke in terror. He told no one. The details were not frightening during the day. In the dark they left him shaking. They'll disappear when I'm at Fontfroide, he'd told himself.

Then he arrived at Fontfroide. If it were possible to fall in love with a place, Jacques Fournier had fallen in love with the abbey, from its twenty-five barns holding cows and goats that gave milk to feed the monks to its vineyards providing the communion wine.

The only part he didn't love was the dormitory where he slept with the other monks. It was neither the uncomfortable bed nor the snoring, but the thought that his body would betray him by expelling fluid that showed sexual pleasure. He wanted to touch himself, but he was able to forgo lust. Priests and monks had to be pure. This had not happened before he'd gone home, but now images of his childhood friends' wives with their breasts, swaying hips and female smells haunted him.

He regretted there was less physical work at Fontfroide because lay brothers did most of the farmwork. Exhaustion could quell sinful thoughts. Physical work had kept him thin: now his regained weight brought back memories of his fat childhood.

What brought him joy was his time in the library reading the words of the great philosophers, studying his Greek, Latin, Hebrew and Aramaic. He absorbed the beautiful sentences the same way soft cloth absorbed water. Even the pagan Romans and Greeks put together words that made his heart sing. God forgive him for his sin of pride for his ease in learning.

If he suffered pride, he also confessed his jealousy regularly to his rival Jean de Beaune, the son of a noble family whose mind was as sharp as Jacques's. Despite the required silent times, they tried to best each other. More than once Uncle Arnaud chastised them both equally, assigning them prayers to be said as they lay prone on the cold chapel floor. Even then they tried to out-pray each other.

The nightmare had happened less often in the four years he'd lived in Fontfroide. The weekly appearances became monthly until he no longer thought of it—until now. Jacques sat straight up in bed. Snores almost drowned out the rain battering the roof. Below in the kitchen next to the refectory, he heard pots and pans clang as lay brothers prepared the first meal of the day. Why had the nightmare come back? What had he done wrong?

No point in going back to sleep. At any minute the first prayer bells of the day would ring. If there had been any light in the room, he would have been able to see his breath. The cold didn't bother him. It was the dream, the nightmare, in which he had to abandon monastic life. It was the same as the last time: the details were as familiar as the rosary: Uncle Arnaud summoned him and without words showed him the door, locking the gate behind him. Jacques pounded on the gate, grabbed the rope to the summoning bell. When he pulled it, the clapper fell to the ground.

Others would come, ring it and the bell sounded clear. The newcomers would gain admittance, but if Jacques tried to push through the gate, it slammed in his face.

He tried other monasteries but they too barred him saying he wasn't good enough. As he waited for the others to wake, he tried to put the dream out of his mind.

Today was his twenty-first birthday. He had almost forgotten. Birthdays were not celebrated. He kept track of dates the same way he memorized verbs and declensions in other languages. He'd memorized the entire Bible in Latin.

This day evolved like every other: he made his bed without a wrinkle, splashed water on his face and joined his brothers for first prayers. Breakfast at the refectory was fresh-baked bread and a bowl of milk eaten while a brother read the first daily lesson.

His physical hunger and soul satisfied, Jacques went to the library to work on a fragment sent from Lyon to see if the Fontfroide monks, who were famous for their scholarship, could decipher it. The words were Aramaic and told of a man wanted for causing an uprising in the temple. It was his job to prove that it wasn't Christ. The man described couldn't be his Lord. Christ was beautiful, but the man was described as hunchbacked, dark and ugly to a point that people shut their eyes lest he mesmerize them with what were described as eyes that penetrated their souls. His speeches were not unlike some that Christ made, but not identical. The problem with fragments is that the sources were impossible to establish as were the motives of the writers.

If the authorities were searching for Christ in the fragment, wouldn't it be written in Latin not Aramaic? Still the ancient letters swam in front of his eyes. He touched the parchment. Amazing that it had existed at about the same time his Lord, Jesus Christ, had walked the earth. Maybe Christ had touched it, walked by it. That was too much fantasy. He dipped his pen into the ink to write his report to send to Lyon.

Jean de Beaune sat next to him translating a Greek text into Latin. When he concentrated his tongue escaped the corner of his mouth. Jean insisted on finding exactly the right word, the most beautiful. His translations flowed in a way that Jacques's never would. Jean's words carried the heart and soul of the original. Jacques's were dull.

A knock at the library door caused both men to look up. A lay brother, new to the monastery and not yet a teenager, entered. His teeth overlapped making him look foolish. "The abbot wants to see you."

"Which one of us?" de Beaune asked.

"Whichever one is Jacques?"

"You must have done something wrong," de Beaune said.

"Which will give you great pleasure."

On the way to his uncle's office Jacques wondered if he had overlooked something that he could be reprimanded for. That he was the nephew of the abbot gave him no relief. In fact, Uncle Arnaud was quicker to punish him than the others. Perhaps it would be a comment on his birthday.

Jacques knocked.

"Enter." Uncle Arnaud stood behind the table that served as his desk. Its legs, the size of tree trunks, had been carved to show the tortures of hell: demons, their faces distorted, hacked at the sinners with axes. Wood flames burned bodies without consuming them.

Uncle Arnaud turned toward his nephew. "Jacques, you're leaving Fontfroide."

Jacques sunk to the stool in front of the table. What could he have done to be banished? "Is this a joke?"

"No joke, I assure you." The eyes weren't cold but warm, much like his sister's, Jacques's mother.

"What have I done to displease you? In God's and all the saints' names please, please tell me." Jacques debated kneeling in front of his uncle, but he could not trust himself to move. He could hear the gate shut. He imagined ringing a bell that made no sound.

Uncle Arnaud smiled. "You've done nothing wrong. Remember I promised your mother I would guide your career. You're like my own son spiritually and emotionally."

Jacques wasn't sure where his uncle stopped and his abbot began. His voice shook. "You've done well, Uncle Arnaud. You've been my father confessor, but I go back to the original question. How have I offended you to banish me?" Christ pleading to God on the cross could not have been more sincere, Jacques thought, then feared, he would have to confess for putting his problem on the same level as the Lord's.

Uncle Arnaud crossed the short span from behind the table to the stool where his nephew sat. "It's not what you've done, it's what we want you to do."

"We?"

"Before I tell you how I reached this decision, let me say you're going to Paris to study theology. It's a great honor."

Jacques grappled for words to express his appreciation for all his uncle's backing while refusing to go without showing ingratitude. He stood and paced as much as he could within the limited space, his leather sandals silent on the thick red rug, the only rug in the monastery. "I don't want to leave."

"That is not your choice."

The more he tried to convince his uncle to let him stay, the more Uncle Arnaud insisted and the more Jacques heard his dream gate lock behind him. Arnaud came up to his nephew, now a full head taller, and pushed him down on the stool. His morning breath was stale. "You are acting like you think that I awoke this morning and said to myself, 'Let's send Jacques to Paris.' "

"I only know you want to throw me out."

Arnaud looked heavenward as if God would transmit a message on how to handle this.

Jacques knew his uncle could order him out, lock the door and he would be on his way, Bible and baggage. By resisting he was breaking his vow of obedience.

"Consider this, Jacques. Your Latin is perfect, your Greek wonderful. You know Aramaic as well as three French dialects all without fault. Your theology has surpassed that of your teachers, the ultimate compliment for a student. Yet . . . yet your mind has not reached its limits."

Jacques felt his face warm. Compliments were not something he received. No one said, "You prayed extra well today."

"That's not the only reason. The other is based on a dream."

A dream? A dream? He would live his nightmare for someone else's dream? Decisions by dreams were for uneducated peasants, not for clerics and not for abbots. Although abbots were not required to explain their decisions to the monks under them, his uncle loaded his decisions with more facts than were needed. Once his uncle had said, "Although unquestioning obedience is good, informed obedience is even better. Remember that Jacques, when you become an abbot."

Jacques had no ambition to become an abbot, but he resisted saying that.

Uncle Arnaud returned to his stool behind his table and folded his hands over his stomach, a sign he was going to go off on a tangent. Jacques resisted the urge to shake him.

"I don't have to tell you why our Cistercian order was

founded by Saint Jean-Paul de Clarvaux almost two hundred years ago."

Uncle Arnaud often told people what he didn't have to tell them. Jacques thought maybe he could shorten the lecture. "He wanted to rectify the sins that existed in . . ."

". . . he wanted to rectify the sins that existed in the abbeys. It was on his visit here that Fontfroide became Cistercian."

Jacques listened again to the monastery's history, when each building had been constructed, how each abbot had been selected. When his uncle paused for breath, he tried to interrupt. "I don't understand what this has to do with my exile to Paris."

"Jacques, Jacques. It's about temptation. You were prepared for the priesthood from the moment of your birth. It's easy to be godly if evil has never tested you."

Jacques opened his mouth then shut it then opened it. "Are you suggesting I find what the devil has on offer?"

Arnaud shook his head. "Well, yes; not quite in the way you asked the question, however." He waved his hand as if to sweep the suggestion into its own oblivion.

"Let me tell my dream. Actually there were three. All were quite similar. They started about a year ago. The devil kept drawing you away from the Church. You were in Paris. Like all dreams, some of the small details faded with the morning. However, the important thing is you won the battle. The encounter strengthened your faith."

Jacques had no idea what to say.

"Therefore, we decided to send you to Paris."

"We?"

"Remember Jacques de Voye de Cahors?"

The name was familiar. A visit from someone to his home in Saverdun when he was six. His mother had rushed out to buy lamb from the butcher to prepare a better meal than the soup she had planned for the family. "Isn't he a third cousin on my mother's side?"

"One and the same."

"He's a priest at . . . at . . ."

"Cahors still. Only he's now a bishop. We met last month and discussed how you can best serve the Church. Your brilliant mind, and it's the best mind I've ever encountered, cannot be adequately fed here. You must go to Paris for your mind and more importantly for your soul."

Paris: another city, another world. "I want to stay."

"There's more to being God's representative on earth than hiding behind walls. Now leave me alone."

The topic remained buried for several days. Jacques continued his library work, but he was so lacking in concentration that he asked to be assigned to cleaning out stables, which left him so physically exhausted that it was the only night he slept through since the confrontation with his uncle.

The next week his uncle summoned him. One foot was not in the door before he was asked if his nephew had changed his mind. Jacques said no.

"Go meditate rather than work outside. And wash. You stink of horse manure."

Jacques meditated until his knees ached. His prayers asked for understanding of what was being demanded of him. Why was he being denied the role of contemplative? The scholar? To punish himself he slept on the floor.

The songs from the chapel woke the rooster who crowed his displeasure. Jacques sympathized with the bird. The idea of the unhappy rooster stayed with him at breakfast. The bird followed nature's rules in the same way monks followed Saint Benedict's. As he ate his porridge, he tried to listen to the reader drone the lesson. The topic was The Rule guiding the abbey each moment of the day. Unlike the rooster, Jacques could select to break The

Rule. The rooster would never wake and not crow.

Later he entered the library. On his bench was the slate he used to write out phrases before committing them to parchment. He scratched the words:

Your wish is mine.

J

He carried the slate to his uncle's unlocked office and placed it in the middle of the table where his uncle would find it when he entered.

CHAPTER 16

For the hundredth time, Marie-Claude Du Pont was looking through the evidence gathered at the dig, hoping she would see something that she had missed before. There wasn't much besides the body: no fingerprints other than those on the dig, no witnesses, nothing that stood out. The key used to lock the body in the shed had disappeared. The murder weapon was probably in the Seine by now. How she despised cases like this.

The worst part was still ahead of her. She had to inform the victim's mother, but each time she'd tried, there was no one home.

Staying in the station wasn't getting her anywhere. She wanted to talk with those on the dig again. She traced down the man that had bolted, although she had to call the leader of the dig to get the address, in a run-down section of Aulnay-sous-bois, thirteen kilometers northeast from the center of Paris.

The area was relatively calm now, but in 2005 riots had broken out. Philippe lived neither in the more run-down sections nor the area where the upper-middle class made their homes on tree-lined streets. The entrance to the apartment building had not seen a new coat of paint for several decades. One look at the elevator and she decided to walk up the three flights of what once might have been an elegant staircase. The carpet on the staircase was clean but ragged.

She found Philippe in his studio flat with only a bed, table and two chairs. A board, resting on a sawhorse, held a hot plate next to an antique soapstone sink. A door probably led to a toilet. Philippe sank back on his bed. She guessed he was nursing a hangover based on his smell. She also guessed that the other man in the room, who was probably in his thirties and dressed in ironed khakis and a short-sleeved blue shirt, might be Philippe's AA sponsor.

Her guess was right. Philippe introduced the man. "This is Etienne Bonnet, my AA sponsor."

So much for the anonymous part of AA, Marie-Claude thought. When Etienne offered to leave, Philippe had said he might as well stay since he had nothing to hide from Etienne: however, he had nothing to offer Madame Du Pont either.

The more they talked the more Marie-Claude wrote Philippe off as an alcoholic trying to fight his way back, but too ineffectual to kill. He had an alibi. After he left the site, he had helped another neighbor look for her missing cat. The neighbor came in with the cat in her arms and verified the story. It put Philippe back in his neighborhood before Amelie could have been shot.

"What did you think of Amelie?" Marie-Claude asked after the neighbor and cat disappeared back to their own apartment.

"A spoiled brat with the hots for Luca." When Marie-Claude frowned, he added, "I'm sorry she was murdered. I'm sorry her life was cut short, but I've seen so many young women like her. Predatory."

Misogynist flashed through her mind.

"Take Jacqueline and Laure. They were both serious about the work. They'll make good archeologists, and I've nothing but respect for them."

Okay, maybe not a misogynist, Marie-Claude reassessed her earlier opinion. "And Annie Young?"

"Speaks amazing French, especially for an American, even if she does have a Swiss accent, but I didn't get much chance to know her. She'd only just arrived and spent most of the day in the shed catching up on the backlog of documentation."

Marie-Claude headed back to 36. No sooner had she settled down with a cup of coffee, when her telephone rang. It was two of the three young women from the dig asking if they could talk to her.

"Do you want to meet me, or should I come to you?" If they had evidence to give, the police station might be intimidating. If they were on their own territory, they might be more forthcoming. "Hey Gilles, come with me."

The only other detective in the room looked up. "Sure, *Patronne.*"

Finding parking in the Marais was always a challenge. Even with police rights she couldn't leave the cruiser in the middle of the street, but she could pull it up on the sidewalk.

Marie-Claude and Gilles found Jacqueline and Laure sitting at a table belonging to Le Petit Prince tearoom, with a drawing of the Saint-Exupéry character on the window. They had been walking by when Marie-Claude recognized the two young women. The tearoom was new and didn't seem to fit into the neighborhood. The women were dressed in jeans and T-shirts. They stood and shook the detectives' hands before pushing two tables together.

Since she hadn't had time for breakfast in her rush to get her son to the crèche, she ordered a *petit déjeuner* of a *tartine,* orange juice and coffee. Gilles only wanted coffee.

"I imagine you'll be glad to get back to work," Marie-Claude said.

"A lot of the work is tedious: it's the hope of finding something that keeps us going," Jacqueline said. "When will the site be cleared?"

"I'm going to release it this afternoon. You may want to check in with your boss."

The waitress brought their food and coffee.

Marie-Claude waited for the girls who fidgeted in their seats to say something. When they didn't she asked, "Were you close to Amelie?" They had told her they had shared a flat in Montpellier.

"How do you mean close?" Laure spoke.

"Good friends, do a lot of stuff together, go shopping, et cetera," Marie-Claude said.

Jacqueline and Laure looked at each other. Laure was the one spoke. "We didn't really like her all that much. When she told us at the end of the school year she was going to get an apartment by herself next year, we were glad."

"We wouldn't have asked her to leave or anything," Jacqueline said. "It's hard to explain, but she didn't fit in. We've had other roommates that have worked out better."

"It's nothing specific, but there's something else you might want to consider."

Marie-Claude said nothing.

"We think she might have been sleeping with Luca."

"Why do you think that?"

"Amelie had a certain way about her when she was with a man or wanted one. It was more than flirting. She found excuses to be in the shed with the door closed," Jacqueline said.

"But to be fair to Luca, whenever she closed the door, Luca opened it fairly quickly," Laure said.

"So you think that, maybe, Luca wasn't as interested in her as she was with him?" Gilles spoke for the first time.

"Or he wanted to keep an affair a secret. I don't know it as a fact, but I think he's separated from his wife."

Marie-Claude already knew that. The American girl had told Marie-Claude that, but obviously he hadn't shared the information with the rest of his team. It might be worthwhile to do a

DNA test just in case he was the father of the baby. "Did you know Amelie was pregnant?" By their reaction, Marie-Claude knew they had not.

CHAPTER 17

The light streaming through the window woke Philippe. He was still slightly drunk. He reached for the bottle next to his bed. Empty. As were three others. Oh, God, how long had it been: two, three days? The alcoholic haze had been so wonderful after his weeks of sobriety: the letting go: the not caring about anything.

Poor Etienne. Philippe had lied to him when he told his sponsor that he would be all right. His sponsor was good. He worked the AA program. But right now, Philippe didn't want the sharpness of not having alcohol in his system.

He was close enough to being sober to realize that his room stank of sweat and absinthe where the last remains of a bottle had spilled on the floor. He would have to get up and go out for more if he wanted to continue in the haze.

He reached into the pocket of his pants that he was still wearing. The bracelet? Had he lost the bracelet?

Staggering out of bed he went over to the table, the only other piece of furniture besides the chairs and bed in the room. Such a contrast to when he was married, and he and his wife owned a nice three-bedroom flat: one for them, one for his son whom he hadn't seen in years, and one for his library/office filled with books and CDs. His wife had furnished it with antiques she'd culled from various dealers.

Maybe she still lived there.

Maybe she'd remarried.

Maybe his son called the new husband Papa.

None of that mattered. It was all in the past.

His pocketbook, keys, phone, change and the bracelet were on the board next to his hot plate. The room was stifling. He wanted to throw up until he realized that he had already done so, earlier, into a wastepaper basket, and he had to force himself not to vomit again.

The ring of his cell phone pierced his brain. He didn't get many calls, but he had needed the phone when he had been trying to get work, just like he had needed this address, which was one room in a run-down building with its ethnic street gangs of out-of-work kids roaming the street. But compared to the streets where he had been for over a year, it was pretty damned good.

"*Hallo?*"

"Philippe, I'm glad to get you. I tried last night but there was no answer."

"Luca?"

"Who else? We're back on the site. How soon can you get over here?"

Philippe realized that if he showed up, still half drunk and stinking of vomit, this job, probably the last job he would ever be able to get, would be over. How many days had he been drunk? "I made a dentist appointment for this morning. A bit of a toothache. This afternoon?"

"You don't sound so great."

"I took some codeine to kill the pain." Philippe had never lost his ability to lie about his drinking to his parents, to his ex-wife, to his former colleagues. Only sooner or later, they saw through the lies.

"Well, get here when you can. We've gotta make up for lost time."

"I will."

He shut the phone and sank back on the bed. His watch said it was 10:29. God, he wanted a drink. He opened the phone and called his sponsor.

"Philippe? Philippe? Are you in there?" The knocking on the door roused Philippe for the second time that morning. He glanced at his watch: 12:28. Two hours since he'd called Etienne Bonnet. He got up and opened the door.

Etienne stood there dressed in a blue shirt and gray slacks. He looked like the *notaire* that he was. "It's a good thing for you that I didn't have any closings today, and even better that I wasn't on my way to the mountains for a hike." Since becoming sober, Etienne had taken to long walks in the mountains. He was determined to undo some of the damage he'd done to his body with his own drinking that had cost him his marriage and almost his partnership in the firm where he worked. His partners, however, were the ones who had sent him off to a clinic to dry him out. "When did you have your last drink?"

"I'm not sure."

Etienne picked up the absinthe bottles and threw them in the wastepaper basket with the vomit. "Okay, this is going out."

"I need to get to work." Philippe's eyes landed on the bracelet. Etienne would have no idea that he had stolen it. He only wished he knew why he had.

"The site is open again, I know."

"How?"

"It was on TF1's *JT*. Claire Chazel reported on it. Let's face it, a pretty young student volunteer murdered . . . it would make the news."

Etienne pulled clean underwear, slacks and a T-shirt from where they were piled by the only window. "You need a shower."

When he wasn't drinking, Philippe had a great sense of order.

"It's a good thing you don't have to dress up for your job."

Philippe nodded. "What day is it?"

"Friday."

"Merde." He had been drunk since Tuesday. No wonder he felt like shit. The saddest part was he wanted to drink himself unconscious again. That would block out the sight of Amelie's body with the red stain across her chest. He couldn't pretend that he'd liked the girl. She'd mocked him more than once. Before he could think anymore, his sponsor propelled him down the hall into the shower. He would need to get through today. Tomorrow? Tomorrow was another day.

CHAPTER 18

Fontfroide, France, 1305

Jacques's first chore was to buy a horse. His uncle directed him to the nearest horse fair and pressed silver *deniers* in his hands. The coins felt cold. Jacques look at them and realized that he hadn't held a coin since he left his family's home. The abbey protected him from base coin.

He walked to the field where the horse fair was being held. How strange to be in the open with no walls to direct his prayers upward to heaven. The spring sun warmed the field wet from the showers the night before. Mud oozed through the toes of his sandals. About fifty horses, munching on clover, were tethered in the meadow. Buttercups, white laces and poppies had been trampled by hooves and human feet. A buzz of conversation was all around as animal owners swapped news and exchanged insults in between answering buyers' questions.

Jacques wandered between the beasts. He didn't know what he was looking for. His father never bought a horse, only rented them when needed. One animal looked too small, another too big: one seemed friendly, another too old. The one he liked, as much as it was possible for him to like a horse, was too expensive.

Traders tried to convince him of their animals' merits, pointing out teeth, legs. It meant nothing to him. He could recognize something well written or badly written, but he had no idea of what made up a quality mount. In the abbey he did not make choices, not even something as simple as when to go to bed. Everything was prescribed by The Rule. No Rule existed for horse buying.

By midday only ten horses were left. He found a dapple mare, but kept comparing her to others. When he went to purchase her, another man was leading her away.

Back at the abbey, he told his uncle the horses were too old or too costly. When his uncle cocked his head, he confessed, "That's not entirely true. I couldn't decide."

His uncle laughed. "Not a surprise, my boy. Things will get easier when you mix with common folk regularly. I've another idea for your trip to Paris, but I need to make arrangements."

Uncle Arnaud said nothing more for a week. Then he told Jacques to go to the laundry and gather clothing and bed for his trip to start the next morning.

It's happening too soon, Jacques thought as he fell asleep. His nightmare came back: he could feel the rough bell rope in his hand and smell his uncle's fetid breath.

The next morning he stood at the gate with his meager belongings wrapped in a cloth. A purse full of coins was tied at his waist under his clothes to trick the robbers he'd been warned about. It was the money for all next year. The following year more would be sent to the abbey at Royaumont outside Paris for him to retrieve. His uncle said fees had been paid in advance, but he could change professors if he wished to do the necessary negotiations, but that he hoped Jacques would follow his advice on whom to study with.

As he waited for the carter with whom he would ride, one by one the monks came to bid him good-bye. Jean de Beaune was the only one to speak. "I'll miss our debates, Brother."

His uncle wished him luck, reentered the gate and locked it. Jacques looked at the bell as the carter drove up, his cart filled with pots, pans, casks of wine and bits and pieces of furniture to sell along the way. He was maybe Jacques's age, but his skin was leathery from time spent riding in the sun. His hair stuck out in all directions: his beard was patchy. He hopped out of the cart to grab Jacques's bundle. "I'm Robert."

Jacques mounted the wooden bench next to the driver's place. "Wait." He jumped down and rang the bell. It pealed loudly. His uncle, who had almost reached the abbey's entrance, came back, a curious expression on his face.

"I just wanted to thank you, Uncle."

It took Jacques only minutes to discover why even a mortally wounded knight would prefer to die in a field rather than spend his last minutes living in a moving cart. Jacques, although used to dull meals, icy stone pressing against his knees, was not prepared for the bouncing and jostling. The backs of his legs were battered by a beer keg that kept rolling under the seat.

Robert looked over. "If you think this is bad, wait until we get to the rough roads."

The cart was pulled by two horses which Robert had named *Pferd* and *Scheiss*, German for horse and shit, Robert told him. Although Jacques did not know German, he had no reason to doubt the man. Neither did he doubt that the next two weeks of being thrown from side to side would be miserable. Robert was not going directly to Paris, but hither and yon to visit customers. Jacques decided to make the best of it. Somehow this was God's will to make him miserable: who was he to question God?

In talking with Robert, he discovered a good person, a bit chatty after the silent abbey. Robert jumped from topic to topic, story to story, song to song until Jacques felt his brain spin. Since a grunt was a response that satisfied Robert, Jacques was grateful he did not have to come up with comments on everything Robert said.

Over the first three days Jacques met other passengers: a farmer, a milkmaid, a miller and another priest. Whoever hitched a ride jumped on for whatever distance they needed before hopping off with a farewell wave. The fare could be a coin, a few cooked eggs, a carrot. A woman pilgrim was with them for two days and told of traveling shrine to shrine to do penance for sleeping with her neighbor. Her confession was said in the same tone as if she'd said, "I baked bread or did laundry."

At Robert's request, Jacques had changed his monk's frock for normal stockings and tunic. "A monk is too attractive for a robber," was the reason the carter gave. "They think all Cistercians are rich."

When Robert, Jacques and the adulteress settled on pallets for the night, he wondered if husbands were more forgiving of adultery than God. She lay between Robert and himself. She was neither beautiful nor ugly: she had most of her teeth, her skin was smooth, her nose large. Her giggle flowed at Robert's jokes, none of which Jacques found amusing. Her blouse was open to reveal a nipple. Jacques looked away saying a prayer as his penis stiffened. She is not the only sinner, he thought.

Every place they stopped, people greeted Robert as if he were one of them. "That's 'cause I treat my customers right. Never cheat 'em. If they ask for something I don't have, I'll make sure I bring it next time." He reached into his pocket for a wax tablet on which he would sketch the desired item. The man was a good artist. Next to the item he would add something to remind him of the customer: a crutch for a lame woman, a hook for a shoemaker.

As for the route, Robert knew it by heart. "Done this hundreds of times. Start out in Toulouse, stop at Carcassonne, up the coast through Avignon to Lyon, Dijon then Paris."

Avignon was the largest city Jacques had ever seen. Mutilated and wretched creatures, barely human, begged for a crust of bread or a coin. In Saverdun no one ever let someone go hungry. Knowing his coins must last a year or he'd be begging himself, Jacques ignored them. At night he prayed to God for forgiveness at his mean-spiritedness.

When they left a *boulangerie*, a little girl, who reminded him of his sister, looked at him with huge eyes. She was barefoot, her hair in tangles hanging down over her dirty face. She could have been his sister. Jacques broke half his baguette and gave it to her. Without a *merci*, she grabbed it and ran away.

"Good-for-nothings," Robert said when Jacques said at least he'd put something in her stomach. "She probably took it to her mother or father who will eat it all and not give her any."

As they drew closer to Paris they circled the city ending up north of their destination instead of entering from the southeast. Being so close, and yet delayed, annoyed Jacques which Robert brushed aside. "You're going to be here a long time. Whatsa couple of days?"

When it was clear that he would be on the road one more night, Jacques insisted on a comfortable bed. He was tired of the ground or an inn where fleas left him scratching the next day. At the Abbey of Saint Denis dedicated to the patron saint of the village of the same name, the abbot was happy to put them up. Jacques insisted they go to morning Mass. Robert muttered about the problem with religious passengers. "It's good for your soul," Jacques said.

"My soul's fine, thank you." Robert hitched *Pferd* and *Scheiss* to the cart. A light wind ruffled their manes. The cart was empty. The last clay pot had been sold to some woman walking by the abbey.

As they rode toward Paris, Robert chattered as usual. "We've got two roads, dontcha know. The Route Saint Martin is paved, the other . . ."

"Take the paved." He saw two roads so close together and asked why.

Robert shrugged. "Who knows? Someone told me they were both built by Romans."

They passed an orchard full of spring cherries. "Stop." Jacques got out of the cart, picked a handful and got back into the cart.

"They belong to King Philippe," Robert said.

"They belong to God," Jacques said.

Robert flashed a smile. "Our trip has been good for ya. Ya were sourer than a lemon when we started out. Now ya steal cherries."

As they got closer to the city, the smell of the fields and flowering orchards gave way to the stench of too many people living too closely together. Robert pointed out a leper hospital, but that was not the source of the smell. Garbage and human waste were everywhere.

"We'll cross at Le Grand Pont, the main bridge," Robert said. Mills operated under the bridge. Jacques thought he should write his father and tell him about the mills.

The word bridge was an understatement. The edifice was almost a village onto itself. Little houses dotted both sides. Jacques worried the bridge would collapse under the weight of it all.

Men and women were busy convincing walkers and riders to buy, buy, buy whatever they had to sell from clothes, food, trinkets or household items. Robert loaded up on merchandise, negotiating them down to prices his own clients would pay while still leaving him a healthy profit. He used his slate and checked off the things that people wanted.

At the end of the bridge, a toll keeper stood outside a hut demanding money from the line of people waiting to enter the city. When Robert paid, the toll keeper turned it over several times, held it to the light, then motioned them on.

Jacques's head was spinning from the smells, noise and numbers of people. Paris made Avignon look like a village in comparison, and he had thought it was such a big city only a week or so ago.

Another five minutes and Robert stopped the cart. "Brother Jacques. Ya're here."

Jacques took his bundle and walked off toward his future.

CHAPTER 19

Annie stood between the *brasserie* called Le Train Bleu and the tracks where the trains arrived. Had the sleek white TGVs morphed into steam engines, she felt she would be in an impressionist painting. As it was, she thought were the impressionists alive now, they would be painting the TGVs. It didn't matter that she was at the Gare du Lyon and Monet had painted at the Gare Saint Lazare.

The arrival board said the trains were on time. No *grèves* had been called either stopping or delaying the trains as the unions argued for this or that advantage. A disadvantage to living in France was that some group or another was always on strike. At the same time, she admired the ability of the workers not to give in to bad working conditions, a concept she sometimes expressed through clenched teeth when her mail didn't arrive, her doctor's office was closed or other major inconvenience set her on edge.

People streamed down the *quai* pulling suitcases on wheels or lugging backpacks. One woman walked with three small dog wannabes with pointy noses and thick golden coats. One veered left, tripping a man who started screaming at the woman. Annie was so entranced with the mini-drama that she was surprised when from nowhere, someone ran into her.

"I'm here! I'm here!" Gaëlle engulfed Annie totally in her arms. "And I'm starved. Can we eat before we go to Rima's?"

Annie looked at the *brasserie* then at the stairs leading to the

Le Train Bleu's formal restaurant. Treat the girl, she thought. Gaëlle's backpack was no impediment to climbing the graceful stone staircase. The dinner hour was just beginning.

The inside was more elaborate than many palaces with its murals, gold leaf and cherubs. The maître d' seated them on a red leather banquette and gave them menus.

"Annie, can you afford this?"

"To introduce you to Paris, why not?" Annie had always wanted to eat here herself, but always had selected the cheaper *brasserie* below. "How many times do you visit me in Paris?"

The menu was ninety-eight euros, but it had *fois gras* with red marmalade, grilled turbot, raspberry sorbet in champagne to cleanse the palate and a risotto with bird's tongue and asparagus, probably the last of the season, for no restaurant of this quality would ever consider serving a vegetable that wasn't at the peak of its perfection.

Gaëlle pulled out her phone. "*Merde,* the battery's dead. I promised Papa I would call the second I found you."

Annie rummaged into her bag and handed Gaëlle her phone. "You'll have to dial it."

"You already took Papa off speed dial?"

"Call him."

Gaëlle pushed the buttons. "*Je suis arrivée,* Papa. Annie and I are eating at the Le Train Bleu. . . . Fine. . . . Fine . . . no, I didn't talk to strangers . . . she's right here . . . good, not sad at all . . . what do you mean I shouldn't have said that?"

Gaëlle winked at Annie who mouthed, "I'm going to the toilet." Maybe it was childish, but she didn't want to talk to Roger. Of course, when she went back to Argelès it would be hard to avoid him. Maybe she could spend some time at her parents' in Geneva. And then again she'd be off on some assignment soon. There was a certain pleasure in knowing that what she wanted was her only consideration for her next assignment. No worry about getting back on weekends or having a temporary residence where he could visit her with or without Gaëlle.

The food was as good as anyone could have imagined. Gaëlle tried several times to bring up her father until Annie laid down the fork.

"Look, your father and I have broken up. This time I don't think it can be fixed. Neither of us want to put you in the middle, but you are making me feel like I'm in the middle, and I don't like it. I want us to have a great couple of days together. We can see the fireworks on the fourteenth. And we're in walking distance of all the events on the Champs-Elysées."

Gaëlle moved some of her asparagus into a square and put the rice inside, making a food fort.

"You can come with me to the dig." She cocked her head waiting for Gaëlle's response.

A good two minutes passed during which Gaëlle rearranged every morsel of food on her plate. "I guess I want you to get back together."

"I know."

They each concentrated on their meals for several minutes.

"Tell me about the dig," Gaëlle said.

"We aren't sure what we have. There are lots of utensils, more than there would be for an ordinary home which is why we think it might be some kind of inn. We've tried to find out what was there in the thirteen hundreds, but the records aren't complete. In fact there are almost no records from that time in the sense they exist today. They have some old documents from the Merovingian period in 751 AD in the archives and a few bits and pieces here and there. Luca found a map of the area where the dig is from that period, but it shows buildings without any explanation of what they are."

"Luca? He's the one that made Papa mad."

"You'll meet Luca. He's at Rima's apartment because his wife threw him out."

"Are you an item?"

Annie really didn't feel like she was lying when she said no. Last night had been a comforting, one-time thingie, not the beginning of a relationship. She wasn't ready for one with anyone and certainly not with anyone as much of a womanizer as Luca, who still had a wife—even a wife that might be an ex sometime in the future, probably the far future considering the speed with which the French divorce courts moved.

"We could use an extra set of hands on the dig, because one of the volunteers was shot and killed. We've just been allowed back on the site."

"Do they know who did it?"

Annie finished the last of her risotto. At these prices she wasn't leaving a grain behind and since doggie bags didn't exist in France and certainly not in a restaurant like Le Train Bleu, she wanted her money's worth. Would Roger be upset that she would take his daughter to a murder site? Hell, the man was a *flic*. Gaëlle was used to violence. Her own mother had been killed by a man who hated her father for putting him in jail. Crime was part of her life, although murders in Argelès were rare, they did happen. "Not that they've let on."

"Tell me about the vic?"

Definitely a cop's daughter that uses slang for victim, Annie thought. And the murder did get Gaëlle's mind off the topic of her breakup with Roger.

Annie and Gaëlle arrived at the flat the same time Marie-Claude Du Pont was buzzing the intercom. Annie introduced her to Gaëlle.

"Your daughter?"

"I wouldn't mind, but she's my ex-fiancé's child. However,

she's not my ex-friend and is here for the long weekend."

"I've a son about your age," Marie-Claude said.

The three of them would not fit in the elevator together especially with Gaëlle's backpack. "I'll go up first with Gaëlle, then you Detective Du Pont, if that's all right."

Marie-Claude nodded. "Do you know if Luca Martinelli is home?"

"He wasn't there when I went to the train station to pick up Gaëlle. He mentioned he wanted to check out some old maps at the Bibliothèque National, because he couldn't find anything online that suited him." Luca should have done the research before they started the dig, but she remembered that when they were in school, his methods had not been the most organized. Because everything had been so well arranged on the dig, she'd thought he'd changed.

"I can wait."

Annie showed them into the apartment. Marie-Claude sat on the sofa while Gaëlle poked around. "So where do we all sleep?"

"The couch makes up into Luca's bed, as you can see." Annie noticed although he had slept with her last night, he'd gone to the trouble to make it look like as if he'd slept in the living room by leaving his pillows and sheets on the one chair. The man wasn't all bad. In fact he was one of those men who, just when you thought they couldn't get any worse, would do some cute little-boy trick that would appease. "I get Rima's and we have an inflatable mattress for you. It's your call whether you want to spread it out in the kitchen or next to me in the bedroom." She turned to the detective. "Can I get you anything to drink, Detective?"

"Coffee, please."

While Annie was making coffee, Annie heard Marie-Claude question the girl not only about herself, but about how she knew Annie and Luca.

"I never met Luca," Gaëlle was saying as Annie carried a tray in with coffee for them all.

The key turned in the lock and Luca came in. He looked at the three women. "You must be Gaëlle. Annie's talked a lot about you." Then he turned to Marie-Claude. "Do you have any news about Amelie?"

"We are following up on some leads. What I would like to ask you, is could you give me a swab for a DNA test?"

Luca frowned. "I could, but why?"

"There's some evidence we want to cross-check."

He shrugged. "I don't see why not. I've nothing to hide."

CHAPTER 20

Paris, France, 1305

If the world were a poem, Paris would give it meter; if it were a song, Paris would be the melody; if it were a painting Paris would add the color. Jacques had trouble believing he was capable of such eloquence in describing the city in a hundred mind-letters to his uncle that would never see paper. He was a plodder, not a poet.

Albeit, until he entered the city, he had thought of himself as a sophisticated plodder because of all of his reading: the city hid answers to questions he had not even thought to ask. With each passing day he grew more convinced that the city itself would teach him more than the men who sat in rooms doling out the wisdom of the ages. So much so, he procrastinated going to meet any of his recommended teachers, excusing his laxity with the need to acquaint himself with his surroundings before delving into his studies.

He found his own behavior so out of his character, so bizarre, he wondered if maybe an evil spirit had entered his body, but rejected the idea because nothing he was doing was evil. His body responded by rebelling to the same hours he had kept for years. His knees that once bent automatically at each hour of prayer stayed straight. His compromise was to pray silently wherever he was.

He attacked the city as a starving man attacks food. He could not believe how he had had to be pushed to come here. In his ignorance, he would have missed the greatest experience of his life. What else was he missing through ignorance?

He found temporary lodging above a stable. The owner teased him about his accent, the way he said *"oc"* for *"oui."* He followed people on the streets, listening to how they used words, then copied them. He prayed for forgiveness for his sin of pride, because within two days his ability to pick up accents eliminated anyone calling him an outsider.

His first major discovery, the first in a long list, was that the university wasn't a single entity. He had assumed he would find it in a cathedral-like building with wings to house the different disciplines. Instead it was a series of houses along the rue de la Boucherie next to the Seine and near the Saint Julian-le-Pauvre church.

Had his uncle known and forgotten to tell him about the city, or was he an innocent of Parisian ways as well? His uncle had been in Paris, Jacques was sure. He'd ask when he finally returned to Fontfroide, but the desire to rush back had disappeared. Someday he would go willingly—just not yet. Not until he finished what he'd been sent to learn.

The professors lived in their own houses and worked hard to establish their reputations. Anyone hoping to have a student following invested a great deal of money and time on entertainment and free lectures to prospective students.

Many times he passed Alexandre de Bois's, the noted theologian's house. He was to be Jacques's master teacher, preselected by his uncle. De Bois in turn would set up sample lectures with others making probably the same recommendations which had come from his uncle and that bordered on commands.

Jacques stood outside de Bois's door, knowing he should enter and introduce himself, sit on the straw-bedecked floor and begin his lessons, but for once in his adult life, he didn't want to sit and listen to words. He wanted experiences, so he walked away, telling himself that tomorrow or the next day, he would start classes—or maybe next week at the latest.

The geography of Paris confused him until he discovered the river Seine divided the city. It helped him navigate the tiny streets and alleys.

He wondered if Paris ever slept. No matter what time he was out, there was activity. Before dawn, boats landed at the Porte de Grève bringing food to the largest food market, which fed the hordes living in the city proper. Jacques watched a boatman, advanced in years, struggle with two baskets joined by a strap worn around his shoulders. Each basket was the same size as the man.

"May I help?"

"Never turn down help," the man said.

The cover fell off one of the baskets and Jacques saw that it was filled with green beans. "Do you have a shop here?"

"Against the king's law," the boatman said. "Merchants can't leave the city to buy stuff. We gotta bring it in, but we can only sell to the merchants. Even if a customer begged on his knees, it wouldn't be worth my life to say yes."

Non-monastics live by rules, too, Jacques thought. Some made sense. Some confused him. Merchants couldn't open their stalls on Saturday, but had to go to Campanelli, a field near the Porte de Paris. His first Saturday, merchants came into the stables to get horses to pull their carts early in the morning. Jacques followed. He stayed to watch families buy meats, cheeses and vegetables laid out on blankets spread on the ground.

Jacques thought it made sense that bakers couldn't fire their ovens on saints' days or Sundays, but to forbid them to bake on Saturdays made no sense. He'd seen the near riots on Friday evenings as bakers rushed to public ovens to get their bread in before the fires were extinguished until Monday. When he went to Mass on Sunday, he saw those same bakers selling their Friday bread on the steps of the church to worshippers as they left. One of his back teeth fell out after he bit into the stale loaf.

The constant motion exhausted him the first few days. He would retreat to the stable where the stable owner had said he could sleep in the hay, but he knew he couldn't stay there forever. He wandered the cobbled streets with their uneven multicolored stones and dirt paths, when he noticed a Cathedral under construction. "What will that be?" he asked a passing woman.

"Notre Dame," she said without really looking at him.

Buildings were going up everywhere. He heard that King Philippe the Fair wanted to create a sweet-smelling city of intellectual activity and beauty. The possibility of an intellectual center was certainly feasible—he doubted that sweet smelling. There were too many people and too few drains.

In his search for lodgings, he ran into a prejudice against students.

"Rowdy."

"Destructive."

"Immoral."

Parisians clucked their disapproval at him. More doors were slammed in his face than prayers which he would have said in a month. Each night he returned to the stable thinking if a stable was good enough for Christ's birth, it was good enough for him. However, telling himself and believing that he could spend his student years sleeping with horses and a black-and-white milk cow were two different things. So each morning he was up early to knock on doors along the rues de la Boucherie, de Garlance and Orléans: when he failed he widened his search. His luck matched Joseph and Mary when they entered Bethlehem.

On the fifth day, tired, hungry and discouraged, he stopped at a tavern selling meat pastries and wine. The ruby liquid was bitter, but thirst quenching. The meat was stringy and so tough he thought he would never be able to chew it long enough to swallow.

The single room, dark because the only light came from the small doorway, smelled of sour wine and beer. The man taking his order was fat, toothless and surly. His clothes held memories of many meals served over an indefinite period. Determined not to let the owner's mood further destroy his own, Jacques asked, "Good Sir, do you know where I could find a room?"

"Student?"

"Not yet, but I will be. Prior to coming here I was cloistered in a Cistercian abbey in the south."

The man spit into sawdust covering the dirt floor. "Worse. That's why you talk fancy. Fancy words don't mean nothing. Students are students. Trouble. Run out rather than pay their rent. And why do you think I should rent to you?" He leaned over and Jacques recoiled from the garlic breath.

"One reason: I would pay in advance."

The man swatted a fly that had settled on the pastries stacked on the rough, blackened bar with a filthy cloth of no discernable color. "How much ahead?"

"Three months." He suspected the man was fully capable of making a deal then throwing him out after a week, leaving him poorer than he should be.

The man threw his cloth on the bar. "Follow me."

They climbed a narrow wooden staircase. Each stair was double the height of the ones in the abbey. It was as if whoever built the house was trying to save money by putting one stair where two should go. At the top was a dark hallway, smelling no better than the tavern below. A candle might have dispelled the gloom, but the owner was unlikely to waste money on any such luxury. Jacques's eyes grew accustomed to the shadows enough to make out four doors.

"Choose one, they're all empty."

Jacques didn't say he understood the lack of paying guests. He lifted the latch to the first on the left. The doorway was so low he had to bend to enter.

The room was occupied by a girl in need of a bath. A cut ran from the corner of her eye to her snarled raven hair. Had she been clean and dressed in anything but rags she might have been pretty, beautiful even. The color of her eyes reminded Jacques of his mother, but with a major difference. His mother's eyes reflected peace. The woman-child's eyes were those of a cornered animal. Picking up a dirty blanket and clutching it to her breast, she bobbed a curtsy. "Papa, I'm through." Her voice quavered.

"Get out, ya lazy slut."

She scurried out without making eye contact.

The room itself was tiny with a straw mattress, table and stool filling it. The ceiling was so slanted Jacques could only stand up straight as far as the center. A single window had a splintered and pockmarked wooden shutter. In winter he would need a candle for light. However, wood would keep out more cold than oiled paper.

"I'll take it."

"I didn't say ya could have it."

"You will."

"Pay in advance?"

"I said I would. How much?"

"Five sous. A month."

"Five sous? For a cubby hole with filthy straw? A *denier*?"

They bickered.

"Listen, good sir," Jacques said, although the man was no more a sir, good or otherwise, than Jacques was a cow. "You've four vacant rooms. Within a matter of days you'll discover I'm an easy tenant, causing no trouble. Think about it: a guaranteed, worry-free income." He paused to let his logic sink into the man's thick head.

"Three *deniers* a month. Pay now." He thrust out a dirty paw.

"I'll go get the money. Then we'll go to a notary." Jacques did not want the man to think he carried the money on him. Nor did he want him to deny being paid.

The man broke into a belly laugh. "Ya're a smart one, all right."

Maybe I gained some respect, Jacques thought as he moved into his new home. Home was not the correct word. Home was where his mother and father had nourished his body and soul. This place offered only shelter.

He bought fresh straw to restuff the mattress. He spread out his bedding. His spare clothes were folded in the corner. He could have worn his white monk's garb, but decided to dress as a normal man during his time in Paris. If students were disliked, priests were often hated more. Jacques did not understand this hatred.

He scoured the city for a locksmith to outfit the door with a lock and key. The first sound of hammer brought his landlord roaring up the stairs. "Ya ruining my property," he yelled.

"When I leave, you'll be able to rent it for more with a key and lock."

The landlord glowered at them. "Shit! All right. Next time, ask first." He descended into the tavern.

"Charming fellow," the locksmith said.

CHAPTER 21

Gaëlle's first excitement about how cool it would be to work on a dig didn't last long. By eleven she marched into the shed where Annie was describing yet another pan handle or that was what she thought it was. "I'm hot. I smell."

"Do you want to go back to the flat?" Annie asked.

Gaëlle flopped into the free chair. "I just thought it would be more fun: we'd find stuff faster."

"Archeology is tedious," Annie said.

"Maybe you should have warned me."

"I thought you knew."

"Are you sitting in the chair where they found the body?"

"The police took it." Until now, no one, at Luca's request, had talked about Amelie, thinking it would be too much for a teenager.

Annie wondered what she was going to do with Gaëlle for the rest of her stay. Luca wanted to work tomorrow to make up for the time lost when the police closed the site and there was the holiday coming up. Although he had not applied for any of the permits to work during the holiday, he wanted them all to come to work. He told them, if they were chased off, they would be chased off. If no one showed up, they would be that far ahead.

Annie was a volunteer, and she didn't feel badly about not working the weekend. The descriptions could be done next week. "Let's finish the day out, but tomorrow and Sunday, I'm all yours."

"You know what I was thinking?"

Annie knew whenever Gaëlle started off with that phrase, she needed to be alert. She hoped the teenager would suggest a concert, some sightseeing thing.

"I haven't been in Paris since I was ten."

Annie knew that. It was the age when Gaëlle lost her mother. Maybe Gaëlle wanted to look up a long-lost friend. Maybe she wanted to see a Facebook friend.

"I would like to see my grandparents."

Trouble, trouble, trouble, Annie thought. They had wanted no contact with Gaëlle or Roger after their daughter died, something that Annie couldn't understand. Roger maybe, but not Gaëlle. "Do you know where they live?"

"I know where they used to live."

"Is that why you came?"

"I really came to see you. I just got the idea when we were working. Laure was saying how she was going to go to her grandmother's for dinner tomorrow night, and I thought . . . well . . . maybe, they might have changed their mind about me."

"What do you think your father would say?" She knew Roger was angry at his in-laws for their treatment of Gaëlle. He also took an active interest in whomever she saw and where she was at all times. "I'm not opposed, but I'm worried you'll be hurt if they don't want to see you."

Gaëlle undid the clip holding her hair off her neck. It did not fall gracefully as it would in a shampoo ad because it was wet with sweat. Then she put it back up. "They probably will reject me, but I need to know that I tried everything to have a relationship with them." She smiled. "And if they do reject me think of what they'll be missing."

"You're a pretty wise kid," Annie said. "Okay, and Sunday we'll do some really July-fourteenth-holiday-Paris stuff. But we'll finish today here. Deal?"

"Deal."

Before Annie could tell Gaëlle to get back to work, Marino hollered, "I've found something really great."

The team stood from where they were kneeling in their own quadrants as Marino got to his feet. He put his hands behind his back. "Left or right hand?"

"Left?" Jacqueline said.

"Right?" Luca said.

Marino held his left hand out. In it was a small coin. A man was on it holding what looked like a scepter. He wore a crown. Some of the letters were worn or dirt encrusted but the team could make out P L U A C.

"I need to take a picture and e-mail it to the Cabinet des Médailles," Luca said.

"What's that?" Annie asked.

"Only the oldest museum in France going back to the time of King Charles. Maybe the fifteen hundreds, I can't remember exactly," Luca said. "They'll be able to identify it, I hope."

Since there was no running water in the shed, Jacqueline offered her water bottle to wash the coin. Then Luca put it on a dark piece of paper. No one was satisfied with the first five photos, but the sixth, everyone agreed, was worth sending.

Not trusting just to an e-mail, Luca called the museum director to tell him what was coming. The e-mail sent, they decided to break for lunch.

Jérôme greeted them all by asking, "Any word on who killed Amelie?" He did not notice Luca signaling him to be quiet and pointing to Gaëlle. "What a pretty woman she was." He kissed his fingertips as if giving approval a new dish prepared by his chef.

"What's the *plat du jour*?" Marino jumping in impressed Annie. Usually young men don't think of being that considerate. "I'm really hungry," he said causing Annie to wonder if he really was hungry and not trying to change the subject.

At that point Philippe joined them.

"You look like *merde*, a big pile of it," Marino said.

"*Merci pour rien.* I've been suffering with a toothache."

"*Filet de bouef, frites, salade,*" Jérôme said.

Philippe slipped into his seat. Annie noticed his hands were shaking. She started to ask if he were okay, but one look at his face and she decided against it.

"Look what we found." Luca took the coin out of his pocket. "You did a lot of work with coins, didn't you?"

Philippe took it from him. "I know what it is. It comes from the reign of Philippe the Fourth. This is valuable. I suspect it is real gold."

Annie realized that until now what they had found had historical value, but not much monetary value. "We can't leave it in the shed, and you shouldn't be carrying it around."

Luca gave her a look that said that he knew that. "After lunch I'm running it over to the Cabinet des Médailles."

"Just be careful that you don't meet any pickpockets," Philippe said.

As Jérôme brought salads, they heard a phone ringing. They all reached for their mobiles except Annie's whose ring was a croak. Luca's phone was the one.

"This isn't a good time, Crystal," he said as he got up from the table and walked away where no one would hear the conversation.

CHAPTER 22

"Come on, Luca. I'll get the work done." Annie was washing the dishes from breakfast. "Remember I'm a volunteer."

"That's the problem with volunteers: I've nothing with which to threaten you." Luca was leaning in the doorway watching.

Annie handed Gaëlle a dish towel. The flat had no dishwasher and the kitchen was so tiny that leaving dishes out left no working surface for the preparation of even a cup of tea.

The girl automatically started drying and putting dishes away in the small area between the sink and single cupboard. "I'm sorry, Luca, if I'm taking Annie away."

"Don't be. Time with you is limited for her. I have the next two and a half weeks to finish the project, and I'll do it. I always make my deadlines. Besides, the team has to find more stuff before she can write about it."

Annie appreciated his answer, but she had seen his expressions whenever they passed a father with his children, boys or girls. She wondered how Crystal could use the boys as bargaining chips, or at least that is how it seemed from her listening to Luca's half of the phone conversations between him and his wife.

"Do you think you'll turn up more coins like the last one?" Annie knew Luca could always be moved off the subject with a question about work. It had worked when they were at university.

"It would be wonderful, but I can only hope. You should have seen Monsieur Delmar's face when I brought the coin to him."

"Is he the director of the Cabinet des Médailles?" Gaëlle asked. She and Annie had been asleep when Luca came home late last night after leaving the dig.

"Assistant. The director is on holiday this month."

"Paris in July," Gaëlle and Annie said together.

"Who will own the coin?"

"Good question. We were on a dig not using a metal detector, which requires permission under French law, except on beaches. It varies in different countries. In some places it belongs to the finder, like in England. In others the stuff found belongs to the state, like in Germany."

"And in France."

"It's been a political ping-pong game. Under the latest version, the state owns it."

"So they get the coin," Annie said.

"Most likely. I really hope so, because the developers are real scumbags," Luca said.

"Scumbags?" Annie laughed at his Americanism.

"Scumbags. Listen, I got to run." He kissed Annie and Gaëlle on both their cheeks.

"Why did he call them scumbags?" Gaëlle asked when they heard the elevator door close taking Luca to the street.

"He doesn't know that much about them, but I suspect, because of the limited time we have on the dig. He would like to explore every inch of the site until we find everything that is possible to find, probably back to Neanderthal days."

"And that's not going to happen?"

Annie shook her head. "What time do you want to beard your grandparents in their den?"

"How about mid afternoon? We can play tourist before."

The Métro 10 Javel-André Citroën stop opened out onto avenue Emile Zola. Although the *canicule* had passed, it was still July, but the heat was at least dry and bearable. A breeze came off the Seine.

"Are you sure you remember where your grandparents live?" Annie asked. She had put on one of Rima's peasant skirts and her own blouse to meet the formidable couple whom she heard so much about, most of it from Roger and little of it complimentary: coldhearted, snobbish, self-centered. He had always added that he never understood how they could have produced such a wonderful woman as his wife, telling Annie he knew she would never be jealous of a dead woman. He'd been right.

Gaëlle wore jean shorts and a T-shirt. Annie had offered to buy her a dress but Gaëlle said that her grandparents needed to accept her as she was. As much as she would like to interfere, Annie knew if this went badly, it had to be based on decisions that Gaëlle had made so that the girl couldn't say, "I shouldn't have listened to you." At the same time, she wanted her to have as many options as possible. In the same circumstances, Annie wasn't sure she would be as brave as Gaëlle was being to put herself on the line for a possible rejection. Still, maybe they would see what a lovely teenager Gaëlle had become.

They walked away from the Seine and through a small gate where there were several high-rise apartment buildings. "It's this one." Gaëlle stopped. There was a code box, an intercom, but no names. She looked at Annie who shrugged.

"We can wait till someone comes out?"

"We can."

Five minutes, ten minutes passed. Fourteen minutes, when Annie was debating suggesting they pack it in, a young woman appeared at the door struggling with a baby carriage. Gaëlle sprinted forward and held the door first for the woman, then for Annie. They high-fived each other.

Inside there was a lobby with a small fountain, plants and a row of mailboxes.

"Their name?"

"Lassieur." Gäelle ran her finger down the rows of mailboxes. "They're still here. Still on the seventh." She headed for the elevator.

The elevator was modern like the building. No cage, like in old buildings, and with enough room for several people or to carry furniture. There was a gold framed mirror and Gaëlle took out her hairbrush and gave her hair a quick run-through.

"You're beautiful," Annie said. The girl was blossoming into a beauty. She was just out of the gawky stage, but still retained the look of youth.

"You're prejudiced."

"Yup, but I'd think so even if I weren't."

On the seventh floor there were three apartments. Gaëlle went to the left one without checking names. She started to ring the bell, stopped, took a deep breath and pushed.

What seemed like several minutes passed without anything, but just as Gaëlle was about to press the buzzer again, the two women heard footsteps, a lock being turned and the door opened.

The woman standing there was probably in her late sixties with gray hair, arranged in a pageboy. She was in full makeup, a summer plain blue skirt and a matching blouse. She wore pearl earrings and a matching necklace. Her feet had ballerina-style house slippers. Outside shoes were in a rack by the door.

"*Oui?*"

"*C'est moi, grandmère, Gaëlle. Votre petite fille.*"

Annie noticed that Gaëlle had not used the normal *mamie* for her grandmother nor the informal *toi*.

The woman looked at the teenager for a moment. She stood aside to allow them to enter the flat. Annie saw gold-leafed chairs with expensive white brocade upholstery, a leather-lined top on a mahogany desk. The rugs were probably Persian. One complete wall was lined with books, all hardbacks. Another case held both records and CDs. There was no television visible. The third wall of the living room was all windows with elaborately folded and tasseled floor-to-ceiling drapery.

"Sit down. I'll get your *grandpère.*"

She disappeared and returned alone. "He'll be with us in a few minutes." She turned to Annie. "May I ask who you are?"

"Annie Young. I'm a friend of Gaëlle's. She's visiting me for the weekend."

Before the woman could reply, a man entered. He had a full head of gray hair. His slacks had a perfect crease and he wore an ascot at this neck. The apartment was air-conditioned.

"Gaëlle, this is a surprise," he said and sat down. There were no cheek kisses.

"*Grandpère* may I present Annie Young. Annie, this is my *grandpère,* Frédéric Lassieur."

"Gaëlle, a man is presented to the woman, first," Madame Lassieur said.

Annie had to bite her tongue not to say that a lady should not correct a person in front of others.

Madame Lassieur rang a bell and a maid in a black dress and white apron appeared. She did not wear one of those funny white hats that maids in movies did. "Please bring us iced tea."

No one said anything until the maid returned with the iced tea on a silver tray. Next to Annie was an antique table without a coaster. She decided it would be better to hold her glass. The others did the same.

Frédéric Lassieur broke the silence. "What brings you here, Gaëlle?"

"It has been a while since we've had any contact. I thought since I'm your only . . ."

Annie waited for Gaëlle to continue with one of the many scripts they had practiced coming over on the Métro. But the girl couldn't get out any of them. Annie found herself not only agreeing with Roger about his former in-laws, she had to hold down her anger. How did these cold, formal people produce a woman who could create a child such as Gaëlle and give her a start in her life that allowed her to survive her mother's death?

"I suppose you are still living in Southern France; what was the name of the place?" Madame Lassieur asked.

"Argelès-sur-mer."

"Hmm. Catalan country." Madame Lassieur's tone made it sound like they were discussing an African slum.

Annie could hold back no longer, but she kept her tone polite. "Your granddaughter has turned into a brilliant young woman, a good student, bilingual. She has many good friends, does jazz dancing and is on the racquetball team. She's good with computers . . ." She didn't know what to add.

"*Bien, bien.* It is nice you have your own public-relations person," Frédéric Lassieur said.

More silence.

"I do wish you had called to let us know you were coming," Madame Lassieur said. "One does not drop in unexpectedly."

Gaëlle had told Annie she was afraid to call in advance. Whenever her father had done that while they were still in Paris, her grandparents had excuse after excuse on why they would not be available—plus they never offered an alternative time.

"You must have other things to do than sit and talk to two old people." Madame Lassieur stood. Her husband did too.

Annie put her half-drunk glass down on the antique table hoping it would mar the surface.

Neither of them said anything on the ride down in the elevator or during the walk to the Métro station. When they got to La Défense Arche, Annie suggested they get an ice cream in the giant shopping area over the tracks. Gaëlle nodded. She chose a place where they could sit down.

When they were served their two dishes of chocolate-chip ice cream, Annie watched Gaëlle stir the chocolate sauce into the melting ice cream. "Do you want to talk about it?"

"It isn't like I loved them or anything. I mean, I never spent much time with them. When we went over to visit, *Maman* always had to take my toys. My friends' grandparents always had toys stashed in their house." She swirled her spoon through the ice cream. She still hadn't taken a bite.

"But you'd like them to be huggy-type grandparents, the kind on TV series and in books?"

Gaëlle brushed tears from her cheeks and nodded.

"It hurts?"

"It hurts."

"Rejection always does." She tried to think of all the things she might say to Gaëlle to make it better: that those two cold fish weren't worth shedding tears over, that she was better off without them.

"I guess I wanted a connection to my mom. Except for Papa, I don't have anything left of her anymore." She blushed. "I mean you've been wonderful . . ."

"Gaëlle, I've never planned to replace your mother. I am happy to give motherly advice, sisterly advice, friendly advice. I'm happy to do silly things with you, go shopping, see movies, listen to music. We have our relationship, but your mother was your mother."

"I wish she hadn't died. And you know what is really stupid?"

Annie shook her head.

"Since she is dead, I wish you and Papa would get married."

Annie reached out and put her hand over Gaëlle's. She didn't know what to say to that.

CHAPTER 23

Paris, France, 1305

At the abbey Jacques's life had been ruled by bells telling the hours. The bells from Parisian churches did not control his actions. Had someone asked Jacques a week before, if he would ever lose the habit of rising before dawn for prayers, he would have said impossible. Yet, he stayed in bed until mid-morning, thinking that maybe he would postpone beginning his studies even longer. Likewise, he adjusted well to sleeping without his snoring brothers. In fact, he loved the quiet and having his own space where he could shut everyone and everything out.

One day's wandering brought the discovery of baths less than a mile from his lodging. For less than a single coin, he entered a huge hall of contained cubicles. Each had a wooden tub of hot water with a seat. Because it was still morning, there were few customers.

At the abbey bathing involved cold water. Jacques stripped off all his clothes, wrapped himself in a cloth given by an attendant, pulled a blue curtain behind him and climbed into a tub. He'd never before felt warm water up to his neck. Maids kept pulling the curtain aside to offer him food and drink: bread, cherries, wine. He refused them all.

A maid with dark-brown eyes and a smile that kept escaping her lips poured an almond-smelling oil into the water from a metal pitcher before he could refuse. The smell was almost intoxicating.

A young woman, also wrapped only in a cloth, poked her head through the curtain. "May I join you?" When she saw Jacques's face, she said, "If you're going to be prudish, make sure you only come mornings. Never on a Saturday night: people get very drunk and all sorts of things, things that you obviously would not approve of, happen."

"I don't want to know." He reached out to close the curtain. No wonder women were vessels of sin. Imagine being in the water with a woman without her clothes even if her private parts were hidden from view.

God!

Paris was a city of sin beyond imagination. The woman must have been one of the demons his uncle had dreamed about. He'd been tested. He had resisted. He needed to retreat, he thought, as he scrambled into his clothes.

He went directly from the baths to the stable to rent a horse and traveled northwest of the city to the Royaumont Cistercian Abbey without stopping, although he let his horse drink from a stream. He stayed mounted to deprive himself of quenching his own thirst. It was an old horse without much energy and it should not have to suffer for his sins.

The rustle of the trees and birds singing replaced the city babble. He rang the bell at the gate. A young lay brother led him to the abbot.

"I need to pray in the chapel," Jacques said.

Without further comment, the abbot had a lay brother take the guest over the stone path to the chapel.

The silent corridors engulfed Jacques in familiar comfort. The smell of incense welcomed him. He knelt in front of the Blessed Virgin and asked forgiveness. As he looked at the serene face, he did not see Mother Mary, but a young girl wrapped in cloth about to set foot into a tub. He prayed harder.

CHAPTER 24

Marie-Claude Du Pont looked at her sleeping son. Daniel was stretched out next to her. He was in his cowboy pajamas, the sheets thrown off in the summer heat. The late-evening sun, already setting a bit earlier, cast just enough light that she could see the sweat on his forehead. Perhaps it wasn't the best thing to lay down with him nights until he fell asleep, but if she didn't he would keep getting up. Part of her admitted she liked the closeness. Would he remember it when he grew up? Probably not.

Raphaël, her older son, off to holiday camp as a counselor for the summer, didn't remember that she had read to him every night for the first six years of his life. She threatened to reread the books to him, but earned only one of those *"Maman,"* remarks stretched out in several syllables.

The problem with lying down with Daniel was she often fell asleep herself, but tonight she could not. As slowly as possible she slipped her arm out from under her son's head. Where it had rested, her arm was sticky from his sweat. He rolled over on his side and stuck his thumb in his mouth as she left the room, drawing the door to, but not closing it tightly. In case he had a nightmare, she wanted to be able to hear him.

She poured herself a glass of wine and settled at her desk with her files. July was an awful month. They were understaffed because of people on holiday. Next month she would have her revenge. She'd booked her family into a campground with a lake, baking and pottery classes, tennis courts and evening entertainments. Daniel's father had introduced her to camping with the promise if it rained they could go to a motel, and she was surprised how much, with the exception of erecting the tent, that she'd loved it.

Next month was still two weeks away. There were several cases which her team was working. A man was pulled out of the Seine: was it murder or suicide? He was successful enough that his death made the first page on *Le Figaro* and *La Libération,* but not important enough that the powers that be were pressuring them. Or maybe they, too, were on vacation. Two teenagers died in a knife fight. That was ready to close out. All she needed to do was write the final report.

It was the young and pregnant archeologist's death that was puzzling. There were no fingerprints. Blood didn't spatter. The shot was so close that there were powder burns on Amelie's clothing. And, because she was sitting in a thickly padded office chair, she'd bled out into the upholstery.

The shed had been locked from the outside and the keys not found. They were probably Amelie's because she had no keys—car, house, dig—on her. Marie-Claude had to get Amelie's landlord to let the police team into the room the victim had rented in the fourteenth *arrondissement.*

A search of her room produced what anyone would expect of a student holing up in Paris for the summer: a couple pairs of jeans, T-shirts, underwear, makeup, books on archeology but also two romance novels, the latest *Paris Match* with the Spanish royal family on the cover, papers and notes related to the dig and her laptop.

Her laptop was a hodgepodge of papers she'd written. Her Facebook page revealed a series of cyberspace friends, but nothing unusual. She didn't seem to play any computer games but some of her Facebook friends were engrossed in that Farmville game that Raphaël played some nights until the early hours of the morning, when Marie-Claude would have to yell at him to go to bed. At least it wasn't some shoot-em-all game.

No clues as to who might be the father of the baby, which could be a motive for her death.

Amelie blogged the events on the dig but those were technical. Damn her for not being one of those people who gave away too much of her personal life.

Her downloaded photos were partially of the dig and some of parties she'd gone to.

Amelie's mother still had not returned from wherever she went, although Marie-Claude had left a note in the LaFollette mailbox to call the Département. She couldn't imagine how she would feel if she returned from a holiday to discover one of her sons had been dead for most of the time she was enjoying herself. She shivered: she couldn't imagine outliving either of her boys.

Amelie's pocketbook had an ATM card, and her bank records showed she lived as most impoverished students—close to the bone. No man was keeping her, so the theory of a married lover, Luca Martinelli or someone else, might or might not be true. If she had one, he was cheap in mistress support, but then again, it was only the upper classes that supported mistresses with apartment, jewels and clothes. Or maybe it was mostly in the movies.

The notes from the interviews didn't produce a lot. The people did not either hate or particularly like Amelie. They thought her lazy, but she could be fun. She wondered if Marino had been interested in her as potential lover.

Oh, my God, she thought. Why didn't I make the connection before. Marino's last name. Wagnier. It was the same as the developer. And she still hadn't questioned him.

Philippe, she'd ruled out as a potential murderer. He obviously had a drinking problem, but he seemed to be trying to beat it, at least temporarily.

Annie Young, who barely had a chance to meet Amelie, had no reason to want her dead.

Which left Luca. A look at Amelie's call records showed an inordinate number of phone calls to and from his cell. At first they were of long duration, but in the last two weeks, they were all to him, and they only lasted a minute or two.

Luca admitted sleeping with her and justified it by saying he was separated from his wife. A visit to the apartment where the couple had lived had only proved that the wife was on vacation and had been away during the night of the murder, according to neighbors. Meanwhile, Luca was bunked in with Annie Young. That they had been lovers over a decade before might be important or might not.

Marie-Claude sighed. Some cases were so easy. The spouse was responsible or a parent for an honor killing if it were some ethnic background that believed in honor killings. Or a business partner. The longer she went without any real leads the less chance she or anyone would find the killer. Some cases fell into place so easily; others were harder, and some would never be solved. She didn't want this to be one of the unsolved ones.

Marie-Claude sighed again. As a detective, she felt she owed something to the victims in her caseload: she wanted to see the murderers pay for what they did. When it was a young, beautiful woman with her life before her, she felt even worse.

The sun had set. She switched off the lamp and headed for her own bed.

CHAPTER 25

Marie-Claude pulled up in front of Marino Wagnier's house in Neuilly. The house was a two-story brick with an iron fence. Bushes of some type hid the first story from people walking by. The neighborhood was not that far from where Nicholas Sarkozy had lived before becoming the French president. The neighborhood was for the well-off, not the filthy rich. There was a bell by the gate which she pushed.

Marino answered the intercom and buzzed her in. He was barefoot and bare-chested. "Can I get you something cool?" he asked after ushering her into the living room, just off the entryway.

"Just water."

"With or without gas?"

"Tap will do."

While he was in the kitchen, she used the time to look around the living room. The furniture was of a quality that was meant to last. The setting was formal. A grand piano was in one corner near the floor-to-ceiling windows. Through the sheer curtains she could see a well-tended garden in back filled with high flowers. Her knowledge of flora was nonexistent.

Marino returned with a tray and two glasses of ice water. "Cooling, no calories. What do you want to ask me?"

"I'd like to know if you are any relation to the developer?"

"Not that I know of. Why?"

"Same last name."

"Interesting. Just a coincidence. My father works for TF1. I can't imagine him in construction. And he was an only child, so no uncles or cousins. *Nada.*"

One of Marie-Claude's questioning techniques was to jump from subject to subject to keep the questionee off guard. "Do you know of anyone who would have hated Amelie enough to kill her?"

"No."

"Where do you go to school?"

"Ecole de Commerce in Toulouse."

"How does that fit in with an archeological dig?"

"Ideally, I would like to be the director of a museum. I did a lot of talking to get this gig. Strangely enough, there weren't that many volunteers, but that might have been because they didn't have time to really get the word out. Or it could be all that hard work for no money in the broiling sun—discomfort doesn't appeal to a lot of students."

"Will it help—the dig work—in getting a job?"

"Won't hurt. Museum posts are really hard to come by. But more interesting, though, than a regular company where I always would have to think of the bottom line."

Marie-Claude did not tell him, he would always be thinking of funding. He would discover that for himself. "What did you think of Amelie?"

"I know she wasn't particularly liked by any of us, mainly because she was a user. When she put on the charm, one would wonder if perhaps user was the wrong conclusion, but then she'd do something."

"Like what?"

He shrugged. "Take credit for something I found. But she only did it once, because I called her on it."

"How did she react?"

"That was part of her charm. She laughed and made a joke about it."

"Did you have a romantic interest in her?"

Before he could answer, the front door opened. "Hey, lover boy," a voice called. "The cats are still away, and this mouse is ready to play." A young man walked in wearing makeup.

Damn it, Marie-Claude thought. I missed that one. "I guess that answers my last question."

Marino's skin was too dark to show a blush, but he kept his eyes away from Marie-Claude's. "You won't tell my parents. If they knew and knew what I did when they were on holiday . . ."

"I don't see any reason to share this information with anyone."

CHAPTER 26

Paris, France, 1305

Jacques's resolve to submerge himself in work was plagued by the lack of a forced routine. Unlike the abbey where there were no choices for him to make, now there were too many. He could sleep as late as he wanted, go to class or not, study or not. He did not consider the lack of discipline a blessing and constantly berated himself for breaking his own rules.

By October he congratulated himself for doing better. Mornings he forced himself out of bed to break the fast, albeit well after the cock crowed. The tavern owner's daughter, Madeleine, served him bread or porridge. When the tavern owner did not hover over his daughter, the portions were larger.

He never gave a name to the tavern owner. The man was so disgusting he didn't deserve a name that would elevate him to a high plane, one that made him human. At the same time, he wondered if the tavern owner was another demon for him to master, for surely if the man had a soul, it was well hidden. The best he could do was to add the tavern owner to his prayers.

After eating, he left for his daily classes. Professor de Bois had recommended two professors, one for philosophy, the other for logic. They encouraged him in his project to research the life and writings of Saint Jean-Paul. Jacques saw the irony in his own lack of discipline in comparison to The Rule of Saint Jean-Paul.

Most mornings his first stop was the library with its tens of thousands texts. Wooden covers protected their pages which held the secrets of God, man and the universe. As a student he could rent books for so much per print column multiplied by the days he had the book in his possession. If he used the books without removing them from the library, there was no charge. Jacques was constantly battling between his meager pocketbook and his desire to own copies of the books he read.

He might have taken a vow of poverty, but to have so much writing at his fingertips was a wealth that left him feeling faint. He promised himself that he would donate these books to the Fontfroide library when he finished his Parisian exile. The vow was a balm to his soul. He thought of them as passing through his hands to enrich future monks at his abbey. As soon as he borrowed a book, he rushed to the copyist, who for a rather hefty fee began copying the books letter by letter. Sometimes, Jacques only required part of the text, and that saved him a coin or two. The first copyists he tried were unsatisfactory, making too many errors, thus negating the value of the finished work.

Then de Bois recommended Anton. His fee was higher, but there were no battles about misspellings or incomplete phrases. Anton did not make mistakes.

Watching the copyist immerse himself in his work was such a pleasure that Jacques often asked to sit and watch while the man moved his armed chair to the right position and angled the flat board on which he put the original. Neither man spoke as Anton mixed colored powders to create the right-hued ink. No matter how closely Jacques looked, he could never tell where one day's copy ended and the next one began.

"Parchment?" Anton would ask each time he started to copy a new book.

Jacques would nod. Although it was more expensive, the book would be of better quality. Anton prepared the material by scarping it with his awl. His manuscripts were works of arts with first letters drawn with flourishes. Sometimes he would do drawings of leaves, flowers or animals in the margins and told Jacques although he should charge for the artwork, he wouldn't. Anton could not bear releasing any book that was anything less than perfect, and part of perfection was beauty.

This October morning as the leaves were just beginning to give up their holds on trees, Jacques stopped at Anton's to pick up Saint Jean-Paul's *de Grandios Superiae et Huliatatis* to add to his *Apology*. With these two manuscripts he could work at home, without limiting himself to the hours the library was open. He liked the idea of saving money by putting several books between the same wooden covers. He resisted the vanity of covering the wood with leather.

The bell above the shop tinkled. The copyist and Jacques exchanged greetings. Anton handed Jacques the book for a final examination.

He chose random pages for comparison. Not a letter was out of place. Anton's copy was better than the original, which has been thumbed through by numerous students over the years. "Perfect."

Anton picked up his pen and wrote "Finished, Thank God" on the bottom of the last page.

Jacques headed to class. He had to channel all his will not to roam the streets, hide out in the library or watch Madeleine going about her chores at the tavern.

He found the last of his obsessions the hardest to believe. Of all his vows he thought chastity would be the easiest. Not that he had broken the vow in reality. At night it was all he could do not to grab himself seeking relief from the desire that swelled his organ until he ached. How could he let himself fall into a state of sin for a girl? And for such a girl at that—his landlord's daughter whom the scoundrel sold to his customers along with his bad beer and sour wine. His mind and his body seemed to be functioning independently of each other and he had no idea how to stop it.

Chapter 27

Annie was tired after she got off the bus and walked to Rima's flat. She had risen early to find that Luca had slipped out even earlier, leaving a note that he wanted to get to the site because he had a feeling it would be a wonderful day for finds. Annie remembered Luca always had talked about *feelings* when they dated: when he turned a corner he would have a feeling they would find a great restaurant or when it was rainy, he was positive that it would clear. Usually he was right, but Annie had suspected that he might have read restaurant reviews in advance and directed her there with the foreknowledge of what they would find. And she never accused him of checking the weather forecast before venturing forth with his own, but she'd considered it.

The flat was in chaos after the holiday. She had had no desire to take her precious time with Gaëlle to do housekeeping. Although Rima had said nothing about coming back for another three weeks, she'd been known to show up before unexpectedly. Annie could imagine what it would be like if she just walked in.

Annie spent ten minutes looking for her watch. The only way to find stuff at this point was to clean. So before going to the dig, she did, putting all related papers together and hanging up the clothes and putting away the dry laundry. She washed all the dishes and emptied the trash. She wondered how a man as intelligent as Luca was not able to put a dish in the sink or realize that the trash bin was full and needed to be carried downstairs. A man as strong as he was should be able to hang a towel on a towel rack instead of letting it stay wherever it fell.

All day she had been extra busy. Luca's feelings were correct as the team began to unearth bricks that were probably part of a chimney from the arrangement. Besides writing up the finds of the previous days she helped with the digging.

Luca had left them early. He wanted an extension on the dig, something he thought he might have a thirty-percent chance of getting if they could prove there was a real room that could be excavated, but not within the time frame assigned to their project. The owner of the site would scream at the idea, he said, which was of no surprise to any of the team.

If that didn't work, he might try to use the coin. There could be others. The news of the coin had not been released to the press, for fear of the site being robbed by people hoping to find their own gold.

Returning to the flat, Annie found the elevator out of order, again. The new paint it had been given since her last visit had done nothing to improve its reliability. She walked up the six flights. Opening the door, she gasped. Luca's papers were all over the apartment. His boots, socks and working clothes were just dropped where he had taken them off. He must have been looking for something, because several books were on the couch. Luca, however, wasn't there.

Annie went into the kitchen. Luca had cooked his own lunch, leaving the clean stove splattered with grease. The dishes were on the little table in front of the stool where one could eat in the kitchen. Onion peelings were left in the sink, not in the compost container.

The door opened and Luca walked in. Before he could say anything Annie demanded, "Why in hell can't you clean up after yourself?"

"Thank you, I had a very productive meeting with the Département des Antiquités."

"I'm glad. Do you realize how long I spent this morning, cleaning this space up?"

"I thought it looked better."

Annie imagined throwing a dirty dish at him. Instead she took a deep breath. "Sit down, please and tell me why you can't put things away? Why if you peel an onion, you can't put the peelings in the container that is just next to the sink instead of the sink?"

Luca walked into the kitchen. "I suppose I never thought of it."

"Never thought of it?"

"Not really." He walked back to the living room. "Have you ever gone into a showroom at a furniture store?"

"Of course?"

"And everything looks perfect?"

She nodded.

"But it isn't real." He swept his hand over the flat. "This is real. It shows people live here."

"It shows pigs live here."

Luca walked over to Annie and put his arms around her. "Annie, Annie, Annie."

"Your old snuggle-her-out-of-her-snit trick is not going to work."

"What's a snit?" He tilted her chin but kissed her forehead.

"It's not going to work. I'm taking a shower."

In winter Annie loved hot showers letting the heat melt into her bones, but in the summer, it was more lukewarm or even cool water. After being on the dig all day, she was sweaty and dusty. She shampooed the grit out of her hair.

The bathroom door opened and Luca, now naked, slipped into the shower. The water had relaxed her enough to accept his kisses and then she found herself kissing back. A pang of guilt about Roger ran into the drain along with the water. She and Roger were finished. And even if he'd had a point about her going away for a nonwork project, she still wanted the freedom to come and go as she wished. Luca wasn't anyone important to her. If Luca had sex with her tonight, and she couldn't call it making love, tomorrow it could be anyone else with an available vagina.

"Luca, stop it."

He did. "Can't blame a man for trying. It would have been fun."

The water poured down on both of them but they still could hear the doorbell. Annie grabbed one of Rima's orange bath sheets and wrapped it around herself before walking the ten steps to the door without shutting the bathroom door which was visible from the front door. When she opened it Roger stood there. The neighbor, Dorothy something or other, was walking down the hall to her flat.

Roger could see Luca come out of the shower and reach for a towel.

"It didn't take you long to replace me," he said as he turned and headed back to the elevator.

"ROGER!"

The only answer was the sound of his footsteps growing fainter as he neared the bottom of the staircase.

Annie padded back to the flat. Dorothy was still fiddling with her key. Annie didn't say anything to her as she shut the door. Luca's expression was closer to triumphant than contrite, and of no condolence value.

"I'm sorry that happened, but why didn't you shut the bathroom door?" He still wore only his towel. He held his arms out to Annie and she went into them.

CHAPTER 28

Annie was sitting in the shed writing about parts of a dish they had found. Jacqueline had been able to put the dish together. Nothing was missing. It was the first complete piece found. The rest of the team, with the exception of Luca, who had been called to the Département des Antiquités for the permit that would allow them two more weeks to work, was still excavating the chimney. The telephone call that the extension had been granted had come in about two hours before and Luca had bolted out of there as fast as he could.

"I think we should celebrate tonight," Marino said. "Go out for a nice dinner, champagne, maybe some dancing." He grabbed Laure and swung her around in the dirt. She tripped on the string marking one of the quadrants. Instead of being angry she laughed, "You're an idiot."

"But he's our idiot," Jacqueline said.

Philippe as usual said nothing. Annie thought he was looking better and his hands weren't shaking.

A police car pulled up and parked above the dig. Marie-Claude Du Pont emerged. They hadn't seen her for several days.

"Can we help you?" Annie asked.

"I want to talk to Luca."

"He should be back at any time," Annie said.

Except he wasn't. Marie-Claude gave up but asked that he call her.

The team left a note in the shed saying where they had gone for the celebration.

CHAPTER 29

Marie-Claude Du Pont took a chance that Amelie's mother might have come home from vacation since she had to drive by the flat on her way back to the station. When she knocked and the door opened, she knew that her time hadn't been wasted. As much as she had wished that her partner was with her to break the news, at least that task would soon be over.

The flat had a closed-up smell. Although everything was neurotically neat right down to the curtain folds all being identical in position and the tassels exactly the same length, everything had dust on it. A huge pile of mail, probably with Marie-Claude's card and request to call the station in it, was on the table to the right of the entry door, and a suitcase was just at the entrance to the living room.

Marie-Claude showed her credentials and asked if she could come in.

Amelie's mother stood aside and then pointed to the living room and indicated that Marie-Claude should sit.

"You're Amelie LaFollette's mother?"

The woman nodded. "I'm Elisabeth LaFollette." She was an older version of her daughter, blonde streaks in honey-colored hair, hazel eyes, good skin. Based on Amelie's age, Marie-Claude guessed the mother might be in her mid-forties, but she appeared younger. Marie-Claude had always hated that phrase—she looked younger than X age—because there was such variation on how people looked at any age based on genetics, lifestyle and environment that it made the statement worthless.

"Please forgive how I look. I just arrived on the overnight train."

The woman looked fine for having just arrived on a train. She was wearing white pants and a white blouse that showed off her figure. Her hair had been combed. She was one of those women that didn't really need makeup. "This can't be good."

Marie-Claude had learned that it was better not to delay in delivering bad news. The recipient knew something bad was coming, and prolonging the unknown raised more anxiety as their mind wandered over all the possibilities, each more horrible than the one before. Let the person know what they were dealing with up front. "I'm sorry, but your daughter is dead. She was murdered a week ago."

Madame LaFollette sat straight in her chair, both feet on the ground. She didn't say anything.

"May I get you a glass of water, anything?" Marie-Claude asked to break the silence after several minutes passed. This woman, when told her child was dead, was calmer than anyone she'd ever seen in similar circumstances.

Elisabeth shook her head. "How did it happen?"

"She was shot."

"*Tiens*. Do you need me to identify the body?" Her tone was the same as if she were asking about going to a film that night or could someone please bring in the groceries.

Marie-Claude found her reaction one of the strangest she'd come across and again she wished one of her team were with her so they could assess it afterwards. "Luca Martinelli, the leader of the archeological dig your daughter was working on, did it officially. However, the entire group was there when she, your daughter, was found so there never was any doubt." She didn't add any details such as the shed having been locked.

Elisabeth LaFollette nodded and sat for a while longer. "What happens next?"

Here Marie-Claude was more comfortable giving out information. "Since we've completed our investigation, you can make arrangements with a funeral home. I'll give you the address of the morgue, but the funeral home probably knows it already." Why wasn't the woman crying? This wasn't even normal shock.

"*Merci.* I suppose you think I'm a cold fish?"

Marie-Claude did not want to answer that.

"My daughter was a problem almost from the day she was born. I don't mean drugs and things like that, but she was a manipulative liar. At four she told her father I beat her and she had bruises. Later we learned that she had given them to herself."

"That must have been difficult."

"As a teenager, she accused him of molesting her. We were divorced by then. I didn't believe her. My ex and I may have parted ways, and if someone else had said it, I might have believed that person, but not Amelie."

"You don't think your husband might have done it?"

"Pierre? He's living in Japan. After our divorce he moved there and sells used tractors and other equipment like that. He's too busy to come back to kill Amelie. Beside, he's happily remarried."

Marie had meant molested their daughter, but she let the answer to the unasked question go for the moment. What intrigued her was that Madame LaFollette did not act resentful of her ex-husband's happiness.

"My ex was fair with me. We drifted apart. He wanted to go to Japan. I didn't want to leave my friends and my work here."

"What do you do?"

"I own a real-estate office. I love my work."

Marie-Claude wrote rapidly in her notebook. "What else can you tell me about your daughter?"

"I could say she was beautiful and smart. Those things would be true too. And she could be really considerate, especially when she wanted something." Madame LaFollette leaned forward in her chair so her head tilted toward Marie-Claude, as if they were schoolgirls exchanging secrets. "Amelie was responsible for the breakup of my neighbors' marriage at the last place I lived. She had an affair with the husband when she was seventeen. He was twenty-five."

"Was she ever into drugs?"

"That wasn't ever part of the problem. She was a good student, a bit on the lazy side. She was able to convince her friends to do some of her work. But she always got eights and nines on her own even when she found herself forced to do her own stuff. Plus, unless you knew what she was really like, you would love her. She was funny and she seemed so considerate, but it was a trap she set for others."

Marie-Claude wasn't sure how to respond. Never had she seen this reaction from what seemed like an ordinary *bourgeois* mother.

"Did she suffer?"

"Death was almost instantaneous."

"That's good."

"What else can you tell me about your daughter, her friends, people who might hate her enough to kill her?"

"Amelie moved out when she started university. At the *lycée* she never brought any friends home. She had to have some because she would go out nights and weekends, although she was always back by curfew."

"That doesn't sound like a teenager out of control."

"Amelie would look like she was obeying the rules. But one never knew what she was really doing." Elisabeth LaFollette sighed. "Years ago I saw an American movie, *The Bad Seed*. We had some friends who were American and they showed it to us on DVD. We were all great fans of movies from the fifties and my ex and I would find French films for them and they'd find American ones for us."

"I don't know it."

"It's about a child serial killer who is so sweet that no one could believe she was capable of such evil."

"Are you saying your daughter . . ."

". . . is a killer? No, but I'm saying Amelie was amoral. That might be a little strong, but she is, was, a total egoist who only cares about herself."

Marie-Claude noticed that the woman never called Amelie "my daughter."

"Are you in touch with her father?"

"We haven't spoken much since Amelie left home. I told him to stop the child support since I wasn't giving her any money either. Before she said he'd attacked her, he tried to be a good father, but once he was accused of molesting her, he stopped having anything to do with her."

"Was there any chance there might be some truth in what Amelie said?" Sometimes it helped to come back to the same question over and over.

Elisabeth LaFollette grimaced. "I know there are mothers who are in denial about fathers abusing their daughters. Pierre and I had disagreements, but they were mostly about how much he worked. Amelie should have been more careful in her stories. The time period she accused her father he was on a business trip in Asia."

Elisabeth LaFollette stood up. "I don't want to be rude, but I really would like to take a shower. The *wagon lit* was hot and the air-conditioning had two settings: none and insufficient."

On one of her visiting cards, Marie-Claude wrote out the

morgue information. "If you would give me contact for Amelie's father, it would be helpful." She wanted to avoid the terms ex or daughter. She wondered if Elisabeth LaFollette would break down after she left. How a mother could make her peace with not loving her children no matter what they did, she wasn't sure. Her boys, especially Raphaël, could drive her crazy, but she couldn't imagine not loving him to bits.

What would the father be like?

She would only be able to judge by a phone call unless she met him and that meant he would have to come to the funeral.

"Do you think your ex-husband will come to Paris?"

"I don't know." Elisabeth LaFollette wrote down his name and number on her own business card and handed it to Marie-Claude. "I'll tell him as soon as you leave. But here's his information for you to talk to him yourself."

Marie-Claude looked at the card. It had a picture of a nice house on it. "I notice you kept your married name. That's rather unusual."

"Business. My real-estate agency carries my name. I was known professionally by LaFollette." She shrugged.

Marie-Claire understood. She had gone back to her maiden name twice and all the paperwork was nothing but a pain.

"He's remarried. He called me last year right before the ceremony so I would hear about the marriage from him first. Rather considerate, don't you think?"

Monsieur LaFollette was called to the telephone by the woman who answered the phone in a language that Marie-Claude assumed was Japanese. She sat at her desk, drumming her fingers as she waited for him. If delivering the news of someone's death in person was terrible, it was far worse to do it by telephone. She was grateful to Madame LaFollette for doing it ahead of her own telephone call to this stranger on the other side of the world.

"Your ex-wife gave me your number," she said after introducing yourself.

"She told me you might be calling." His accent was Parisian. "I'm still trying to absorb it all."

Marie-Claude offered the traditional condolences, knowing her words wouldn't do anything at all to soothe the emotions aroused.

"*Merci.* My wife said she told you about my daughter's accusations. Needless to say, that ended our relationship. I've put it all behind me. I try and remember her as the sweet little girl I read bedtime stories to, but it is hard."

"Will you be coming for the funeral?"

"I asked Elisabeth if that would help her. She said no, and that is the only reason I can think for coming. My first wife was not a bad woman. We both wanted different things." He sighed. "People say a divorce is always a failure. She and I had fourteen good years together where we were in sync. I don't see that as a failure, especially when our divorce was such a success."

Marie-Claude found his attitude interesting. She did not feel her marriages or her divorces were successes at all. "When was the last time you were in Paris?"

"About eighteen months ago. On business. And I didn't see Amelie or Elisabeth." He paused and Marie-Claude let the silence hang there. "I know it is a cliché, but I've moved on, built a new life here, a good life: my own business, a new wife, a son who is two months old. I know it sounds harsh, but . . ."

Marie-Claude debated asking for more information. What his business was, what contacts he still had in France. The desire was more from her lack of a suspect than any real suspicions. All her instincts told her that Monsieur LaFollette had truly moved on and killing his daughter either by coming to France which could be checked or by hiring someone seemed remote.

"When was the last time you talked to your daughter?"

"I really can't remember. Elisabeth told me she said that you know my daughter accused me of molesting her."

"*Oui.* It must have been hard for you."

"It was. One of the final things that broke Elisabeth and me up was her saying that Amelie was a liar and a manipulator. I defended her. Amelie was angry at me because I wouldn't send her to New York on a trip by herself so she made up the story. I realized that my ex-wife was right about our daughter. I apologized to Elisabeth, but by that time, it was the proverbial straw for the proverbial camel's back."

The story about why the couple broke up might vary slightly, but Marie-Claude knew that was normal. She apologized for the telephone call and hung up, but she put the phone number where she might find it if she should need it again.

CHAPTER 30

Paris, France, 1305

A week before the Feast of the Lord's birth, Jacques located an Aramaic teacher. That and de Bois's class kept him sane. He was faced with a situation he never expected to encounter and one that was not typical for scholars.

Students were divided between those who preferred lectures so they could drift off to sleep, especially if they'd been carousing the night before, and those who loved to participate in debates. De Bois encouraged the latter. Some were so lively that fistfights would break out.

Days when he was involved in his studies, Jacques was able to shove Madeleine from his thoughts. She was his problem.

At night, when he returned to his lodgings, she greeted him at the tavern's door. She served his supper such as it was. Sometimes instead of gruel, it might be meat pie or a root vegetable. As winter wore on, the vegetables deteriorated until Jacques fought bugs for his meal. A glass of wine, usually sour, washed it all down.

As he ate he felt her eyes watching him, even when the tavern was full. Her father encouraged her to handle the men and charged extra for it. Sometimes the man and Madeleine disappeared upstairs. Jacques read shame in her eyes.

He decided that man, in general, was a weak creature. He was weak. He pretended that as a priest, he was caring for her lost soul then berated himself for lying to himself.

One night he was more tired than usual. The debate in de Bois's class had turned into a fistfight, with the teacher's table being smashed and a knife being drawn before de Bois could calm his students. Jacques stayed to help the professor fix the damage to the room. They continued the debate as they worked, leaving Jacques mentally drained.

The tavern was full that night. Jacques got the dregs of a watered-down stew. Several customers were drunk. Madeleine ducked around one man who kept shoving his hand up her skirt. Although Jacques knew he should go upstairs, he didn't want to leave her unprotected. The drunk gave the tavern keeper some money and staggered over to her. He took her arm, but she pushed him away.

The tavern owner growled something, but she shook her head. He raised his hand to strike her.

Jacques grabbed the tavern owner and shoved him through the door. Outside, the cold air felt like a slap against his skin. Clouds hid any light from stars or moon. The men could barely see each other. "You won't hit your daughter again," Jacques said.

"Says who?" The voice was slurred from sampling stock.

"Me."

"I can tell ya to get out."

"We've a contract. Let me repeat: if you do not treat your daughter better, I will beat you until you hurt so bad you'll wish you were dead. If you treat her right I'll increase my rent."

The tavern owner, although bulky, was fat, slow, allergic to pain and greedy.

"Notice I did this outside where no one knows our deal. You won't have to be ashamed in front of your clients." Jacques walked back inside.

Madeleine looked at him with wet eyes. Her tears had left

little streams down her dirty cheeks.

"He'll leave you alone," Jacques said.

Madeleine grabbed his hand and kissed it. Jacques pulled it back. He was not a pope or cardinal whose ring needed kissing.

He went to his room and opened the book that he had plans to analyze that night. His candle flickered in the dark from the wind blowing through the shutter slats. He shivered.

Her lips were so soft.

He gave up any idea of studying and settled on his mattress, pulling the blanket up to his neck. Tomorrow he would write his parents for cloth to hang on the windows to keep out the drafts. Although he tried to plan the letter, soft lips kept filling his thoughts instead.

The next morning when Jacques left his room and locked it for breakfast, the tavern owner growled no more than usual. Madeleine was washing the tables. She grabbed Jacques's hand and put it to her breast.

He pulled back. Would it be necessary to find different rooms since he was hated by the father and worshipped by the daughter? And if he did leave, there would be no one here to protect her.

CHAPTER 31

Anton Wagnier slammed down the telephone. *Merde! Merde! Merde!* The Département des Antiquités was giving the fucking archeologists two more weeks because they found some damned chimney and they thought they could find the structure of a building. Everything had been ready to start August first. He had figured the cost down the last *centime* and if he lost his crew it would be hard to find a new one, Crédit Paris could call in the loans and he would be bankrupt. He wasn't some big-time construction company, but one who had done well with building houses and renovating old apartment buildings for resale.

He didn't dare tell his wife about the delay.

She'd been against his going out on his own.

She'd been against him putting their house up as partial security.

She'd been against him borrowing from her parents to top off what the bank was loaning.

She was a cautious *fonctionnaire,* always playing it safe in her safe government job with the Département de Justice. Her salary wouldn't begin to cover their expenses: plus she'd warned him, if he were to fail, their marriage would be over. He had known when he married her, she was risk-averse, but he thought that might balance his love of pushing everything to the limit; make him look at things more carefully. Of course the fact that they wanted to make love constantly played a bigger part in the reason he married her. Her parents were so Catholic that there was no way they could live together without being married. In fact, her father had taken him aside on the morning of their wedding and told him how lucky he was to be getting a twenty-three-year-old virgin.

And he had looked at this project carefully, but he had not built in the time to turn his future restaurant and office building into a bloody dig into the past. That was all right for Greece, Rome or Egypt, but not for Paris. Goddamn it, the city had had people living on it for centuries. Sure there was stuff, but let it be found when his building fell down. It could wait for future generations.

He debated going out to the site and seeing if he could persuade the head of the dig to quit. Maybe he could pay him off. How much could an archeologist earn anyway? A whole year's income would be cheap at the price. Much better than his losing everything.

CHAPTER 32

When Annie woke in the morning, the shower wasn't running and there were no kitchen sounds. Maybe Luca had snuck out early. She hadn't heard him come in last night, but having had just under too much champagne and making sure Philippe got home safely after he had had too much to drink, she'd fallen into bed and slept soundly. The street noises, footsteps from the flat upstairs, people walking by in the hall—none of it had disturbed her.

At least she had no headache, a sign either that she hadn't been really drunk last night or that the champagne was of a better quality than they thought. She called out for Luca.

No answer.

She wandered into the living room. The couch was still a couch. Nothing had changed from last night. Maybe Luca had gotten lucky and found a woman's bed with a participant who didn't say no. For a moment she felt jealous: no, not jealous—just a reminder that Luca was like a leaf blowing down the street on a windy day. No one could count on him for shade. In a way she loved him as an old friend, as a man passionate about his work, as a person who was warm and funny. If and when she finally settled down, she would want someone more like Roger, stable, who faced responsibilities not with a joke or a smile but with the intention of acting as a truthful, responsible adult.

★ ★ ★ ★ ★

Luca did not show up at the dig. However, the team worked as if he were there. The chimney they had discovered was almost completely intact—only a few bricks were missing. A bread oven was uncovered.

The heat had returned full force. Marino now being the only male on site did most of the heavier digging. Alexander had quit saying he wanted to go back to Toulouse. Philippe was probably too hung over to come to work. Jacqueline and Laure knelt in their quadrants sifting the dirt in case there were small items worth saving. They all hoped for another gold coin.

Because they were down so many volunteers, Annie helped with the digging until her arms and shoulders ached. Her T-shirt was as wet as if she'd been caught in the rain. The sun was merciless. She threw down her shovel. "I'll be back."

She climbed out of the hole and walked to the restaurant where they usually ate.

The cook was arranging fish, meat and vegetables on ice in the window making a gourmet painting. Jérôme was setting the tables laying down orange placemats and sticking orange napkins in the water glass. "Annie, you're too early for lunch."

"We're roasting on the site," she said. "If you put barbecue sauce on us, and cannibals came by, we could be served on a platter with one of your fine wines."

"I never serve my best customers to others," Jérôme said. "What can I do for you?"

"I wonder if you had a spare umbrella that we could set up to give us a little shade."

Jérôme shook his head, but indicated Annie should follow him. Since there were restaurants in all the old buildings side by side on this street that had been occupied by the same buildings since the Middle Ages, all the restaurant owners, chefs and waitstaff knew each other. When they went out onto the street calling to customers to convince them to come in, they would insult the other restaurants while building up their own.

"We've the freshest salmon. It just walked into the kitchen five minutes ago."

"Don't listen to him. The fish was wheeled in from an old-age home."

After the restaurants closed down and all was cleaned up, sometimes the waiters or chefs or owners would get together, have a drink and talk about the customers, good and bad. Jérôme went to five restaurants before he found an unused umbrella.

"It has a small tear. I hadn't gotten around to throwing it out," said Costos, the owner, bringing a green umbrella and its stand from the store behind the kitchen.

"Would you be upset if we eat at Costos to thank him?" Annie asked.

"One meal, one meal only." Jérôme helped her carry the umbrella to the dig and set it up so it provided some shade for Marino as he dug.

Periodically during the day one of the other team members would call Luca's cell. He never answered.

CHAPTER 33

Roger Perret was staying at a small hotel in the fifteenth *arrondissement*. It was a true old-fashioned French hotel with pillows that were like a large, long roll, hard and uncomfortable. To get to his room he had to walk through a small plant-bedecked courtyard and up three flights of stairs. There was no elevator.

The bathtub was square and when Roger sat on the porcelain seat inside, the water came up to his armpits.

The bathwater cooled his body but not his temper. Annie had replaced him with a former lover in just a few days. He had believed that she loved him more than that.

He knew he should go back to Argelès, but he had fought for a five-day holiday in the busiest season and five days he would take. Gaëlle was off to a holiday camp. As she had stomped off to her friend's mother's car, her last words were, "Make up with Annie. You were wrong."

Maybe he was wrong to use the word *forbid* with Annie. He didn't think he was wrong to resent her going away on a nonpaying assignment.

He was back in Paris for the first time since he and Gaëlle had moved south after his wife was killed by one of the criminals he'd put into prison. He'd grown up in the fifteenth. He and his wife had lived there all through their marriage. The buildings were the same as he remembered, but the stores were different. He had walked by his grammar school, but he didn't go near the apartment building where he had been so happy with his wife and daughter.

He had hoped when he stormed down the stairs away from Annie she would telephone him. His cell remained quiet. No text messages, no calls, nothing. He had made a move. She needed to make the next one.

For all the years he had lived in Paris he had never played tourist. He wasn't sure what he should do this hot, hot day. Go see Napoleon's tomb? Climb the Eifel Tower? No—it was too hot.

Maybe he should go back to the station, the old 36, where he had worked. How many of the same people were still there? Some were sure to have been promoted, quit or retired. He'd never really associated with his coworkers. When he had free time he'd wanted to spend it with his wife and daughter. His old chef had called him the first Christmas after he'd moved south; then there was no more contact.

He got out of his bath, put on a pair of lightweight khaki pants and a white short-sleeve shirt and headed to the quai des Orfèvres. The Métro at that time of day was not as crowded as it would have been at rush hour, but even with the summer holidays, people waited. The curved walls were covered with posters advertising a trip to the Seychelles, eyeglasses, a do-it-yourself store, a Florent Pagny concert, a new bookstore, FNAC. When he'd lived in Paris he'd never really noticed the posters. He was always rushing because of the case he was working on or to get home to be with his wife and daughter or to some school event.

He walked along the *quai*. Gray buildings were to his left and the Seine was to his right. A boat, not one of the tourist boats, but a houseboat, floated down the river. Usually they were docked in one place. He and his wife knew a couple who lived on a houseboat, which was romantic in good weather and damp during the long, cloudy Paris winters.

The receptionist at 36 looked up. "May I help you?"

"I wonder if I could see Raymond Baille?" He hoped his old chef was still there. The man was too young to retire, but injuries and burnout made more than one chef leave their posts.

"And you are?"

"Roger Perret. I used to . . ."

"Oh, my God! Roger! It's me, Angelina. Don't you remember?" The woman rushed from behind the counter and grabbed and hugged him. When he'd worked there, she'd looked older, overweight. This woman could have been her younger sister.

"You look wonderful." He refrained from asking what happened.

"I met a wonderful man, took off about twenty kilos and redesigned myself." She asked about his daughter and how he liked the south of France. Finally she called Baille, who rushed out. He kissed Roger on both cheeks and led him into the office.

They exchanged news of family and cases.

"Argelès not too tame for you?"

"Sometimes, but with Gaëlle . . ."

"Ever consider coming back?"

"Sometimes, but again with my daughter . . ." Why did he say that? Paris was his past.

"If you ever want to, I'll move the bureaucrats to get you back. You were one of the best."

Roger wasn't sure that was still the case. Most of what he dealt with was petty kid crime, drunken tourists, a car fatality or two. In his time in that Catalan village, he had only investigated three murders and one of those was a knifing between two drunks along what was called a river that ran through town even though it had no water eleven months of the year.

They were interrupted by a knock, and a woman entered.

"Marie-Claude, I want you to meet one of my old staff here." Baille finished the introductions and the two exchanged the normal pleasantries until Marie-Claude's cell went off.

"*Merde.* They found another body in the little courtyard at Saint Julien-le-Pauvre. It was in a Dumpster. A shooting, according to the person who called it in."

"Go girl." After she left, Baille said, "She's one of my best, too, now that you're gone."

When Roger finished talking with Baille, he ran into two other men with whom he had worked. There were still about eight people from the old days, but they were on holiday, Baille had told him. It was strange being there. The computers had been updated. When he peeked into the conference room he saw white boards with pictures of people and notes for various cases. He didn't go into the interrogation area.

To be back at 36 was like watching a surreal movie. Things were almost familiar—yet not. He was anxious to get out. Leaving 36, he stopped, not sure where to go. He headed toward Notre Dame. He hadn't been in the church since he'd investigated a murder there. He left the church and wandered along the Seine where all the booksellers had their stands. Some sold magazines. The dealer that only sold old *Paris Match* magazines was still there. Roger's wife used to collect issues on the deaths of famous people. Displayed was the cover of the issue featuring the death of Claude François in 1978. Had she still been alive, he would have bought it for her.

Paris was not a good place for him to be: too many memories. He needed to go home: home to Argelès. Home to Gaëlle. And he should be going home to Annie.

He glanced at his watch. He had time to check out of his hotel and to buy a ticket for the night train leaving from the Gare d'Austerlitz.

CHAPTER 34

Paris, France, 1305

When Jacques left his room the morning after his fight with the tavern owner over Madeleine he wondered if he would need to find another room.

When he returned that night the tavern was full again. Jacques slipped undetected to his room. He pounded on his mattress to smooth out the straw and fell asleep, but woke to the sound of smashing wood. He sat straight up.

Shouts.

Bangs.

A scream.

He opened his door to see the tavern owner on the floor. Another man was on top of him. Jacques assumed he was a paying guest because a door was open to the room across the hall. The stranger was pummeling the tavern owner with both fists. Jacques grabbed his stool and hit the man with it, giving the tavern owner time to push his attacker off. The man lay on his back for a moment, stunned.

The tavern owner went into the room and gathered the man's things.

The stranger staggered to his feet, pulled a knife and was heading toward the tavern owner, but Jacques grabbed his arm and bent it behind his back. The knife fell to the floor. The tavern owner turned. Between them they were able to subdue the man and throw him out into the night.

The tavern owner slumped on a bench inside the tavern. "Not bad for a student." He yelled at his daughter. "Bring us some wine, and don't charge him for it."

CHAPTER 35

So that was the famous Roger Perret, Marie-Claude Du Pont thought after she had been introduced. His solve-record was legendary as was the story of his wife's death and his ultimate decision to leave Paris. Handsome man.

Stop it, she told herself. Two marriages were enough. Since her divorce even dating was out of the question. If she had free time and if her sons were occupied elsewhere, she preferred to stay home with a good book or a good DVD. If she went out it was with one of her girlfriends from forever. Not that there were many but Sophie and Marielle had been her friends together from the *lycée* and had shared marriages, divorces, kids, shopping, movies, gabfests, picnics and everything else imaginable. Not that they saw each other all that often because they were caught up in their own lives, but they knew they were just a phone call away from each other if they were needed for the good or the bad.

Marc, one of the younger officers, walked over to her. "Hey *Patronne*, we've another body. Dumpster near Saint Julien-le-Pauvre." She didn't tell him she already knew.

She tossed him the keys to the Panda. "You drive."

They had to park a bit away from the church: it was much too congested to park where she would have liked. The Dumpster was turned over inside a small courtyard with an iron fence around it. The only other thing in the courtyard next to the thirteenth-century church was a tree. The Dumpster did not seem to belong to any particular restaurant. Logically the church was too far from any eating place for a Dumpster of that size.

Sprawling among the fish skeletons and vegetable peelings was a maggot-covered body of what had been a beautiful man, not handsome but beautiful. His open gray eyes had long lashes, and his hair waved over his collar. His chest was covered with blood. He looked familiar to her, but she couldn't quite place him. She met so many people, that in itself, it was understandable.

"There's not enough blood to say he was shot in the Dumpster," Marc said. But someone could have shot him and put him in it."

She looked at the ground. The *flics* had not disturbed the wheel marks in the dust.

"It must have been wheeled from someplace else," Marc said.

That was exactly what Marie-Claude had thought. A new medical examiner arrived, a young woman that Marie-Claude had only met a couple of times. She was new, just out of medical school. What was her name? Lillian something? No, Florence something. A photographer was with her.

"Anyone touch anything?" Florence asked.

"Someone turned over the Dumpster. That had to be recently because it's not a secluded area. A corpse would be noticed but it was under all the garbage."

"Or maybe someone turned the Dumpster over to hide the body," Marie-Claude said.

The *flics*, who had arrived first, finished roping off the street. Tourists and locals alike were gawking. A reporter from TF1 that Marie-Claude knew ducked under the tape. Marie-Claude told Marc to push him back but to do it politely because there was a camera crew behind him. God, they were fast. Or maybe they were just having lunch nearby. So far there was no one from France2, 3, 4, 5, 24 or M6, but there would be.

"No one wanted to hide his identity," Florence said, holding up a wallet. When Marie-Claude started to reach for the rubber gloves she always carried, Florence said, "I'll look." She opened it. "His name is Luca Martinelli."

"Jesus, Mary, Joseph. From the dig," Marie-Claude said. Two people from one site killed. That put a whole different slant on the situation, but she wasn't sure what it was.

CHAPTER 36

Annie expected Luca to be home when she let herself into the apartment. She would have called out, but the place was so tiny, a half a dozen steps and she could see not only wasn't he there, he hadn't been there. Once again she tried his cell phone, and once again she got the *messagerie*. "It's Annie again, Luca. I'm getting worried."

Now what? She tried his old apartment. This time she got Crystal's message, and she didn't want to leave a message with her. A hang-up on the telephone wouldn't arouse as much suspicion in a jealous wife as a woman's voice, even though she had met Crystal. If Luca had persuaded his wife to give him another chance, a message from a woman whom he had been sharing a flat with would not be diplomatic at best.

Tonight she was bone tired having spent more of the day digging than writing up anything. Without Amelie, Luca, Alexander and Philippe the crew needed as many hands as possible.

The next thing was what to do about dinner. A glance in the freezer showed that they had emptied out everything Rima had cooked. Before she left, she would restock the freezer with meals, just not Middle Eastern: spaghetti sauce, a beef stew, maybe a lentil dish. She would need to check the Internet for recipes. Rima was not one of those people who would only eat her own nationality's dishes, but she only cooked them, which was fine with her friends who enjoyed eating her preparations.

She could go to McDos, the Japanese takeout, or get a pizza

and bring something back to eat in front of the television. Then there would be no major cleanup, and she could curl up in front of the television and watch a variety show. She was too tired to listen to one of the celebrity shows where they all talked at once about nothing much. However, she was much too dirty to go out as she was—even for takeaways.

She turned on the shower. The water left little mud rivers down her body, but she felt her muscles relax. After drying herself off but leaving her hair wet, she put on a sundress, grabbed her purse and opened the door. Standing in front of the door was Marie-Claude Du Pont, her hand poised just before the bell. "Hello?"

"Hello," the detective replied. "May I come in?"

"I was just going out to get some dinner. I'm starved. Do you want to walk with me?"

The neighbor Dorothy Richardson got off the elevator and walked toward her own door.

"Not really. I've bad news. We've found a body. It was Luca Martinelli."

"Oh, my God," Dorothy interrupted. "Was that the man who was so angry the other night?"

Annie couldn't take in that Luca wasn't alive. "What? Luca? A body?"

"I said a body. I'm sorry but he's dead."

"How?"

"May I come in?" She turned to Dorothy who had moved closer. "I'd like to talk to you a bit later. Which apartment is yours?"

Dorothy pointed to her door. "Luca was which man? The one staying with you or the one who was so mad to find you with another man?"

Annie wanted to scream shut up as she noticed Marie-Claude's face. It read motive, motive, motive.

"Luca was the one staying here." She beckoned the detective into the flat. Then she herself sat because she wasn't sure she could stand any longer. "Luca? Dead?" The words didn't make any sense.

"I listened to your messages on his cell phone."

"When he didn't come home, when he didn't show up at work, I was worried. I thought maybe he got lucky last night, but his staying away from the site was really strange. Late, yes, he could have gone to the Département des Antiquités first thing, but he wouldn't have been there all day."

"Are you lovers?"

Annie was taken back at the direct question. "Not really."

"Not really?"

"At university. Then one night, more by accident." When she saw Marie-Claude's raised eyebrow, she continued. "Sex by opportunity, hot night, few clothes, memories? You understand?"

Marie-Claude nodded that she did. "And what about this other man?"

"My ex-fiancé. He showed up as I was getting out of the shower. Luca was also there but not really dressed, and Roger jumped to the conclusion we'd been having sex. He took off before I could explain."

Annie knew well enough that this would make Roger a suspect, but he wouldn't have killed Luca. He was still haunted by the criminal that he had killed when he still worked in Paris. "I know what you're thinking, but Roger would never kill someone. He's a *flic* himself."

"I'm not saying that he did, but being a *flic* isn't proof of innocence. We've had some of our own kill in domestic-violence cases. Is he in Paris?"

"I haven't seen him since he left here, so I really don't know. He's easy to find. He works in Argelès for the police. I'm sure you've the number in some directory."

Marie-Claude started to say something then stopped.

Noticing, Annie wondered if she should say something, decided first not to then changed her mind. "Is something wrong? Besides Luca's death?"

Marie-Claude shook her head.

"Do you have any idea how I can get ahold of Martinelli's wife? We found his cell phone with her number on speed dial, but she doesn't seem to be picking up."

"I know she's on holiday with the kids at her mother's. I don't know where that is. Somewhere outside of Toulouse. And I don't know her mother's name."

Marie-Claude looked at her watch.

"You look tired."

"It's been a long day. I'll be at the site tomorrow to talk to the others. I would appreciate it if you didn't talk to them before I tell them, although I can't forbid it."

"I won't. We aren't close friends, but it would be nice if they had another few hours without knowing about this murder."

"I never said he was murdered."

Shit, Annie thought, of course she didn't. "But you wouldn't be here if he died of natural causes would you?"

Marie-Claude almost smiled. "I still would have to notify the family. You're the closest thing we have to tracing it down."

Annie almost smiled back. "But they would send the ordinary police, not the head of a murder-investigation team, if it were natural. And there's Luca's connection to the dig."

Marie-Claude nodded and rubbed her temples.

"I suppose my once being engaged to a man who used to work where you work, gives me an insider's knowledge."

Marie-Claude frowned. "Who was that?"

"Roger Perret. Did you know him?"

"My God, I met him for the first time today. I didn't make the connection."

And although Annie knew that the detective had let her professional demeanor slip, she could read the exhaustion in her face and felt sorry for her. "Do you want a cup of tea?"

Marie-Claude drew herself up as if looking for inner strength. "Thank you, I need to get home. Officially my shift ended three hours ago." She turned to go.

Annie stood holding the door. "Roger is the last person to kill anyone willingly. He once told me how he'd killed someone while on duty, and he still feels guilty about it. That was years ago."

"I'll be out at the dig tomorrow first thing." Marie-Claude walked toward the elevator.

Annie stared at the closed door. She heard Marie-Claude's footsteps heading to the elevator, a silent pause then the sound of the elevator arriving, the door opening and closing and the last whir as it descended.

She went to the couch. Luca's pillow was on top of the throw cushions. She picked it up and hugged it to her chest. The other night both their heads has been on it and it carried the smell of his aftershave lotion.

She wasn't in love with Luca. She'd never been in love with him, but she respected him professionally and she had enjoyed him as a friend, not the kind you see regularly, but when you do, you pick up where you left off. Then she cried.

CHAPTER 37

Paris, France, 1306

January brought rain and fog. Jacques Fournier's bones felt cold as he studied in his room, when he walked the streets and when he sat in class.

Twelfth night, instead of bringing gifts to the Christ child, brought a thick drizzle mixed with smoke from thousands of chimneys. Jacques huddled under his cloak as he propelled himself through the muddy streets. A few horses clip-clopped by him. A wagon splashed him, traveling too fast for the narrow road. He jumped back and fell against a door opening into a small shop.

An old woman flashed a toothless grin. "Most people just walk in. May I help you?"

Jacques struggled to his feet. "I'm sorry to disturb you."

"You didn't. Business is bad on days like this. Would you like some hot cider?" She pointed to a fireplace with a kettle hanging over a small fire. "I like chatting with people, especially the young." She ladled cider into two cracked bowls. "Give me your cloak, child." She whisked it off of him and headed to the fire where she spread it over a stool then handed him a rag. "Dry yourself."

Before Jacques left he knew that her husband had run the shop until his death a few months before. She lived behind the shop front. The building was a hovel, but perfect for her she said. Eking out a living selling buttons, ribbons and thread satisfied her. Her ribbons were wound on spools. Jacques saw that one spool captured the summer sun. "I'd like a length of that ribbon."

"Go on with you. You got no need for a ribbon."

"I'm offering it as a gift to a friend."

"You sure you don't just feel sorry for an old lady on a horrible winter night?"

"Talking with you has been a pleasure, not to mention how good the hot cider was." He put the ribbon between the covers of the book he had been carrying under his cloak. As he put it on, he realized the garment was totally dry for the first time in days. His room was too damp and too cold for anything to dry properly. Outside the rain had turned to sleet. He skidded his way back to the tavern, landing once on his backside.

As soon as he entered the tavern, he made his way to the fire, which was spluttering from water dripping down the chimney, and held his hands out to warm them. "Raw out," he said to Madeleine and the tavern owner, the only two people there. He was not surprised that customers preferred to be at home on a night that was getting worse.

"Goddamned weather is bad for business. This keeps up and I'll starve to death," said the tavern owner as he disappeared into his own quarters.

Madeleine wiped down the tables.

"I talked to a woman today. She was selling something I thought you might like."

The rag stopped moving. She tilted her head as she looked at him. "I never had a gift. What do I say?"

"Try thank you."

"Thank you." She rubbed the rag where she'd cleaned a moment before.

"You don't know if you'll like it."

She worked on the table with more concentration that ever before. Jacques realized how embarrassed she was. "Do you want to guess what it is?"

She shook her head. The cloth moved back and forth. The uneven wooden tabletop was all she would look at. She dug at a hole with her finger where food had lodged in a crack.

He turned his back to pull the ribbon from the book. Crumbling it in his hands and putting them behind his back, he stood in front of her. "If you don't want to guess what it is, at least guess which hand it's in."

Her eyes left the table: she turned slowly toward him. A butterfly would have tapped his left arm harder. He held out his empty left hand.

She sat.

"Try the other one."

"What if it's empty?" Her lips trembled.

"Try anyway."

She did. The ribbon fell from his hand into hers. She put one hand over her mouth, and then held the ribbon with the other. "What a beautiful yellow." Standing on tiptoe, she brushed his cheek with her lips and danced over to the only candle to admire the ribbon in light.

"Wear it to keep your hair out of your eyes." He took the ribbon from her and turned her around and tied it in place. Although he wanted to suggest she wear a wimple or at least a head cloth, he resisted.

Madeleine was never again without the ribbon. Three days later Jacques brought her a comb and the snarls in her hair were replaced by waves.

As his studies became more intense, he spent more time at the library, more time in his room going over the texts. And although he told himself that he had no more time for poor waifs, he still couldn't stop himself from thinking about her.

CHAPTER 38

Roger watched the night train pull into Gare d'Austerlitz. After double-checking his ticket he found his sleeping car. A young couple speaking German were in the top bunks, the middle two bunks were empty as were the two bottom. He'd reserved a bottom.

A red plaid blanket, pillow and a sheet that was sewn in such a way one had to get into it like a sleeping bag were on each of the empty bunks. Roger quickly made up his bed, stashed his overnight bag under the bunk and climbed in. The older cars could have very efficient air-conditioning in January and equally efficient heating in July, but this was a brand-new TGV.

He wanted to be home. The bunk was harder than his mattress on his own bed and far narrower. If he were two inches taller, he would have had to sleep in a fetal position, but he could just stretch out with his head grazing one end of the bunk and his feet the other. By morning he was sure that the other bunks would be filled. In summer, people were always going south for holiday, but this was not August 1, the biggest travel day of the year when half the country went home and the other half set out for vacation. Well, half was a bit over the top, but a good majority.

The young couple was whispering among themselves. He hoped they wouldn't talk all night, but they asked him in French if it was okay to put out the light whose switch was over the door frame. Roger said it was. He heard them trying to find a position as they whispered *Guten Nacht* and *Ich liebe dich* to one another.

As he lay there he felt the train begin to move. The rocking always put him to sleep. If there wasn't too much talking or people coming and going, he normally would sleep quite well. But . . . but this night all he could think of was he wished he hadn't come to Paris. Part of it was he had stirred memories he would have preferred remained buried. And the other was Annie. Just thinking of them together made him mad. The man was sexy and handsome and Italian. Luca was Annie's age, not fifteen years older like Roger was. He felt a lot older that night.

The train pulled into Argelès-sur-mer at 5:37 in the morning. Roger hoped there would be a taxi because his house was too far to walk, and even if the police would ignore his own car illegally parked too long by the station, he didn't like to take advantage of his position.

There were no taxis. Well, he could go to the tearoom/ *boulangerie,* where the baker would have been baking for the last two hours to make sure the good citizens and tourists had fresh bread, brioche and croissants for their breakfasts.

The smell of flowers and pine trees hit him. The morning was already hot. A garbage truck rumbled by the front of the station as Roger walked toward the village center.

A police car pulled up driven by officer Boulet, one of the stupidest policemen he had ever had the displeasure of working with. Boulet's father, an ex-mayor, was now a quadriplegic after trying to kill Annie over a nonexistent treasure. He had also murdered the local priest. The *flic* rolled down the window. The air-conditioning inside hit Roger in the face.

"Get in, *Patron.* Thirty-six called you about a murder and I've been meeting every train since then. They want you to telephone a Detective Marie-Claude Du Pont."

Dear God, he thought, don't let anything have happened to Annie. "Take me directly to the station."

CHAPTER 39

The dig team was down to the three women and Marino. Philippe had checked himself into rehab. They sat on the edge of the steps of the shed as they went over and over the two deaths. The normal can't-believe-its were intensified by the ages of the deceased and the fact they had both been murdered. No one on the dig to this point had ever known anyone who was killed deliberately. And, now, within a week, two people had been killed by someone.

"What should we do?" Laure asked. Her face was swollen from crying. Tears filled her eyes and she brushed them away. "I thought I was through crying. That detective woman must have thought I was in love with Luca the way I bawled in front of her."

Annie didn't say that the detective was interested in her possible sexual relationship with Luca, but then Luca was a man on the prowl, so if she looked at women who had slept or wanted to sleep with Luca, the list would keep her busy for a long time. Annie had a dislike for silly men, those who constantly made innuendos, but Luca wasn't like that. She believed he genuinely loved women, not just in bed. Some men, she noticed, claimed to love women, but they would be the first to manipulate. Luca never manipulated. He was forthright. I want to sleep with you. And he might press, but never force. Or he used to press. It was still hard for her to think of him in the past tense.

"What should we do about the project?" Laure repeated.

"We've no boss."

"One of us should call the Département des Antiquités. Let them know that Luca is dead, although I suspect that Detective Du Pont will be calling them, anyway. And in the meantime we need to keep working. For Luca. And there still might be . . . *merde.*"

"What?" Jacqueline asked. She did not look as if she'd been crying. Her relationship to Luca had always been professional. Once she had asked Annie if she were the only woman in the world that Luca hadn't made a pass at. Annie had said there were probably one or two more including Mother Theresa, but then added that Jacqueline gave off *don't-think-about-it* vibes. "It's not like I want him to, it's just that I don't want to be considered unattractive." Annie had reassured her that she was attractive.

They all looked up. The mobile unit of TF1 was parked at the top of the dig and a reporter and a cameraman scrambled down. The reporter was one that Annie had seen any number of times on television talking earnestly into a microphone about whatever story he was covering. He was in his early thirties, one of those who were up and coming and getting better and better assignments. He often interviewed politicians, but this was July in a nonelection cycle and almost all the politicians were in the south of France or up in the mountains. She tried to remember his name but she couldn't.

He was wearing makeup. Jacqueline, Laure and Marino all stood up as he came over to them. "I'm from TF1 and we are doing a story on the Medieval Murders."

"The murders took place last week, not in medieval times," Annie said.

"But they took place on the site of a medieval building." He flashed a smile then let it fade. "It must be hard on you, losing two of your coworkers."

At least he wasn't one of those reporters who stuck a mike in someone's face and asked a grieving mother, "How did you feel when they discovered your daughter's body sliced and diced?"

As Laure started crying, the cameraman started shooting. Annie shoved her hand in front of the lens. "Please don't. This has been hard enough."

"Just answer a few questions. Please. About the project."

Unlike the others, Annie had enough corporate experience to not speak beyond her authority which was nonexistent. "I suggest you go to the Département des Antiquités. They're in charge of the project." She took her hand away from the lens when the cameraman lowered his camera.

"Do you think that the murder had anything to do with the treasure?" the reporter asked.

"What treasure?" Jacqueline asked ignoring Annie's hand signal to shut up.

"We heard there were many gold coins unearthed."

"There were not many gold coins found," Annie said. She didn't say there was only one found so she wasn't lying just using phrasing that implied something different. She wondered if the reporter were sharp enough to pick that up. Before he could, she noticed that the cameraman was walking around shooting the site, but his camera was lower than normal shooting position. She went up and again put her hand over the lens. "*S'il vous plaît,* leave."

The reporter and cameraman climbed out of the hole. Annie watched them stop at the top. The reporter fixed his hair, adjusted his makeup and stood so that the cameraman could stand on a crate he had pulled from god knows where and get part of the dig. What he said into the microphone, Annie couldn't hear with the normal street noises.

"Let's get to work and wait for further instructions," she said.

They worked for over an hour unearthing a few pieces of pottery and bones which they decided were from chickens and maybe a lamb or goat. They would not be sure without testing or showing them to someone more acquainted with animal remains.

No one felt like a lunch break, but they took one anyway. When they got back, a woman in her forties dressed in jeans, boots and T-shirt was standing in the hole. "Who are you and what are you doing?" Annie asked.

"I'm Sophie Martin, and I've been assigned to take over from Monsieur Martinelli." She shook hands with everyone. "I know this must have been hell for you having two team members killed. I would understand if you wanted to quit, but I hope you don't."

"Did you think we had when you came and no one was here?" Annie asked.

Sophie nodded. "Also I wondered . . ."

". . . if we were afraid we would be next?" Jacqueline asked. Her face was dirty. In fact all of them had dirty faces and arms, although their hands were clean from washing in the restaurant before lunch. Their clothes were dust-caked.

"That too," Sophie said. "But I see you went right ahead today."

"Dedicated volunteers," Marino said.

"We really would like you to finish the project. It looks like we've got some interesting things here, and I would hate to see it stop."

They exchanged looks and one by one said they were in. "After all," Jacqueline said, "for us students this is great experience for our CVs." Laure nodded.

Sophie looked at Annie. "And you?"

She wasn't sure what to answer. "I started out to help an old friend and do something different. But I know Luca was dedicated to the project, so I think this is the way I can best honor his memory." It sounded stilted to her, but in a way she meant it. If any of the others had been behind the murder, she wanted to be around to unveil them.

CHAPTER 40

A slight breeze rippled the palm trees lining the parking lot by the Argelès train station. Gendarme Boulet stood next to the car, but he could tell him nothing about why 36 wanted to talk to him. Roger Perret swallowed his worry about Annie. In her wallet, she carried an in-case-of-accident-notify card with her parents' names on it.

He and Annie had fought about it. He'd wanted it to be him. David and Susan Young would have notified him immediately if something had happened to their only daughter. He doubted that the Youngs would be nasty to him just because he and Annie had broken up. They had developed a friendship. He was closer in age to her parents then he was to Annie. Sometimes her parents told her that she was being unreasonable in her treatment of him, which usually pissed her off. And he was sure at some point they would reach out to Gaëlle, for they had become her surrogate grandparents.

"If something happens to me in Argelès, you'll know about it," Annie had always said.

"But you're away so much," he'd said.

"Then I want my parents to break it to you. Supposing someone got Gaëlle on the phone and it was some clod without an inch of tact who told her."

He saw her reasoning, but he still felt as if he were being relegated to second place and he also felt stupid for feeling that way. In any case 36 would never contact him over Annie. He probably left something at the station when he was visiting yesterday.

"I'm going home and shower and then I'll call when I get to the station," he told Boulet who shrugged.

"You're the *Patron*."

I am, Roger thought.

"*Merci* for telephoning," Marie-Claude Du Pont said when she came to the phone. "I don't know if you remember, but we met yesterday."

"You've got brown hair, wear it shoulder length and there's a wave that you can't quite control. You were wearing a light beige linen-looking pantsuit with a brown short-sleeve blouse."

"Good observation."

"I'm a *flic* too. Did I leave something behind?" He'd checked for his wallet and cell, but he didn't check to see if something had fallen out of his wallet before he called. Probably from a bad night's sleep in the moving *wagon lit*. And the trip to Paris had been upsetting, not just in terms of seeing Annie, but in raising his fears that this time he had really lost her. He did not regret the life he lived in Paris, in fact he had cherished his wife and loved his work at the time, but they were the past and that's where he wanted to return them.

"We'd like you to come back."

"Excuse me?" The last thing he wanted was another long train ride.

"We need to discuss a crime with you."

"What sort of crime?"

"I'd prefer to talk in person."

"And I prefer some professional courtesy here."

There was silence. "We are investigating a murder."

Roger understood the phrase; his heart stood still. "Has anything happened to an Annie Young?"

"Madame Young is fine."

"I'll be happy to answer any questions right now." He knew she would want to see his face and body language. "Or you can come down here." He knew that 36 was too careful with travel budgets to make a trip to the south of France in vacation season a reality. "And can you tell me who was murdered?"

Another silence then a sigh. "Luca Martinelli."

"Luca?"

"Where were you the night before last?"

"At my hotel." He added the name and address.

"And were you with anyone?"

"No."

"We know you were angry when you saw your ex-fiancée with Luca."

Of course he was angry, or a better word would be hurt. "Annie and I have had our ups and downs, and this is a down time, but I expect we'll work it out."

"And wouldn't her affair with Luca reduce your chances?"

He didn't want to answer that question, not at all.

CHAPTER 41

Paris, France, 1306

On Purification Sunday, the first in February, the tavern was closed. Jacques had been cooped up in his room trying to decipher a passage from a contemporary of Saint Paul. The writer sounded resentful of the saint, although Paul hadn't been a saint then.

Jacques decided he needed a walk.

As he entered the tavern on his way out, he saw Madeleine emptying the fireplace ashes. The smell of smoke from dead fires and wine hung in the air, more apparent now that there were no longer smelly people sitting at the tables. Her yellow ribbon was no longer crisp. "Ya want something to eat?"

"I was going for a walk. Want to come?" The words were out of his mouth before the thought of them.

"I have to ask my father."

"Two *deniers*," the tavern owner said. He had come into the room with an armful of wood that he dumped next to the fireplace.

"I want to take her for a walk, not use her body." Jacques kept his voice pleasant, although it was an effort.

The tavern owner snorted. "All priests are alike. They fuck when they can."

Jacques hit him with a flurry of arguments until the consent came grudgingly on condition that Madeleine finish her chores.

"Not good enough," he said each time she completed something. "Again."

Jacques went upstairs to wait. It was mid afternoon when she knocked. He let her in. She stood by the door, her arms behind her back. One of the books caught her eye and she opened the cover. She traced the letters with her fingers.

He cringed, thinking she would dirty the page, but he said nothing.

"I can't read." It was the first thing she'd ever said to him on her own initiative that didn't involve asking if he were hungry or thirsty.

"Most people can't."

She seemed to accept that. They put on their cloaks and went out. The sky was blue, but they could see their breath. Instead of walking next to him, she lagged behind until he took her hand and pulled her up to him and didn't let go. They trekked in silence for less than ten minutes to reach the river Seine.

She clapped her hands. "I've heard about the river. I've never seen it." She bolted and ran down the bank and stuck her hand in the water, but pulled it out even faster. "It's so cold." Her eyes, bigger than normal, took in something that he saw every day. He resisted rubbing her hand to warm it.

She wiped her hand on her cloak. "Why do ya want to be a man of God?"

"It's a long story." He told her about his difficult birth, his father running to the church and offering his son as a priest if only his wife would live. And after that he told her of his mother's determination that his father's vow be carried out.

When he'd finished, she let out a long sigh. "Your father made a vow to God: mine made one to the devil."

There were hundreds of questions he wanted to ask her, but he was afraid of increasing her discomfort. He remembered the nights he had heard sounds of passion from her room, followed by her crying. He'd heard her father yell and the sounds of flesh on flesh. "Why do you let him do it to you, your father? Mistreat you?"

She shrugged.

"You've a choice."

She whirled around until she stood in front of him, anger written in her eyes. Her lower lip jutted out. "Always the priest, ain't ya?"

"You could enter a convent?"

She laughed, not a normal laugh, but one that was hard and dry. "The sisters would love to take in a tavern whore."

"Don't call yourself that."

"Why not? That's what I am."

"Jesus Christ was kind to a prostitute. Mary Magdalene. Her name is almost like yours."

"Jesus Christ ain't got nothing to do with me."

Blasphemy. Certainly understandable, though, that she would think that. Try as hard as he could, he couldn't get her to change her mind. Finally he said, "Christ loves you whether you want him to or not."

She put her finger against his lips. "Don't tell my father. He'd charge him a coin." They resumed walking along the river where not that many people walked. They passed boats and barges pulled up along the bank. River grasses were knee-high stalks that crunched when they stepped on them.

Madeleine burst ahead of him and bent down to retrieve something that Jacques couldn't make out until she walked back to him and held out a mud-encrusted gold bracelet shaped like a rope.

"Someone must have dropped it." What a stupid thing to say, Jacques thought. No one would put a bracelet there. "I imagine it's yours now. There's no way we can find the owner."

Madeleine's eyes went from the bracelet to Jacques's eyes

then back to the bracelet. She dipped it into the river and dried it on her cloak before putting it on her wrist and holding it so the sun beamed off the metal. "It's so beautiful."

As they walked along, she kept holding out her wrist to admire it. "My hands are so ugly."

"Your hands are graceful," Jacques said.

"I'll have to hide the bracelet from my father. He'd sell it."

He knew she was right. "I could keep it in my room. There's a lose floorboard, and I lock the door."

She broke into a laugh. "And I will know it is safe. You living in the tavern has been such a help to me. My father doesn't beat me anymore when you're around."

He resisted taking her into his arms as they continued walking in silence until they reached King Philippe's palace.

She stopped. "It's huge."

"You've never been by here?"

"I've only been around the tavern's neighborhood. Now I've seen the world."

They crossed to the Île de Cité at the Petit Pont. The bells of Notre Dame chimed. Although the church wasn't finished, Mass was being held in a part that had been completed. He dragged her in and she went, but he saw she didn't know what to do. The sacrament meant nothing to her, but she copied him when he knelt.

As night fell, they returned to the tavern. At the entrance, she brushed her lips across his cheek. He inhaled her smell, mustiness combined with the cold coming off her cloak. "This was the best day of my life."

In his room, Jacques relived the day. He wished he could teach her the beauty of the Mass. He wished . . . no, he decided not to even think of that.

CHAPTER 42

Sophie Martin was a better dig manager than Luca had been. She worked harder, joked less but praised more quickly. She had them concentrating on the area around the fireplace, saying she wasn't sure they would be able to finish before their deadline, but the fireplace area was the most likely place to find cooking tools and pottery.

She was right. They unearthed an iron spit, a big iron pot and bones from many different animals.

"They kept the garbage in the house," Laure said. Her face was covered with dust, more than the others, because she'd been down the hole that had been dug around the fireplace. The other quadrants had been abandoned. She handed up another shard.

"Maybe they had spareribs," Jacqueline said.

"Has anyone checked to see what was here?" Sophie asked.

"I tried," Annie said. "Deeds don't go that far back. We identified the building as being about the time of Philippe the Fourth, because of the coin we found. That means we are on the outskirts of the university area, so a private home, a hostel perhaps." Her phone rang.

"Take it," Sophie said.

Annie looked at the number. *Merde.* Roger. She walked to the shed.

"Don't hang up" was his response to her *"Oui, hallo."*

"I'm usually not that rude."

That made the others look up, so she walked a little further away and turned her back on the dig team. "What's up? Are you still in Paris?"

"I'm in Argelès, but I've decided to come back to Paris, and I was wondering if I could stay with you?" When Annie didn't say anything, "It's important." When she still didn't say anything, he added, "They want to question me about Luca's murder."

"Luca's murder? They couldn't think . . ."

"That woman detective wonders if I killed him in a jealous rage, although she didn't say so directly. At first I thought that I wouldn't come up, but I'd answer any questions. Now I think I can clear it up better, if I walk into the station."

Annie wasn't sure she wanted him in the flat with her, but then again, she wasn't sure she didn't.

"My God, look what we've found."

"Come. Let me know when you get in. Gotta run." She shut the phone and walked over to the dig.

Laure was standing over what looked like the skeleton of a very small human skull.

"Oh, my God." Jacqueline's dirty hands covered her mouth. "What do we do?"

"Call the police," Marino said, "although I suspect that they won't be interested in a seven-hundred-year-old corpse."

Annie took out her phone and dialed because she'd entered Marie-Claude's number on her speed dial. She explained what they'd found, how deeply it had been buried and that there had been at least two buildings over it during the centuries from the time they were currently excavating and the present day. "It's really discolored," Annie added.

"I'm still sending a medical examiner over," Marie-Claude said.

CHAPTER 43

What a day. Marie-Claude circled the *crèche* three times before pulling her car up on the sidewalk. Unlike most days, she wasn't the last parent to show up. Today, she had promised herself, she would leave work to spend some quality time with Daniel.

It had been a hard, hard day. She'd finally finished questioning all of Amelie's acquaintances. She had found no friends. People described her as beautiful, intelligent, lazy, fun, man-hungry. More than one young woman had complained that she'd gone after their boyfriend. One woman said that was a deal breaker for her because it had told her more about her *mec* than it did about Amelie. None of them seem to be angry enough to shoot her.

Then Annie Young had called from the dig about a baby skeleton. Marie-Claude had sent a medical examiner who reported that even without testing he knew it was very, very old. Since Marie-Claude had enough to do with modern murders, a skeleton from the fourteenth century held little interest for her. No, make that absolutely no interest.

Roger Perret had telephoned and apologized for being so rude during his earlier call and said that he was coming back to Paris and he'd see her tomorrow.

It was one of those beautiful summer evenings in Paris when the temperature was just right. She wondered about picking up some salads from Monoprix and taking them to the park for a picnic with Daniel. With her older son still at holiday camp, she would be able to focus just on her baby, although he was rapidly becoming a boy.

Inside the *crèche* there was silence. Marie-Claude walked to the back where there was a courtyard where she found the children running through a rotating sprinkler. Silence was replaced with screams as the water poured over the small bodies.

Daniel ignored her until she grabbed him before he ran back into the water. He kicked and screamed as she tried to get him back into his shorts and T-shirt. Giving up, she threw him over her shoulder. Her blouse was wet where his bathing suit touched it.

In the car he fell asleep mid-whine. At home he pushed her hand away when she tried to shake him awake. She carried him into the apartment building. Once in her own flat, she dropped him on his bed. She suspected he would sleep till morning. As good as the *crèche* was, he often came home so tired and cranky that the only thing to do was to put him to bed.

She went into the kitchen. No way could she sneak out to Monoprix for anything to eat. She didn't even dare go next door to the Chinese restaurant in case Daniel woke.

The *frigo* had little to offer: two eggs, wilted coriander, one celery stick. On the counter was an apple. She guessed that would make a salad if there were any mayonnaise left. There was.

With the salad, such as it was, and a glass of wine, she went out on her balcony which overlooked a small park. A few parents were watching their children go down the slide. Mostly they were couples. She half wished she had a mate. But then again, if she were married, she would probably be struggling to fix a real meal for him. Her desperation salad would not satisfy any man she knew, and it would be pure fantasy to think that some man would prepare the dinner for her. At least none in her life so far would have. If she ever found a new man, she would put him through a culinary test before getting in too deep.

The balcony held a chair and table. She found a two-month-old copy of *Express* which she had not had time to read. The evening, although different than she planned, might not be so terrible after all. The tension began to leave her body as she fantasized a nice soak in the tub, a few candles on the side, maybe some Bach playing. Her love of classical music was something that she'd always kept secret from her coworkers who were more into pop music.

Her telephone rang. *Merde!*

She found her purse.

"Franck, here," the assistant medical examiner said.

"What's up?"

"Well, my wife was in a bitch of a mood this morning, and I didn't particularly want to go home, so instead I decided to do the autopsy on the Martinelli corpse. You'll never guess what I found." Franck loved guessing games.

Marie-Claude did not, so she said nothing.

"*Ça va, ça va.* You don't want to play. I'll tell you anyway. The gun that killed Martinelli also killed the other woman on the dig."

CHAPTER 44

Paris, France, 1306

Sunday walks became a ritual for Jacques and Madeleine. On Mondays and Tuesdays, Jacques thought about everything they had said and done. On Wednesdays he began counting the days until Sunday. He fantasized that she became a nun and later an abbess. He would be an abbot and they would confer about abbey/convent problems, always finding brilliant solutions.

In his fantasy, Madeleine would have not only learned to read, but she would have learned other languages, although it would have been difficult. He would have helped her with declensions and verbs, and although she made mistakes on some of her translations, overall she did remarkably well considering her late start.

When he offered to teach her to read, she always found a reason not to go ahead with the lessons: she needed to cook for the evening's customers, there was cleaning to do, the light wasn't good enough. Mostly she wanted to go out for their walks, and that he understood. For her, being away from the tavern had to be a freedom that she had never known before, he imagined.

He tried to think of new places to take her: they would walk by one of the king's palaces. He pointed out the gargoyles and explained how they drained the rain. They passed many of the barbershops run by women. "If I could cut hair, I could be free of my father," she said. "But, it is too late to be an apprentice and I'd never have enough money to open a shop."

She stopped suddenly. "Unless I sold the bracelet: do you think it would be enough?"

Jacques had no idea of the cost of an apprenticeship nor what the cost of opening a shop would be. "I could find out for you."

They walked further. "No, don't bother. Look. We're at the river." She rushed ahead for she loved crossing the Seine on the bridges that had many shops.

Sometimes he would buy her a meal in a tavern that was better run than her father's. "Do you think he would appreciate it if you tried to make some improvements?" Jacques asked.

She looked at him as if he were crazy. "Tell my father anything? Do you really think that's possible?"

One Sunday she had packed some bread and cheese and he had picked up two apples from the *marché*. The weather was warm enough, that he spread his cloak over a large stone along the riverbank. The water, a dirty brown, was higher than usual from two weeks of almost constant rain. Had they not found the stone, his cloak would have been soaked if he'd spread the material on the muddy ground. He lifted Madeleine onto the rock. The food was placed next to her, but there was not enough room for him to sit as well.

She unwrapped the stale bread from the piece of cloth and brought out the mold-covered cheese. With a knife she cut off the bad parts. He took the knife from her and cut the two apples into four pieces and gave half of each to her. "In case one apple is sweeter than the other, we will have equal pleasure," he said. But the pleasure he really wanted to share with her would mean breaking his vows.

And he refused to dwell on the image of a serpent tempting Eve with an apple.

CHAPTER 45

Annie could barely stay awake on the Métro. Every now and then she would open her eyes when they came to a stop and would see the wall-to-ceiling posters advertising eyeglasses, books, vacations and DIY stores. Then she would shut them until the next stop, grateful that this was the line that had chosen to not go on *grève*. Had the workers struck, she would have opted for a taxi and hang the cost.

Her watch told her it was almost 21:33, late to be coming home from the dig. But once the medical examiner had told them the baby skeleton was not of interest and Sophie had said that she would do all the paperwork on the find, they had carefully used brushes to clean the skeleton and put it in the shed, probably treating it with more respect than the person who had buried it near the fireplace.

Although the commuting crowd were most likely eating their dinners, there were still enough people occupying the cars, but not so many she couldn't find a seat without anyone around her. Because she was dirty and sweaty, other passengers kept their distance.

At La Défense Arche, the 144 bus was not due for another thirty-two minutes. She could walk it in less than that. As she passed the Chinese café, she saw they were just closing. She motioned she would like to buy something and Monsieur Wang, whom she had gotten to know, nodded that yes, he would still serve her.

213

Good. Her energy to cook was nonexistent.

Armed with food for at least two nights, she made her way to Rima's flat. With each step she fantasized a shower and bed. The elevator creaked its way to the fifth floor. As she stepped out she saw Roger sitting on the floor in front of the door. He scrambled to his feet.

"Your neighbor, Dorothy something or other, said I could wait with her, but I didn't really want to," he said as he kissed her on both cheeks. That was saying he accepted he was there not as a lover, but as her friend.

"You're looking good," she said.

"You're looking dirty."

"You know how to sweet-talk a girl." She told him of the skeleton find and the deadlines they were under as she unlocked the door and put the food on the kitchen countertop.

"You take a shower," he said. "I'll set up dinner. How did you know I'd be here? I didn't say when I'd arrive."

"I didn't. The guy was closing. He gave me everything at half price so I took double." She rummaged through her suitcase, which she'd never unpacked, for clean underwear.

"I've a confession. I called you from the train. If you hadn't said I could stay, I'd have found a hotel, but I would much rather be here."

"Hmmm." She shut the two bathroom doors, the one leading to the bedroom and the other to the living room. Were they still a couple, she'd have left them open, although considering how dirty and tired she felt, this was not a night she'd have invited him to join her.

The water washed not only the dirt away, but some of the ache in her muscles from bending over. This was the first project she'd ever undertaken where she did the work as well as the translation and writing. However, the physical labor helped erase her thoughts about Luca.

As she shampooed her hair, she felt the grit under her fingers. It took a long rinse before it felt really clean.

What the hell was she going to put on? She'd been planning to slip on her pajamas, a shorts-and-tank-top set. Roger might take that as an invitation—one that she was not issuing. She could get dressed again, but she didn't want to. Why had she said yes, he could stay? Dumb, dumb, dumb.

As she toweled her hair then used her pick through the mass of curls to unsnarl it, she heard him moving back and forth from the kitchen. The table, pulled from the wall, was followed by the rattle of cutlery and plates. The same thing had happened one night with Luca setting up dinner while she showered.

Poor Luca. Her eyes filled and she brushed the tears away with the back of her hand. She had no pretensions of being in love with him, more like being in like with him. He was so loveable in a good-hearted rogue sort of way. He'd added color to her life a couple of times, but he was no one to be serious about. For serious, she needed someone stable like Roger. Put that thought right out of your head, girl, she told herself.

Damn if she would let Roger's presence force her into clothes. She put on the pajama set and opened the door.

The table had been properly set.

"I couldn't find any chopsticks."

"No problem."

He pulled out her chair and then seated himself before starting to dish out the food between the two of them. He paused with his egg roll midair. "Perhaps you want to serve yourself."

Annie had been relieved not to decide. "As long as I don't have to eat everything you put on my plate." She took the first bite, thinking she wasn't all that hungry, but by the third, she realized she was famished. "How's Gaëlle?"

"Happy to be with her friends. At one of the campgrounds, there's a new Irish kid whom she fancies. And him her."

"And you're not doing the worrywart-father routine this time?"

"I'm trying to be cool, mainly because he's only there until the weekend."

Annie debated saying a lot could happen in the three days before the weekend. Her role had been to run interference between the teenager and her ex-fiancé, but that was no longer her place. If Roger was learning to loosen up slightly, she didn't want to ruin any chances for Gaëlle in the future. She had more faith in the girl's common sense than Roger did. He'd never been a teenage girl. His experience as a cop often made him worry about the needless, while not understanding the real. She left it at "Good."

"I'm heading over to 36 in the morning. I know I'm a person of interest, because they thought I might have been jealous of Luca."

"You were, the way you ran out of here."

"No, I wasn't." He took several mouthfuls of fried rice. "Well, maybe a little."

Annie smiled. He didn't lie about being on the train when he called, he didn't lie about jealousy. Despite all their problems, one thing she had always appreciated about Roger was his honesty: his wanting to control her whereabouts was another thing. And his nerve to forbid her doing something was totally unacceptable. Had he said that he wished she wouldn't go on the dig, she might have accepted that—or not. At least they could have done some negotiating, but she was not a child to be forbidden anything by him or anyone else.

CHAPTER 46

Marie-Claude made it into 36 early. Because Daniel had fallen asleep so early, he'd been up early. They'd had a breakfast where she'd cut his bread into the shape of a man and a dog. He dunked them into his bowl of chocolate milk as she made up a story about them, a silly story, where the dog talked and the man barked. Not the quality time she'd wanted the night before, but quality time nevertheless.

The drive into work took less time. She was ahead of the traffic, and the traffic was holiday light. Not only that, there was a parking place in front of the door. This might be a good day yet. Inside there were the usually rustlings of a shift change: people walking out, people walking in, notes being exchanged.

"Go to Raymond's office," the receptionist said. "Stop frowning, nothing wrong. You can get coffee on the way."

Coffee in hand, Marie-Claude entered her boss's office. Through his office window she saw a man sitting with his back to the glass. She knocked and entered without waiting for the okay. The man swiveled around. It was Roger Perret.

He was a good-looking man, still in excellent physical shape. Men graying at the temples, with hair curling slightly over their collars, had always been a turn-on for her. Enough of that. She wondered if he were the type of man that might cook dinner for his wife. "I'm sorry you made the trip for nothing. I had thought you were a person of interest, but you've been exonerated by the evidence."

"What evidence?" Raymond and Roger asked at the same time.

"The medical examiner called me last night. The same weapon killed both people associated with the dig. Roger, you weren't in Paris at the time of the first killing. Of course, you could have hired someone, but you would have had no motive to kill the woman."

"It's hard to put a contract out on someone I didn't even know existed," Roger said.

Raymond broke into a smile. "I knew you were barking up the wrong tree with that one, Marie-Claude. Roger wouldn't hurt a fly if he could help it."

God, why did her chef always have to talk in clichés? Still, he was one of the best bosses she'd ever had. He didn't play games.

"Roger," Raymond said. "Why don't you stay up here for a few days and work on the case with Marie-Claude. It might do you good to get out of that backwater. Get back to the cutting edge."

"It's summer. The village has gone from about eight thousand to fifty thousand people."

"And if I know you, your team is trained to handle it all," Raymond said. "Two weeks maximum?"

Roger smiled. "Two weeks, but I'll leave earlier if everything is solved. You going to do the paperwork?"

After they left the chief, Marie-Claude briefed Roger. He asked all the right questions, including, "Who benefits if the dig shuts down early?"

"The developer-to-be."

"Let's go see him," he said.

"I hope you don't mind riding with a woman. I'm not sure you're insured for our cars here."

"Not at all. I like being a passenger."

He had a killer smile. Calm down, she told herself. He lives at the bottom of the country. He has an ex-fiancée, a brand-new ex-fiancée. She didn't have time to get involved with anyone, much less someone just off a relationship. Since the breakup of her marriage, she vowed she would stay single. She certainly didn't want to drag men into her bedroom with the boys around. She'd seen too much damage when there was *oncle* Philippe, *oncle* Michel, *oncle* so-and-so. Kids would get attached and then the man would disappear. And she didn't even want to think of the Oedipus issues. None of that didn't mean she couldn't enjoy looking.

CHAPTER 47

Paris, France, 1306

May 1, 1306, was one of those days in Jacques Fournier's life that would always represent a major change. There were a few others: the day he left for Boulbonne, his first day at Fontfroide, the day he took his final vows. None were as major as May 1, because all the other changes had left him striding along his intended path.

He woke with a start. The room was totally dark. Someone was next to him. He wouldn't put it past the tavern owner to rent out part of his bed without telling him. Some nights, he was so tired he forgot to lock his door. Or it was too much work, for the lock was sticky and it could take several minutes for the key's position to budge. Although he didn't like to admit it, he hated the feeling of being trapped inside. He slipped out of bed and opened the shutters.

The full moon reflected on Madeleine, her hair spread out to make a curly, black halo, her face more of a child than a woman. She moved and opened her eyes.

"What are you doing here?"

She sat up. "I was lonely. I thought ya might be too." She patted the place that he had just left.

"I can't. It would be a sin."

"We ain't going to do nothing. I just feel better when ya're near me."

As if Satan had stolen his will, he went back under the covers, grateful he wore a nightshirt. She wore nothing. After much prayer on his part, they slept entwined.

Throughout May, one or two times a week, he would wake to find her there. He knew he could lock the door, but he never did now, didn't even try. He told himself that the lock would be too much work. He also told himself, as long as he did not commit a sexual act, his soul would be safe. He told himself over and over, knowing he was lying to himself.

CHAPTER 48

Marie-Claude Du Pont hopped into the driver's side of the police car. As she maneuvered around the streets, Roger decided that Marie-Claude was a good driver and any uncertainty about women driver *flics* was latent chauvinism. He certainly hadn't missed the Parisian traffic although in summer the roads into Argelès could be bumper-to-bumper. Roger noticed she was checking the rearview and side-view mirrors just about the right amount. She didn't turn to him as she talked. Although the traffic was summer-light, it was still Paris with intersections where cars seemed to be going every which way.

"I hope you forgive me for suspecting you."

"It was normal. Ex-fiancé finds his ex with another . . ."

". . . man. Jealous rage and all that."

When Marie-Claude smiled, Roger thought how very attractive she was. Of course, he had never stopped appreciating women all the time he was with Annie, but he'd never acted on it. Still, it was too soon to think of another woman. Gaëlle was not ready to accept that he and Annie were finished; the logistics of dating a Parisian *flic* were too complicated and there were hundreds of reasons not to follow up on his urge. His old boss had told him that Marie-Claude was free after a painful divorce. He wondered if she would be one of those women that raged on about the horribleness of the ex.

"Exes can be a pain, but the healthiest thing is to get mad and get over it. Jealousy is usually about the great time you imagine someone else is having and in reality their life is never as great as you imagine," she said circling the same block. "Like all the times you see a white-haired man with a trophy wife and screaming kids in McDos: you can just bet he left a woman his own age and all the problems of raising a family to find himself right back in the same problems."

Roger had only been half listening as he scanned the road. "If you're looking for a parking place, two o'clock."

She turned the wheel so fast to enter the parking spot that he listed toward her. If it were not for his seat belt he would have been in her lap. "But the ex-wife is probably picturing them having great sex and when she learns about the new baby, she thinks the child sleeps through the night and changes its own diapers."

Roger thought how being a widower was so different from being divorced.

"Besides, hatred takes up too much energy." She shut off the engine.

He laughed. "Okay, enough philosophy on breakups: what are we trying to accomplish here?"

"As far as we can tell, the person with the most to lose at this point is Anton Wagnier. He owns the building site. This is his first big project."

"And what did he do before?"

"Smaller projects, mostly renovations." She reached for the door handle at the same time he did.

"How old?" he asked.

"Fifty-two."

"Old enough to want one last chance to go for something special, but also old enough to worry about the risk of losing everything and not having the time to recoup," he said.

They got out of the car and walked by a kiosk, one of those round metal buildings which tourists so loved. He spied a paper.

"Stop." Roger grabbed and paid for a newspaper.

"Do you often have news attacks?" she asked.

"The headline caught my eyes. 'Meurtres du Moyen Age.' I was hoping that it didn't refer to the dig. Listen."

He read, "Two people have been killed on an archeological worksite in the last two weeks. The first, Amelie LaFollette, 23, was an archeological student at the University of Montpellier. Her body was found Tuesday morning in the locked shed used by the team as an office.

"The second victim, who officially has not been named by the police, is thought to be the supervisor of the project, Luca Martinelli, 35. Police said they were withholding releasing the name pending notification of next of kin, according to an unnamed source. Martinelli was working for the Département des Antiquités, as a consultant, and is also a professor at the Sorbonne.

"Other members of the team are excavating what they think is a fourteenth-century *relais*.

"Unconfirmed sources report that a valuable piece of gold was found at the site raising the possibility of more treasure items still to be found and a possible motive for the murder."

Roger stopped reading. "*Merde,* they'll need twenty-four-hour security now."

Marie-Claude took her cell and told her chef just that. "Okay, you've seen it." She clicked off the phone. "The men were already on the way over. Good. I would hate to think any of the others are in danger." She turned to Roger. "That gold coin . . . I wonder where they learned about it?"

Roger's thoughts were all of Annie, not coins. She could be killed, if there was someone out to shoot enough members of the team to stop the dig or to look for gold. At least he'd be staying with her nights. Maybe he could volunteer to be part of the dig to keep her safe.

"You're worried about your ex?" Marie-Claude asked.

"She has a way of finding trouble," he said. "One of our problems is she's not like your average woman who wants to go shopping. She gets more excited about an old document instead of a new dress."

They had arrived at a three-story apartment with six doorbells. There was one for Michel Wagnier Enterprises. Marie-Claude pushed it. The front door gave a click and they pushed their way in. The building was old, renovated perhaps thirty years before, yet it still had a cared-for look. The windows had no fingerprints, the hallway floor was spotless. The paint was not chipped, although it was dingy.

A middle-aged secretary answered Wagnier's door. Her office was furnished with flat-pack desks and filing cabinets, but everything was a matching fake oak. The desks had the obligatory computers, all laptops. The secretary's IN and OUT boxes had papers that were neatly stacked, with more in the out than the in. A single rose was in a bud vase.

Marie-Claude showed her badge and asked to see Monsieur Wagnier.

"He's not in," she declared, but simultaneously the door opened and a man in his mid-fifties entered. He wore light linen pants, a short-sleeve shirt and no tie or socks. "What can I do for you? I'm Michel Wagnier."

As soon as he discovered the identities of his visitors he invited them into his office which had the same furniture as the secretary. It was slightly larger, with a window that looked out onto the street where people were walking by. The neighborhood was half residential, half commercial, but the ground floors of the area were offices for real-estate agents, attorneys and doctors. It was neither upscale nor down.

In one corner of Wagnier's office was an architect's mockup of a three-story building. Wagnier saw their eyes go to it. "That's the place I want to build on the site of the Meurtres du Moyen Age," he said.

Roger and Marie-Claude glanced at each other with a look that said Wagnier had read the same news article they had.

"I'm worried. I'm working on a shoestring budget, and if you want, I can show you. I've tenants lined up but the premises have to be ready by a certain date or I pay penalties. I suspect you think of me as a person of interest."

"We're looking at all possibilities," Marie-Claude said.

"Well, having the dig delayed by the murders achieves the exact opposite of my best interest." He opened a drawer and pulled out the newspaper, the same one Roger had just bought. "This does nothing to encourage people to rent from me either. The restaurant that is planning to open—they called about canceling their lease. I can see their point: the idea of dead people can hurt their business unless it wants to play on the macabre—come eat where people died, meet their ghosts."

Roger thought he had a point.

"I'm willing to answer any questions that you might have."

For almost a half hour they went over financials, how he acquired the building. His alibi for both murders was that he was with his wife and friends. During the estimated period for Martinelli's death, he'd been home playing with his grandkids, people had come in for a barbecue. He'd driven his grand-daughters to the *crèche* this morning. His daughter and her two little girls were living with them, as was his son. He then had gone back home to pick up his wife, whom he later dropped off at the hospital for some blood work, and gone to the office, where his secretary could say what time he'd arrived. In between, he did not have time to kill anyone, much less move a body.

"How did you know the body was moved?" Roger asked.

"It's in the paper." Wagnier threw the paper at Roger, but not nastily. "Second page, paragraph four. When I read it, I thought *merde*, another delay. And I told the other *flic* who asked me about the first murder that I went camping with friends in the forêt de Fontainebleu for a couple of days. We both keep caravans out there so we can get away without having to go far."

Roger would have thought a man of his age would prefer a more comfortable getaway.

"And I suppose your friends will back you up," Marie-Claude said.

"It would be hard to get all those people to lie for me."

They thanked him and left.

"You didn't say don't leave the city," he called after them.

Once in the car they looked at each other.

"Motive, half and half," Marie-Claude said. "He's right that murder would cause delays he can ill afford."

"Alibi?" Roger asked.

"Seems to be ironclad, but we should check it anyway."

"But not the first thing. How about Martinelli's wife?"

"She's been on holiday and we've been trying to reach her. Not much luck there. *Mon Dieu*, I hate Julys when everyone is on holiday unless it's me."

"And I hate Julys because everyone's on holiday where I'm working. Same for Augusts."

Marie-Claude's phone rang. Using her free hand she opened it up. "Okay, I'll go over there." She snapped the phone shut, and as she reached for the key in the ignition, she asked, "The morgue. Do you want to go over there?"

Roger shook his head. "I think I'd rather go to the dig."

"Worried about your ex?"

"You got it in one," he said.

CHAPTER 49

They had brushed the last bit of dirt from the baby's skeleton and lifted it into a small wooden box that Jacqueline had bought. They tried to keep the bones in formation. Both Jacqueline and Laure had insisted on finding a proper box for it.

"I don't care if the baby's been dead seven days or seven hundred years. It deserves respect." Marino had rolled his eyes, but all the other women agreed. "What do we do with it?"

"Turn it over to the Département along with everything else," Sophie told them, "since the coroner doesn't want it."

"I wish we could give it a proper burial," Laure said.

"Maybe it had one." Jacqueline looked as if she could cry at any moment.

"I doubt it. It looks like it was buried near the hearth to get rid of it," Sophie said. "There were horrible people back then too that didn't give a damn about human life."

"And I thought it was such a religious age with the Catholic Church the only religion despite a heresy or two." Jacqueline used the back of her hand to wipe away a tear, leaving a dirt streak near her eye.

Laure patted her on the shoulder. "You're such a softie."

Annie went back into the shed to do more documentation work, just as Roger appeared at the door. He was dressed in new jeans and a T-shirt. "I thought you could use a pair of hands."

"If this is an attempt to make up with me . . ."

He stepped in and closed the door. "I'm supposed to be observing everyone for 36," he said. "Help me out here."

She looked at him skeptically.

"Okay, okay. I admit, I don't like the idea of us not being together, but when have I ever forced you to do anything you didn't want to do?"

"Define force. Does it include temper tantrums and sulking? *Forbidding?*"

"What do you want for dinner? I'll treat. They say the way to a girl's heart is through her stomach."

"More likely it is saving her from cooking. We can pick up some falafel on our way to the Métro."

CHAPTER 50

Madeleine's frequent appearances in Jacques's bed gave him physical, emotional and spiritual torment. If his uncle were with him, he would confess, make his penance and tell her no. He did not consider he could go into any church for his confession. No matter how badly he felt, he could never make himself say no, never lock his door against her. The fact that he only held her didn't help him. His sin was in wanting. His sin was in loving to sleep with her in his arms.

As surely as the season changed from spring to summer, the inevitable happened. He found his hand move on its own from her shoulder to her breast, then over her little belly to the wiry hair between her thighs. He held onto it feeling its coarseness, surprised it was there. He'd never imagined women had hair there. He was sure that they would be clean and pure unlike men. Perhaps it was just Madeleine.

She guided his hand into her soft place, her wet place. He withdrew his hand. He tried to think if he had ever seen a woman naked. A woman in the bath he went to when he was first in Paris had begun to disrobe, but he'd stopped her, saving himself. His mother was always clothed. There was the baby sister of one of his friends, who had been on a bed as she was being dressed back in Saverdun. He couldn't have been much more than four or five at the time. The girl was still not walking.

He had stared, thinking she was missing a vital part.

Until then he hadn't thought much about what made the difference between boys and girls, men and women. It was just there: women were mothers, men fathers. They wore different clothes. He and his friends sometimes peed in the woods. His mother told him that girls were made differently from boys, but since he was going to be a priest, it wasn't important.

"But how do they pee?" he'd persisted. She'd laughed and told him, "Girls manage that activity quite nicely."

Madeleine gave him little kisses up and down his body. When he went to push her away, his hand touched her breast again. She covered his hand before he could pull it away. The skin was so soft. No wonder infants enjoyed suckling their mothers.

She crawled on top of him. Moonlight peeked through the shutter slats, ribboning her breast. She touched his face then put her nipple in his mouth. "Taste it," she whispered.

Her nipples, so much larger than his, grew hard under his tongue. There was no milk, but that was just mothers who could give milk like cows, although they gave milk long after giving birth.

Madeleine smelled of sweat and fish.

Ambrosia!

Witchcraft!

His body ached. As she reached for his organ, huge and hot and put it inside her, he spewed into her body: a sin, but it was a sin bringing a wonderful relief. The sin drowned out the release. Jumping out of bed he cried, "My God, what have I done?" He paced up and down the small space between the bed and table.

She had propped her head on her elbow as she watched him, her face twisted in confusion. "Nothing. Ya did nothing wrong— only what all men love to do. Women too." Her arms reached out to welcome him back.

Jacques's entire body shook. He turned his back on the room and opened the shutters. He rested his hands on the table and stared out the window. Her simplicity made her think the act was not the same as the thought. An evil thought is an evil deed. Explaining the difference would be useless. When he turned back to look at her, he saw her face, furrowed and without any understanding of what she had done wrong. Her confusion caused him pain. He hurt her, hurt himself, damaged his soul. Damaged her soul.

He sat on the edge of the bed. When she reached for him, he pushed her back, but not roughly. He lifted a strand of her hair from her face and put his finger to her lips. Her eyes were wide open as he took her hand. He sat there, holding it until sleep overtook her.

To the melody of her soft breathing, he watched the waning moon. Although the weather was warm, he was chilly. Self-realization cleared his vision.

Monks are chaste.

He was a monk.

Therefore, he was chaste.

A simple syllogism . . . no alternative . . . no bargains to make . . . there was right . . . there was wrong . . . no almost right . . . sin is sin.

The pain began in earnest the next morning when he faced Madeleine. She woke and rubbed her eyes as a small child might. Bad news did not improve with delay. He told her.

She sat up, grabbing the cover to hide her breasts. "What da ya mean? I can't come to ya room anymore?" Tears ran from her eyes.

Her tears were like acid cutting groves in his heart. No wonder Eve tempted Adam. She probably cried until he ate the apple. Women's tears were a thousand, no, a million times more powerful than any sword. They endangered Adam and thus all mankind. They endangered him.

"It's a mortal sin. If I spend more time with you, my soul and yours will be in danger for eternity."

She scrambled out of bed and knelt naked in front of him. "Don't do this to me. Don't leave me."

He looked over her head out the window to the apple tree that bore small green hard knobs. "I'll have to move. I can't stand the pain of seeing you every day."

"I thought ya loved me."

God help me, he thought. "As God as my witness, I do, but I'm pledged to Him."

"Then God be damned." She ran naked from the room slamming the door behind her.

CHAPTER 51

Crystal Martinelli shoved the tomatoes from her brother's garden, along with a red pepper, balsamic vinegar, lemon juice, coriander and a cucumber into the food processor and let it smoosh up together. She wore shorts, was barefoot and had her hair clipped back off her face, which shone with sweat. The house had taken on the heat of the day, despite the shutters being closed.

It was quiet.

She'd sent her boys to a holiday camp where their father couldn't reach them. He hadn't known where they were which was more than fine with her. She wished that he never would have any future contact with them, the lying son of a bitch. His kids were where he would hurt most.

This was her childhood home where she had come as a newborn to join her parents and brother. It had been built about forty years ago on a *lotissement* in Castanet, a Toulouse suburb. All the houses were the same terra-cotta color, most were the same design, but over the decades an addition here, a garden there, a different wall, gave the neighborhood a less conformist look if one ignored that all the surrounding streets had the names of French artists.

The boys had liked being at their grandmother's, because it was more spacious than their Paris flat, but she still shipped them off. She had never asked how her sister-in-law liked living in her mother-in-law's home. Crystal did notice that Elodie had made some changes, but every time Crystal was there she still felt as if she should go up to her old room and start her homework.

Her brother Jean-Paul, her only sibling, had been grateful to Crystal for agreeing to spend the month here so he and his wife and their two daughters could escape to the sea.

The gazpacho was done. Crystal put it in the freezer so it would be cold enough when they sat down to eat, not that it mattered to her mother, who would probably eat tissues if they were put on a plate in front of her.

The kitchen doorbell rang for that was the door closest to the street. Few people went around to the living room. The house had been placed on the lot a strange way.

When Crystal answered it, she saw two *flics*, one in his blue uniform, one in a lightweight beige suit. They showed her their badges, although she had never really seen a genuine police badge.

"Crystal Martinelli?" the one in the suit asked.

She nodded.

"May we come in?"

Crystal led them through the kitchen and around the corner to the living room. They perched on the *clic clac*, the sofa bed which allowed for extra guests . . . not that there were any these days. The *clic clac* had to have been Elodie's idea as a replacement for a two-seater which had been impossible to be comfortable on.

It was where Crystal had taken to sleeping nights so she could hear if her mother crept down the stairs. She took one of the straight-backed chairs that had been decoupaged. Her mother, who had always tried to find this or that antique for the house, had picked them up at an auction. That was before her memory started going.

An auction was the first clue something was wrong with her

mother when she had come home from one on the bus. The problem was she'd driven her car and had forgotten that she'd done so.

At the time Crystal's father had been alive. Perhaps taking care of his failing wife had shortened his life, but his heart attack brought a quick end. At the time of their father's death Elodie and Jean-Paul rented their own home on the other side of Castanet, but within two months they'd moved in to oversee the daily care of the old woman—if you could call sixty-two old. Crystal knew lots of women in their sixties who were still working or leading full and normal lives.

"We have some bad news for you," the suited one said.

"Something has happened to my kids?" She managed, somehow, to speak the unthinkable, the unspeakable.

"Your husband," the uniformed man said.

Crystal frowned. "What about him?"

"He was murdered."

All she could think to say was "That's not possible."

They told her it was not only possible it really had happened. "The Paris police asked that we notify you and ask some questions." The one in the suit leaned forward. "This must be a terrible shock."

Crystal was not sure how she should act. "I suppose you know we were estranged." Before she could say anything else her mother wandered in, her blouse undone and one boob hanging out of her bra. One side of her gray hair—which had been combed earlier—was flat from where she had lain on it, the other tousled. Her mother who had always presented herself with every hair in place and who would immediately change her clothes if she found a microscopic spot on anything she was wearing. Crystal jumped and adjusted her mother's clothing, a dark skirt and a white blouse, which Crystal had washed and ironed but now bore stains from lunch.

The policemen had the courtesy to avert their eyes. They excused Crystal who led her mother to the dining-room table, where she put down two plates and gave her a bag of beans to sort. These beans had been sorted too often to be counted, but Elodie had discovered that it seemed to make the older woman happy and, more importantly, it distracted her.

Crystal walked back into the living room. "I'm usually in Paris, and my brother who is a dentist and my sister-in-law who is a nurse usually take care of her. But they needed to get away for a couple of weeks of normal life."

"I understand," said the suited *flic*. "My father kept my mother home as long as he could, but then it got too much for him. How long have you been here?"

"Three weeks. I can't even leave her alone to go shopping, so I take her. She seems to enjoy the outings."

Crystal put her hands up to her face. "Do they need someone to identify the body?"

"It's already been done by his boss. You said you and your husband were separated," the uniformed *flic* said.

"My husband was a terrible womanizer. I got tired of it. If you have his cell phone, you'll hear several nasty calls from me." She was quiet for a moment. "Of course *you* wouldn't have. It must be in Paris."

"You were angry with him." The suited *flic* took over the questioning.

"Angry doesn't cover it. We could have had such a wonderful family life, but he kept catting around. He was never abusive to me. He was great with the boys. Coming down here gave me a chance to think of what I wanted, and it was a divorce."

"Did he want a divorce?"

"He said he didn't."

"Do you think the two of you might have gotten back together?"

"We'll never know, will we?" There was a crash in the dining room. The white spotted blue metal plate of beans had fallen to the floor. The old woman's crying turned into a wail. "I'm coming, *Maman*," Crystal said.

The *flics* followed her and helped pick up the beans.

"How long will you be here?" This was from the uniformed cop.

The suited cop patted the old woman's arm. "You're doing a good job with the beans." His voice was soft and he spoke slowly as if addressing a small child.

Crystal's mother smiled. If anyone were looking, they would think she was normal. She leaned forward and whispered, "I hope the cook doesn't get too annoyed that I spilled the beans." She indicated that the cook was Crystal.

"I'm sure she won't, Madame," the suited *flic* said.

"Will you tell her it was an accident?"

He nodded then started moving the beans around the plate. Crystal's mother also started moving the beans. The *flics* stepped away from the old woman and back into the living room. Crystal sat so she could watch her mother through the doorway.

"How long are you here for, Madame Martinelli?" the uniformed cop repeated.

"My brother and his wife and children are not due back for another week and a half. My kids are coming back from camp at the end of next week."

"Maybe you should ask your brother to come back earlier," the suited *flic* said.

"I don't know where he is." Crystal found the ability to let a few tears fall from her eyes. "I suppose this changes everything, doesn't it? What will I tell my boys?"

"It will be hard, Madame," the suited *flic* said.

She rubbed the back of her hand against her cheek to rub away her tears. "Excuse me." She went into the toilet off the entryway and returned with a tissue and blew her nose. "At least I don't have to tell Luca's parents. They passed away several years ago."

"Yes, Madame," the suited *flic* said.

Before Crystal could say anything more, Crystal's mother wandered into the living room. "Who are you?" she asked, but before either policeman could speak, Crystal held up her hand. "Just friends of mine, *Maman.*"

"And you?" she looked at Crystal, but before she could answer her mother asked, "Where's Jean-Paul?"

"He'll be back soon. Are you hungry?"

"Do we have any bananas?"

Crystal excused herself and brought back a banana peeled and cut into rounds with toothpicks. "Let me put on the television." She settled her mother in a chair and pulled up a tray in front of her. The program was a children's cartoon made in Japan. "Let's move into the kitchen," she said to the *flics*. The only place to sit was one stool against a board where someone could sit to peel carrots or potatoes. No one took it. Instead Crystal leaned against the refrigerator, and the *flics* stood in front of her.

"I'm taking care of my mother until my brother comes back from holiday. As you can see she can't be left alone." She swallowed a sob. "It's so horrible to see her like this."

The suited *flic* nodded. "I lost my mother twice, once to the disease and once when she died."

"Do you feel guilty?" Crystal asked. "Guilty you couldn't help her? Guilty that you wanted to shake her back to whom she once was?"

The suited *flic* nodded.

"I escape to Paris most of the time. It's my brother and sister-in-law handling this, and I don't know how they do it, but since the beginning of July, I've been here because, as I said, she can't be left alone even for a minute." She looked down at her feet. "I already told you that."

The two *flics* exchanged looks that Crystal thought said, alibi.

"Do you know when the body will be released? Luca had no family left so it will be up to me to arrange the funeral . . . and . . . everything."

"No, Madame," the suited *flic* said making Crystal wonder if the other one had been told to talk as little as possible. "But here's a number in Paris to call. Ask for Marie-Claude Du Pont. She's in charge."

Something crashed in the living room. All three looked toward the wall between the two rooms.

"Go ahead, we'll let ourselves out," said the suited *flic*.

CHAPTER 52

Annie and Roger, having overslept, were late getting to the dig. They had talked into the early morning going over the same old, same old. The only conclusion they agreed on, with almost a smile, was that they were both too stubborn and with that stubbornness it was doubtful that a marriage was possible. Yet neither was able to deny that they loved each other and Roger had even suggested it was possible to try and be less stubborn. "I'm sure *you'll* succeed if you try," Annie had said. "You're stubborn enough."

On the Métro, they both found pull down seats by the door where they were surrounded by other commuters standing like so many canned sardines. The crowding made conversation impossible, but allowed Annie time to think about their conversation the night before. She wished that he had never *forbidden* her to come to Paris. She was convinced he regretted it even more than she did.

"I'll treat you to a croissant and coffee," Roger offered as they mounted the stairs at Saint Michel.

"We're late," she said.

"But we're volunteers."

"And you're undercover." She raised an eyebrow, because only half of her believed it and half of her was convinced he was trying to protect her from becoming the next victim. Yet she was hungry; a cup of coffee would maybe help her wake up after not enough sleep and she wasn't that eager to dig in the dirt under the hot sun. She was originally supposed to only work on translations, but between the murders and Philippe's disappearance, they needed sweat labor more than they needed brain labor. She felt that the last thing she could do for Luca was to get as much done of the project as possible.

Annie was glad there was some kind of equilibrium between her and Roger now. If one of them started dating someone else, then it would be harder to maintain. Or, she wondered, was she just projecting her feelings? Just because she'd broken off her engagement, didn't mean she'd stop caring. She was just being realistic that this would not work.

The first café they came to had six tables outside. Two were occupied. One man was reading *Le Monde* and a woman was reading from a Kindle. Annie wished she could see the title, because she regularly chose books she'd seen being read on trains, planes or buses, considering if many people were reading something, it might be worth buying.

The waiter, with his white apron below his knees and the string tied about his waist, served their coffee and plunked down a green plastic basket with two croissants in record time. Roger handed her the one that was slightly overcooked, knowing she preferred them and then dunked his normally baked croissant into his coffee.

A few pedestrians walked by, mostly older people and some tourists with cameras around their necks and maps in hands. A couple sat down at the table next to him.

"I suppose we'll have to sell our firstborn child to pay for this coffee," the man said with either a Canadian or American accent—it was too neutral to pinpoint.

Annie could have resisted, but didn't want to. She faked a French accent. "Excuse me, Sir, you have to realize that when you buy coffee in a Paris café you are not just buying the coffee. You are renting real estate. That coffee lets you sit here as long as you want."

The man harrumphed, but the woman, probably his wife, laughed.

Roger spoke to her in French, "I can't believe you did that."

"Believe it."

They lingered at the table partly because the waiter was slow to bring the bill, and partly because sitting side by side on a perfect-weather day was pleasant. Neither seemed to want to break the mood, but when the waiter showed up, Roger paid.

They started toward the dig. As soon as it came into sight, they saw police cars, the medical examiner's car and camera crews from TF1, France2 and France3.

A *flic* stopped them.

"I'm police," Roger said. He pulled out his identification.

At that moment, Marie-Claude Du Pont looked up from the pit. "Let them in, Dennis."

The *flic* stood to one side.

The medical examiner was standing to one side. "You have got to stop unearthing old skeletons. You are using too much of our time." He stomped over to the ladder and climbed up to street level and back to his car slamming the door.

"Another?" Annie and Roger asked together.

"This is of a young woman or a teenager."

"Old?" Roger asked.

"Old," Marie-Claude said.

Sophie came over to them. "They've canceled the dig as of tomorrow. Annie, can you help us pull the reports together? A truck will come to take away what we've found. Do you think you could give us another day here and maybe a couple back at the Département?"

Annie nodded. "Yes."

Marie-Claude came up to them. "I can see the news tonight. More medieval murders. Speculation is growing that there's a connection between deaths centuries ago and those of the past week and so on. Ghouls, the press."

"At least there are no more current deaths," Roger said. He looked at Annie. "I suppose, I can't convince you to come back to Argelès with me?" But before she could answer, he turned to Marie-Claude. "I suppose you'll okay me going back."

"I'd love to have you on the case, but I'll tell Raymond, you're no longer needed here."

"Good, I'll book the train this afternoon. Annie?"

"I want to be here for Luca's funeral."

"We'll go back right after." He took her into her arms and hugged her.

CHAPTER 53

Paris, France, 1307

The day after Jacques Fournier lost his virginity he sat in class, but could remember nothing that was said. He ate at another inn or rather he ordered a meal. When it came, he looked at it. He picked up a hunk of bread and cheese and left, giving it to the first beggar that he saw. He walked the city streets until he was sure everyone was in bed before going home, although where he slept was hardly home. Home was now Fontfroide.

The next morning he left before anyone was awake. He walked along the river until he found a church where Mass was being sung. There he prayed. Even if he were not a monk, Madeleine would not make an appropriate wife. She was a whore, although not by choice. She was unlettered. She was ungodly. She was sweet and kind—and he loved her.

Madeleine did not appear in his room again. He cursed her obedience. They exchanged a few words. He looked for new lodgings, but found nothing. The popularity of students as tenants hadn't changed since he had arrived in Paris. If anything it was worse. Trying to get a refund from the landlord would be useless. He resigned himself to staying where he was.

Sundays became the most dreaded day of the week. The specialness of the day, when they'd taken their walks, had melted away. He left early in the day, her eyes following him out the door if she were up. Not only had he been robbed of what most men and women did naturally, he'd robbed her of those few hours of happiness each week. His favorite words became "if only."

When he walked he was no longer aware of Paris around him. He was too busy making deals with his God to be a better monk.

On Saturday night, to mute his pain, he made the rounds of taverns in the Latin Quarter with four of his fellow students. A classmate might have carried him home, but he wasn't sure. He woke gagging the next morning, but unable to lift his head to throw up. Nothing was left in his stomach from the night before. He lay in his own vomit.

So this was what a hangover felt like. His classmates talked enough about them. He had thought of them as weaklings to overindulge and create their own misery. He now hated himself for his own weakness.

The sun screamed through the open shutters as the tavern owner pounded on his door. When the man opened it, Jacques had never realized how loudly the hinges on the door squeaked.

"Did ya ever tie one on last night. Ya couldn't even walk." He slammed the door behind him. Jacques wondered if he'd proven himself more human in the man's eyes. He probably resented that his tenant had spent money in other taverns.

He rolled over, shut his eyes and wished he could shut out all the noises. Finally he slept. In late afternoon, he woke to Madeleine's whispers from the doorway. "Can I get ya something?"

When he shook his head, even the skin on his body hurt.

She left saying, "Call me if ya need anything."

Jacques fell back into a fitful sleep that lasted all Sunday and Monday. By Tuesday he was no better. Hangovers do not last two days. He was afire. Wine does not give fevers.

Madeleine brought broth, but it came up faster than it went down.

By Friday he could not walk across the room to use the pot. Madeleine found him surrounded by his own filth. His teeth chattered to the point they seemed they could break from the strain. First nothing could warm him, then sweat would run from every pore. Nothing would cool him, not the cool cloths she wrung out and put on his body, nor the freeing of his body from the cover.

She carried on with a basin of water and did the best she could to clean him. The mattress's cloth covering was soaked through with all types of body fluids. Madeleine exchanged the cover with one from the other room and dragged the filthy material outside to soak in a large rainwater-filled barrel.

The mattress's straw filling was wet and stank. She bought new straw from the stable, but her money was so limited, she only had half as much as he'd had before. He could feel the hard floor beneath him.

A doctor came at the girl's request. He was the same age as Jacques and new at doctoring. His newness was the only reason Madeleine could persuade him to come. His fee was a meal that Madeleine stole from her father. She had bundled it into a cloth and slipped it to the doctor as he worked on the patient. The doctor smelled worse than Jacques as he opened his jar of leeches and set them on Jacques's stomach to suck the blood from the sick area.

The doctor had a root that he had dug out of the forest, ground and mixed with alcohol. He did not tell Jacques that he had no idea what it was, but none of his patients had died. He poured a little down Jacques's throat.

Jacques gagged so hard that two of the leeches fell off. Vomit spewed out of his mouth. The doctor jumped aside, but not fast enough.

Madeleine gave him the cloth she had used to bathe Jacques earlier. He dabbed it in water and rubbed the fabric, a rough wool, which merely put the foul liquid deeper into his cloak. Then saying, "Good, it cleaned him out," he packed his things, including the food Madeleine had brought, and left.

Jacques floated in and out of consciousness for several days. He thought he heard, or maybe he dreamed, the tavern owner complaining about the time his daughter spent in the sickroom.

Days melted into nights and back into days. Time was measured by his discomfort. Jacques, who had worried about purging Madeleine from his lust, now concentrated his energy in finding a position where he didn't ache. The room spun without stopping. His ears burned as if someone poured hot oil into them.

Again Madeleine called the doctor. He came, smelling no better than before. Jacques thought his beard was scragglier, but maybe it was a hallucination. His potion was viler. The leeches hurt more.

He had a recurring nightmare. Not the one about being locked out of Fontfroide. In this dream he strolled to class on a foggy, damp day. The cold sank into his bones. Out of the fog, a narrow ray of light drew him in as a moth was pulled into a lighted candle. As he went closer with each step he felt warmer.

Two figures, using the light as a path, wended their way toward him, their arms open. Because the light was behind them, he could not make out their faces, yet he knew they were his mother and Uncle Arnaud.

His dear mother wore wings and a halo. They disappeared as he squinted at the light around her, catching only glimpses of her robe as it flashed in and out of his range of vision. He called after her, then began to run. When he caught up with the woman, it wasn't his mother—it was Madeleine.

"I love you," she hissed, "follow me." He stayed a few steps behind her. When the distance became too great, she stopped to beckon him. They turned and twisted down alleys until he was lost. Giving up, he tried to retrace his steps, but he was blocked by demons. The stench gagged him.

He woke vomiting. Madeleine held a pot with one hand and his head with the other. Spent, he fell back on the mattress.

"I heard ya screamin'. When I came in ya puked."

Too weak to comment, he allowed her to wash him, not caring that she touched him all over. If wanting to feel clean was a sin then let him sin.

When she left he tried to make sense of the dream. Madeleine was too gentle to be in league with the devil, knowingly, but she could be indirectly. Then he remembered his uncle's dream. Madeleine must have been the temptation his uncle had prophesized. He'd fought the battle and won. The fires of passion were nothing compared to the fires of hell. Priests and monks must keep their chastity vows.

CHAPTER 54

Philippe closed the door behind the AA meeting and headed back to his room while his roommate was still in the meeting. He was about ready to check himself out of the rehab center even if they recommended a longer stay. The desire to drink was still there; it would always be there. He loved that click when he went from sober to the first buzz. At the moment, however, his desire for a sober life was even stronger.

He wasn't sure how he was going to get another chance after having blown his job at the dig. Maurice, who had put him forward for this job, might give him one more chance, but he was sure it would only be one.

At least, being in rehab meant that he wasn't a suspect for having killed Luca. What a shock that was. Luca was a great *mec*. A womanizer, for sure, but show him one man that didn't have some weakness. Not possible.

The news was having a wonderful time with their Medieval Murders story. He'd watched the reports on the television in the recreation room. The finding of the baby skeleton and the young woman from the same period just added to it. However, he suspected at any moment the dig would be shut down and the new building would go up. Except for the fireplace, a few dishes, the skeletons and the gold coin, the finds were not a reason that the city would hold up building a new tax-generating property.

That thought brought him back to the bracelet he'd stolen.

Well, not really stolen, because the owner must have died centuries before.

Property was something that had always seemed strange. How can anyone really own anything? When he was eight and was caught stealing candy from a *tabac,* his father had whipped him until his rear end bled. And his father wasn't even drunk at the time. He'd proclaimed his son was not going to be a thief.

He began putting the few things he had brought with him into his backpack: shaving cream, razor, two pairs of shorts, two T-shirts. It was his sponsor that had packed for him. It was his sponsor who would pick him up.

His mind drifted back to the property question. Once, before his drinking got out of control, he and his ex were skiing in Zermatt. They had arrived while it was snowing, but when they got up and opened the shutters the Matterhorn, which had been invisible the night before, was so close that it dominated the window. At the time he'd imagined two mountains talking. One was saying, "What is your name?" The other replied, "Matterhorn, at least for now. The Italians called me Monte Cervino and the French Mont Cervin." Then the two mountains which had been there for millions of years had a good laugh that puny little mankind who lived but a few decades at best could think that they could label them.

And when he and his ex had bought their house, he wondered how they really could own a piece of land that had existed as long at the planet had been swirling around the sun.

None of this helped him resolve what to do about the bracelet. He couldn't walk by the dig and toss it in. The press was all over the site and there were also the security cameras. He couldn't put it into an auction without some kind of backup on where he'd gotten it and the great-great-grandmother story might not work, or then again it might.

He didn't want to say good-bye to his roommate. He just

wanted to get out of the center and back to his own place. He had his life to rebuild again. And if he wanted a drink, he wanted a normal life more—at least he did today. One day at a time, he thought, and picking up his backpack, closed the door behind him.

As he walked by the recreation room, he heard a newscaster Jacques somebody or other, talking about the Medieval Murders. The screen showed the dig. The new-old skeleton that had been found was allegedly of a woman, the reporter on the scene was saying. Marino had already called and told him that. The newscaster turned the story over to a young woman standing with her back to the dig. He could see the small park across the street at Place Paul Painlevée.

Philippe wondered if the bracelet had belonged to her.

"The dig is being closed down because of the murders," the reporter said. Philippe had not seen the woman before. She was young, pretty. She had her whole life in front of her. What did he have? A half-life. He'd used up half his allotted time. He had to figure out how he could use the other half.

When he looked up from the television, his sponsor entered the room.

CHAPTER 55

"I don't want to go to the funeral." Noëllo spoke with the force of any angry youngster.

"I want to go to say good-bye to Papa," Pablo said.

Crystal Martinelli sighed. She tied a black scarf that set off her one black sheath around her neck. This wasn't a fashion show, but she wanted to make sure she looked like a proper, yet attractive, widow in mourning.

"I'm glad he's dead," Noëllo said. "He made you unhappy."

Crystal wanted to say that was a horrid thing to say, except he was right, he had made her unhappy and she was glad too that he could never hurt her again. At least partially glad. It was not nice to be happy about the death of any human being.

On the other hand, never again when Luca was late coming home would she wonder in whose bed he'd been. No more strange perfume on his clothes. Noëllo had always tried to protect her when she and Luca had fought. Even when they sent him upstairs, he would hover at the top of the staircase. Luca had never hit her, but their quarrels had been loud and ugly, and more than once one or the other had thrown a vase, a dish. The only reason they never threw an ashtray was because she banned smoking in the house, not that he smoked.

Pablo, however, was a papa's boy. No puppy ever followed his master closer. But three was too young for a funeral, she thought.

"*S'il te plait Maman.*" Pablo never whined, but his voice was pleading.

She bent down in front of him. He was wearing a pair of shorts that were still too big for him. "Papa isn't there, only his body."

"I want to see him."

"He's in a coffin. It will be closed." Crystal didn't want to see him. She had no idea how the autopsy would have left him, and she wanted to remember him as this beautiful man who'd left her a beautiful young widow. It was his looks that caused half of Luca's problems with women.

"Noëllo, get into your suit."

Maybe it would be better to take Pablo, but first she sat him on her lap. "We will be in a church, and the box with Papa inside will be on the altar. There will be music and people talking. They will say nice things about Papa."

"Can I say anything?"

"You can tell me."

"How he used to make up stories before I went to sleep?"

"Like that, but only grown-ups talk at a funeral. And if you went, you would have to sit still a very long time."

"I would, I promise."

The doorbell rang. When she answered it, her neighbor and best friend Chantal, also dressed in black, was there. "Are you ready?"

"Noëllo doesn't want to go, but Pablo does," Crystal said.

"Let him—Pablo, that is. I'll talk to Noëllo."

"Would you?" When Chantal nodded, Crystal said, "I don't know what I'd do without you."

Chantal put her arms around Crystal. "Look, we've been there for each other for years. Why should this be any different?" She started toward the living room then turned and winked. "Of course, shopping, meals and movies are more fun but we'll get back to that someday."

She walked into the living room where Noëllo sat with his arms crossed and perched on the edge of the couch. Chantal wanted to hug him, but he was at the stage that he thought he was too old for hugs, a change Chantal had noticed in the past couple of months. She loved that the two Martinelli boys often spent time with her, and would claim to anyone who listened that she had no children by choice, but liked to borrow those of other people. "Look, Noëllo, I know you don't want to do this, but trust me. If you don't, you'll be sorry later on. Trust me."

He looked up at her. He had his father's eyes, big and brown with eyelashes so long they looked as if they'd been bought at a cosmetic counter and pasted on.

"All the times I took you places when your mother was working, did I ever lie to you?"

Noëllo shook his head.

The doorbell rang and a young boy's voice was heard. Then nine-year-old Christophe stuck his head into the living room.

"Christophe is going." It was so strange to see her own nephew in a suit. The two boys had been almost inseparable from the days when they were in the *crèche*. Sometimes Chantal felt she had three nephews. Luca has always taken Christophe when he took Noëllo and Pablo someplace, which was often. One thing she could say about her neighbor, he had been a hands-on father, which was why Crystal felt the boys were an effective weapon in the Martinelli marriage wars. Crystal and she had so often strategized how to bring Luca in line. What Chantal never told Crystal was that Luca had made several attempts at an affair with her until she threatened to cut his balls off.

"Go get changed, Noëllo."

The boy heaved a gigantic sigh and slouched out of the room. In the other room the landline rang. Crystal picked it up.

"Crystal, Jean-Paul here. I'm going directly to the church."

His tone said it all. Her brother was none too happy to cut his holiday short to return to Castanet and take up care of their mother. He detested Paris and he hated coming up for the funeral, especially since his wife had stayed behind to watch her mother-in-law. But Crystal also knew that Jean-Paul always did what was the proper thing, and attending his brother-in-law's funeral was the right thing to do.

Crystal also understood that she would receive little emotional support from her brother, not out of meanness, but between his patients and his care of their mother, he had almost no time for his own wife and children. Support came not from husbands or brothers but from friends. She shuddered.

"Are you all right?" Chantal stood in the doorway.

"I just feel terribly alone."

Her friend hugged her. "I'll be right beside you."

CHAPTER 56

Paris, France, 1307

Winter arrived before Jacques Fournier had the strength to even leave his room. When Madeleine knocked he thought she would be carrying his dinner. Instead she arrived empty-handed and announced, "Ya got a guest."

Jean de Beaune stood before him. At first Jacques hoped it was another nightmare, but his rival was there looking in excellent health.

"They told me you were ill. They, by the way, is just your professor de Bois." De Beaune settled on the mattress. "You look half dead."

"I look better than I did. It's been slow." No one at the abbey knew he was ill, unless his professors had sent word, which was unlikely. "Why are you here?"

"I'm going to be studying with you. I've rented the room next to you from your not-so-charming landlord." He gave one of his smirks. "Think of how much pleasure we'll have as we try to out-best each other, the debates we can have."

Jacques had two reactions: no and maybe it was a sign, a messenger to keep him from more sin. Never had he thought he would be grateful to have his intellectual enemy so close.

CHAPTER 57

"Did you find anything?" Roger asked as Annie walked in Rima's door.

She held up a bag and pulled out a black dress. "It won't take me long to change. And I got this for you." She tossed a plain blue tie at him.

Neither of them, when they'd come to Paris, had planned on attending a funeral. While Roger adjusted his tie, Annie slipped into the bedroom to put on the dress she had just bought in the shop a block away. Fortunately, she'd brought a pair of plain black flats and did not have to buy new shoes too. How she hated shopping, but the dress had a straight cut, a simple circular neckline and short sleeves. In the future she could dress it up or dress it down and not have to enter a store for a while.

When she and Roger were a couple, she would have changed in front of him. Now it was too personal. She battled her hair into a chignon and went back into the living room. "Let's go. And thank you for staying and going with me."

The Eglise Catholique Gallicane was in the fifteenth *arrondissement*. Made of gray stone, the narrow building was dominated by a circular cut-glass window. Annie had only discussed religion once with Luca, who called himself a recovering Catholic. Annie remembered vaguely that the Gallicane churches were somewhat autonomous from the pope, going back to the same period of the building they'd been excavating, but she couldn't remember much more about it.

She wasn't sure how Luca would have felt about a traditional funeral in a church that was very French instead of Italian, but of course, he had nothing to say about it. Most of the people there she didn't know, outside of the crew from the dig and Marie-Claude, who came up to them. The *flic* wore dark glasses and a hat.

"Let's sit together," she said to Roger and Annie. She kept her head down until they were inside. "I didn't want *them* to notice me and start asking questions." The *them* were the cameras from the news stations.

Only about sixty people sat in the chapel. She guessed most were from the university or other archeologists with whom he'd worked. Also, there were quite a few women, most of them alone.

"What about his birth family?" Marie-Claude asked. "We couldn't find any parents."

"Dead, before he moved to France." Annie wondered why Marie-Claude hadn't asked her sooner or why Roger hadn't. "I met one of his brothers years ago, but I have no idea where he is."

"His wife told us over the phone that he was estranged from his family. Even she didn't have any information," Marie-Claude said.

Luca had told her that he didn't want to become his parents, never living further than a few blocks from where he'd been born, and constantly being observed by aunts and uncles, but before she could add anything more, a dirge began.

As for finding Martinellis in Rome, there were thousands, and his brother might not have stayed in Rome.

Crystal entered the church, holding on each side the hands of her two little boys. The three-year-old had his hair slicked down and looked terrified. The nine-year-old, at least Annie thought she remembered Luca saying that was their ages, had an I'm-not-here expression on his face, or at least that is how she interpreted it. Crystal wore a lace mantilla over her dark hair. A woman was with her and they walked to the front pew where a man awaited. The man looked a bit like Crystal, and Annie guessed he was probably her brother.

The casket, already on the altar, was covered with flowers.

When the Mass was finished, the casket was taken out by six pallbearers and placed in the waiting hearse.

Crystal stood at the back of the church and thanked people for coming.

"I'm so sorry," Annie said.

Crystal looked her in the eye and put her mouth next to Annie's ear. At first Annie thought she was going to give her the double-cheek kiss, but instead, Crystal whispered, "You were one of his lovers. How many of the women here do you think he fucked?"

It happened so fast Annie thought for a second that she might have imagined it. Then she realized that she hadn't. Watching Crystal move among the attendees, there was a click in Annie's head.

She joined Roger and Marie-Claude who were moving toward a café. They were seated outside the café on three beige and black cane chairs surrounding a small round metal table with three cups of espresso in front of them.

"She killed Luca."

"Ridiculous," Roger said. "She had a perfect alibi. She was hours away taking care of her mother."

"Why do you think that?" Marie-Claude asked.

"Instinct: and I know that doesn't prove anything." She then told him what Crystal had whispered in her ear.

Roger, who often went on instinct, looked at Annie. "I owe you an apology for saying ridiculous. But you can't arrest a person who was nowhere near the crime scene on your feelings. Nor can you do it because they show jealousy."

"I know that. Maybe she hired someone."

"We looked at bank accounts. No unusual payments," Roger said.

"But what about the other victim?" Marie-Claude asked.

"She was one of Luca's lovers. Crystal could have hired someone twice," Annie said. "I saw such anger and hatred in the few seconds when she whispered in my ear, I suspect she wanted to kill me. And when she was talking to others, there was something off."

Roger put his hand over Annie's. *"Chérie."* Before he could say more she frowned.

"She was jealous. She was often irrational when she would call Luca," Annie said. "I could hear her yelling because Luca often put the phone down until she stopped."

"She was in Toulouse," Marie-Claude said. "And if she hated Luca that much, I can't imagine her giving the job to someone else to do."

"How do we know for sure she was there?" Annie said. "Has anyone talked to her mother's neighbors?"

Marie-Claude and Roger exchanged looks. As the *flic* loosened the scarf around her neck and although it added a certain flair to her gray dress, Annie thought the lightweight material could have been responsible for the sweat on her face.

"When are you going back to Argelès?" Marie-Claude asked. Before either of them could answer, her telephone rang.

Annie heard her say, *"Oui . . . oui . . . oui, c'est vrai?* I'm only half surprised. *Merci."*

Marie-Claude clicked her portable shut and blew on her espresso. "That was the result on the DNA tests on Amelie's baby. It wasn't Luca's child."

"Which doesn't prove he didn't have an affair with Amelie,

but does prove he didn't make her pregnant," Roger said. "Did he even know that Amelie was pregnant?"

"If he did, he didn't mention it to me, but then he didn't discuss details about his lovers. He only admitted to having them without naming names."

"How did that conversation come about?" Marie-Claude asked. "I can't imagine you asking when you met him, 'So who've you been sleeping with lately?' "

"The first time I remember discussing his infidelity was when we met up for dinner once when I was in Paris and that was some years ago. Crystal was supposed to have joined us, but he said she was mad at him because she thought he was sleeping with one of his students."

When Roger frowned Annie said, "Don't look like that. I often eat with other males, but that doesn't mean I sleep with them. Besides it was before your time." Her annoyance with Roger was in her tone.

He held up his hands and shook his head as if to say, "I didn't mean anything."

"Of course, I asked him if he were guilty," Annie said. "Luca said that from the beginning of their marriage, Crystal had accused him of sleeping around. He finally decided if he was going to be accused of it, he might as well get the pleasure, but that he didn't sleep with his students. Luca had his own set of ethics and he lived by them."

Marie-Claude nodded. "And back to when are you going home?"

"We were going to buy our train tickets this afternoon." Roger glanced at Annie. "If that's all right with you?"

"It makes sense to travel back together," Annie said.

"Would you consider stopping in Toulouse and talking to Crystal's neighbors?"

"Of course," Roger said. "But will you call the Argelès police and tell them?"

"As soon as I get back to 36," Marie-Claude said.

CHAPTER 58

Roger and Annie stood at the car rental agency counter located not that far from the Toulouse-Matabiau train station. They had walked from the white stretched-out building to the agency to rent a car.

The clerk, a woman in her early thirties, probably unhappy at working on a weekend, handed Roger the keys and pointed to the lot where he could find their rental.

"I've always liked Toulouse." She remembered her three-month contract with Airbus. It was after that contract that she'd taken a mini vacation before her next contract, had ended up in Argelès for some beach time, found her studio, which she called her nest.

As they drove out of the car rental parking lot she looked out the window to see the red brick buildings on the other side of the Canal du Midi, thinking how when she worked here, she'd biked along its banks, past riverboats and shaded by trees. Sometimes she'd ridden all the way to Carcassonne and then taken the train back, marveling how the canal had been built starting in 1667. Since Roger did not share her love of history, nor did he like to hear of what she did when she wasn't in Argelès with him, she kept this to herself. Another reason not to marry him: their different interests.

And yet . . . how many of her married girlfriends shared interests with their spouses? They were not glued to the television sets when their husbands rooted for their favorite football team. Nor did their husbands relish going shopping with them. Husbands and wives often liked different movies, foods, people, books, et cetera, et cetera, et cetera.

What was enough to build a life together?

"Do you know how to get to Castanet?" he asked referring to the suburb of Toulouse where Crystal's mother lived.

"Vaguely. I went to dinner at a girlfriend's a couple of times, but that was at least three years ago. Anyway, I can point you in the direction, and there'll be signs." Besides the directional signs, there were many electoral signs, promoting the Socialists, the Communists, the Greens, the miscellaneous right parties, all who would vie for seats and argue long and hard after the election.

"French politics." Roger pointed at the signs.

"And turn right at the sign for Intermarché." The last time she'd been here, there was a field of sunflowers, but now there were two-story houses.

They drove slowly looking at the names of streets, all with painters' names.

"That's it," Annie said. "Paul Gauguin." The street led into a cul-de-sac. Terra-cotta-colored stucco houses each had fenced-in driveways and garages. Crystal's mother lived at number seven. "Where do we start?"

"Not we. Me. You're not police."

The gates of one house opened and a small blue Renault drove out. A woman was behind the wheel and alone.

Annie hopped out of the rental and signaled to her. "May I bother you for a moment?" She explained they were on special assignment in the murder investigation of Luca Martinelli. Roger had followed her and showed her his badge.

The woman frowned until Roger said, "You can check with 36 if you wish."

She waved her hand, shut off the engine and got out of the car.

"Poor Crystal," the woman said. "I've known her for years. We went to school together. Her husband was adorable but fickle. Even for an Italian. She was lucky she didn't get some disease."

"Did you see her often after she married?" Roger said.

"We would get together when she came down to see her mother, although that was less often because of the Alzheimer's."

"Horrible disease," Annie said.

The woman, who gave her name as Nathalie Landry, nodded. "My father too. Each summer Crystal takes over from her brother and sister-in-law. I go over to her place, because she can't really leave Jeanette alone. Madame Legrand. That was Crystal's maiden name."

"Were you always neighbors?" Roger asked.

"No, I used to live on the other side of the *château*." She pointed to her right. "Crystal's family lived at number eleven."

"You said Crystal can't leave her mother alone?" Roger said.

"When she needs to go shopping and can't take her mother, I stay with her. I do the same for Elodie, that's Jeanette's daughter-in-law. She used to work: now she takes care of her mother-in-law full time, but it also lets her stay home with her kids." Before they could say anything, Nathalie continued. "They've two girls. Crystal has two boys. Have you ever noticed how sometimes that happens in families?"

Roger frowned.

"One sibling has only girls, the other only boys," Nathalie said. "I've two girls and they play with Jean-Paul and Elodie's daughters. Same ages."

"What would happen if the mother *was* left alone?" Annie ignored Roger frowning at her.

"She'd wander off. Poor Elodie was out in the garden, planting flowers in June when Jeanette woke from her nap. They found her at the *boulangerie* in the village still in her slip."

"So there's no way Crystal could be gone for twenty-four hours or more?" Roger asked.

Nathalie shook her head. "Not that I can think of."

"I guess that's all. We're sorry we delayed you." Roger gave Annie one of those knowing looks that always annoyed her.

"Not a problem." Nathalie started to open her car door.

"Just one more thing." Annie felt like Columbo. "When you went to take care of Madame Legrand or go to chat with Crystal, how was it arranged?"

Roger gave her a strange look.

"I waited for her to call. The same with Elodie. If the mother was settled, I didn't want to disturb her. Anyone taking care of Jeanette needs every moment of peace that they can find."

They thanked Nathalie and waved as she drove off.

"Satisfied?" Roger asked.

"No."

CHAPTER 59

Roger sat in the car as Nathalie's car disappeared and looked at Annie. "No? You're not satisfied?"

"No."

"You do realize that I'm not in charge of this investigation."

She nodded. "I'm convinced Crystal killed Luca. She probably killed Amelie, also."

"And do you think she killed those ancient skeletons that your team found?"

Annie wanted to hit him. "Don't be stupid. At least call Marie-Claude for instructions."

He took out his phone and dialed Marie-Claude, who was now on his speed dial. He briefed her, leaving nothing out. Annie noticed that he did not shade anything to either his or her point of view. He didn't say, Annie thinks . . . but did ask, "Do you want us to talk to other neighbors or even Crystal's brother or sister-in-law?"

He listened then said, "You're welcome," clicked off the phone then turned to Annie. "I'm one hundred percent off the case and need to go back to my real job."

Annie wanted to be angry as they rode back to the station to turn the car in to the rental agency and grab the next train to Argelès, but she couldn't be. Just because she *knew* intuitively that Crystal had killed Luca, there was no way to prove it. Okay, she had been wrong. Crystal could not have been in Paris to kill

Amelie and Luca. And where would she find a hired killer anyway?

At least Roger wasn't gloating about her being wrong. He never did gloat, one thing in his favor. If she were to be unreasonable, she would say his not gloating made it difficult for her to gloat when he was wrong.

"Why don't you call Gaëlle and have her meet us at the station. I'll take you both out to dinner." Before Annie could object he added, "You'll have nothing in your studio to eat."

Annie agreed, even though she could have gone out to eat on her own.

Gaëlle was at the platform with her bike as they got off. She hugged Annie first, then her father. The three of them walked to Les Arbres, where two other couples were eating inside rather than on the terra-cotta terrace because of the Tramantane blowing. Marie-France greeted them with the double-cheek kiss. She was a big woman, but very feminine with her strawberry-blonde hair. She wore white slacks, a pink sweater and a scarf with many shades of pink and rose. "I haven't seen either of you for a while."

"We were in Paris," Roger said.

"It better not have been on a honeymoon . . . since I consider myself responsible for bringing you together, I want to be at any wedding ceremony."

"It means we had work projects," Annie said as Marie-France slipped behind the bar to pour two kirs and an Orangina for Gaëlle.

"On the house," she said. "When you do get married, I want the reception to be here."

Annie covered her left hand with her right. So far Marie-France had not noticed she was no longer wearing her engagement ring. She would update her friend later when no one else was around, but she was in no rush to do so because she didn't need a lecture on how perfect their couple was.

When their orders were taken and Marie-France was occupying herself with the other diners, Gaëlle asked, "Does this mean you two are back together?"

"I'm working on it," Roger said at the same time Annie said, *"NO!"*

Gaëlle let out a long sigh. "I do get tired of your breaking up and getting back together, so why don't you just get back together and forget about another breakup."

Marie-France brought three goat-cheese salads.

When she left Gaëlle said, "Do you two have any idea how your unstable relationship could affect my delicate teenage years?"

Annie and Roger exchanged a look then laughed.

"No, really," the teenager said. "If I turn to drugs, it's all your fault. Both of you."

"Eat your salad," Annie said.

Gaëlle put down her fork. "Sometimes I feel like the grown-up here. Annie, you get your nose out of joint when Papa doesn't like you going away. I don't like it when you go away, but that's your work. Papa, you should learn to accept it. And Annie?"

Annie put down her fork too.

"Annie, you have a hissy fit every time Papa doesn't react the way you want him to. This last trip wasn't necessary from a work point of view. You could have explained better why you wanted to do it, come home weekends, looked for a compromise rather than throwing your ring at him. You act more like a teenage brat than I do." With that she stood up. "I'm going to buy a pizza and take it home. Maybe you both should start talking to each other." She walked out of the restaurant and picked up her bike that she had left attached to the pine tree at the end of the terrace.

Neither of them spoke for a full minute.

"Wow," Annie said.

"I guess she told us," Roger said. "Annie, I love you. I still want to marry you."

Annie wanted to say she loved him.

"You love me, too. You know you do. We have all kinds of differences, I know." He wasn't smiling.

"You're a man, I'm a woman. I'm a Third-Culture Kid that really doesn't belong a hundred percent anywhere."

"And I've only lived two places in my life, both in France."

"You spent a short time in the United States on a training course," she said.

"In a dorm with other French police officers. Not a real cross-cultural experience, although we did go to McDos."

"Maybe you're right. It's called Mickey Dees in American English."

When he covered her hand with his she didn't pull away. "Don't change the subject. I know your father's job meant you lived in Holland, Germany and Switzerland. Even now, they hop back and forth between Geneva and Caleb's Landing. That's normal for you. Not for me."

Annie picked up her fork and took a bite of the goat cheese on her salad. The cheese, which had been runny, had congealed.

"You put down little roots here when you bought your studio."

She nodded. "I know that I can always come back here. It won't go away."

He put his hand over hers. "I won't go away either. Can we try again?"

Annie watched another couple come in and sit down at a table near the door. They didn't speak to each other. She looked at Roger, opened her mouth and looked back at the couple.

Still there was no conversation.

His eyes followed hers. The couple ordered and sat in silence. Their eyes never met. Marie-France brought them two glasses of a local red wine. No clinking of glasses.

"Do you think we'd end up like that?" Roger asked.

She and Roger might fight, but they never ran out of things to talk about. Although they had many divergent interests, they shared many: movies, news, Gaëlle, reading, although Roger went more for scientific stuff, while she doted on fiction and history, walks in the mountains, love of animals. He was fascinated by cars, while she thought if she had to own a car, she would have failed somehow, although she didn't know exactly how.

"Annie?"

She looked at him.

"Let's try again. We're better together than apart." Roger said.

"Let's check and see if Gaëlle got home okay. Come back to my place, we've more talking to do, when she isn't around." As much as Annie hated to give in, it felt right.

Marie-France sat down their two plates of *magret de canard*.

"After we eat, of course."

Roger leaned over and kissed her cheek.

"I love watching you lovebirds," Marie-France called from behind the register.

CHAPTER 60

Paris, France, 1307

Jacques returned to his classes. He and Jean de Beaune fought for books, fought to outshine each other in class. Long into the night they debated some finite point. Jacques found it ironic that his rival was a buffer between him and Madeleine, something he could never admit to de Beaune for that would give the new arrival too much power over Jacques.

As winter was beginning to loosen its grip on Paris, when boats were no longer fighting to break free of ice as they brought their cargos to the city, the workload on both students increased.

Jacques was sitting at his desk on a Sunday morning, taking advantage of the open window to bring in light by saving on candles and tapers as he read. He had wrapped himself in both a cloak and blanket to keep from being cold. Jean opened the door without knocking, something that always annoyed Jacques. His nemesis was wrapped in a cloak.

"I was planning to go for a walk. You up to it?"

Jacques touched the parchment in front of him. "I was going to go to Mass later, but I need to finish reading this first."

Jean entered the room and looked over Jacques's shoulder. "Not well written."

"No, but the ideas are sound." The writer was a minor church man who always seemed to get a declension just wrong enough that the meaning had to be fought over. That the man couldn't get the dative and ablative endings right annoyed him. "Maybe we'll meet up later."

After Jean left, Jacques continued to play with the words until the context made sense. A knock broke his concentration.

He opened the door just a crack. Madeleine stood on the other side. Instead of meeting his eyes, she stared at her feet. Although she wore new shoes, they were food splattered. There was a smudge on her left cheek, making a slightly oversized dimple. "Can I come in?"

It had been almost two years since their first walk. God, please don't let her refer to that, he thought. He knew that he'd hurt her, and he didn't want to hurt her more. But she was Eve to his Adam. Eve must have been as beautiful as Madeleine as she walked toward Adam, her soft hand outstretched with a rosy apple.

A ripe apple.

A ripe woman.

What if Adam hadn't bitten into the apple? Supposing he'd only licked it. Would he have been thrown out of the garden only for a time and then allowed back? Jacques had only nibbled at sin. His soul was almost thrown out of the garden.

Poor Adam.

Poor Jacques.

"It's a bad idea," he said.

"For a minute? Just a minute?" She brushed by him and sat on a mattress, her hands folded in her lap, her fingers the object of great attention. "I gotta say it."

He dreaded the next words. If she begged, if she cried for him to reconsider, he would again be tempted. "What?"

She took in a deep breath and then looked up at him. "I've lost ya. Maybe I never had ya. I could've fought another woman. I can't fight your God."

"He's your God, too." The words sounded hollow to him.

She was so beautiful, a temptress. She was sin waiting to happen, but she was also a human being, one whose care had saved his life. He knelt in front of her, taking both of her hands in his. "Madeleine. I belong to the Church. If it were only another woman, you would have won. I want you to know that I love you, but I can't do anything about it."

She put her hand over her mouth and tears filled her eyes. "I don't want to know that. It makes me too sad. Can we be friends?"

He stood and pulled her up and enfolded her in his arms. "I would consider it an honor to be your friend." His cock stiffened. Would the temptation never go away? He would need to fight it all his life or remove himself from it. That was what all priests must do, not give in, not ever.

Madeleine shoved him away and ran from the room.

CHAPTER 61

Annie knocked at Rima's door.

Her friend, wearing an apron and holding a spoon, opened the door and threw her arms around Annie. "You made good time from Gare du Lyon."

"Caught the RER, and the 144 bus was waiting for me at La Défense." Annie sloughed off her laptop case and maneuvered the small suitcase into the tiny apartment. "Everything smells delicious."

"*Fool,* I'm making it because I know you love it, and then there's *tabouli.*" The table had been set. Unlike when she had been there last, the window was closed against the cooler September air. "I was so excited when you said you had a two-week assignment here. I was bummed at missing you in July."

Annie loved how Rima, who had earned her PhD in the States, had picked up American slang, some of which she herself needed translations for, since she so seldom went to the country of her birth. "We'll have plenty of time nights and weekends, even if I'm working and you're teaching."

"Teaching is work," Rima said as she took Annie's coat and hung it in the closet.

"You know what I meant," Annie said.

Over dinner the two women caught up. Yes, Roger and she were back together. They had mentioned a wedding date.

"Mentioned?"

When Annie said, "Can't rush these things," Rima shook her head.

Rima was dating a geology professor, a non-Syrian who was divorced and had two children. "My parents are having half a fit."

"Half a fit?" Annie asked.

"Thrilled that I may have a chance of getting married, horrified that he's not Syrian and worse, he's divorced. Maybe that's two thirds of a fit."

They talked about Rima's class load, her latest research. Annie told her about her assignment to do the manual for a new piece of software here in Paris then take the documents home and translate them into Dutch, German and English.

"Now that's out of the way, tell me about the Medieval Murders," Rima said.

Annie told her about the dig, describing the different people. "I wish we could have finished it."

"I felt so sorry about Luca. I didn't know him all that well when we were all at uni, but it's a horrible way to die," Rima said.

Rima helped Annie turn the sofa into a bed. "Where is the job?"

"Not that far from the dig."

CHAPTER 62

Paris, France, 1307

With Jean de Beaune as protection for his soul, Jacques had no more problems with Madeleine. He delved deeper and deeper into his studies. He and Jean resumed the rituals of the abbey, getting up at three in the morning to pray, read a lesson to each other as they ate bread brought up to their rooms. The tavern owner insisted they be quiet. Praying was not good for tavern business. Jacques wanted to forget Madeleine existed, and half succeeded.

"I think our tavern wench has gone into the baby-making business," Jean said one day as they walked back from their Aramaic class.

"Can't be." Jacques did not want to consider the possibility.

When they entered the tavern, Madeleine was standing behind the bar. "Can we have a glass of wine and something to eat please?" Jacques took a seat near the fireplace.

A few leaves had blown in and snapped under their feet. The dirt floor was seldom swept. Jean reached down to pick one up. "Pretty color. I like this time of year."

Jacques had never really noticed. Where he grew up and in the abbeys, the leaves turned yellow and fell off the tree. He had never thought of them in terms of beauty. He seldom thought of beauty at all. Jean would talk of the taste of food, the marriage of a good wine with a piece of meat.

Jacques felt his fellow student was much too interested in the material, the comforts of life. His family had sent him enough money that he had been able to add many comforts to his room. Jacques's diet improved too, as de Beaune often paid for meals far better than Jacques could afford.

As much as Jacques didn't want to be beholden to de Beaune, temptation for a good-tasting piece of meat and a savory sauce usually won out over his refusals. It was almost a joke between them that Jacques would say no twice then accept.

De Beaune would invite Jacques to friends' houses where there were rich tapestries on the walls. These people were not priests and, in fact, not religious at all. But they were intelligent. They knew the politics of the time, and argued about this or that, something Jacques had never paid attention to.

They discussed music and painting, subjects new to Jacques, but he enjoyed listening. He certainly didn't want to say anything to let on to Jean de Beaune that he was out of his depth. Pride was a sin too. If Uncle Arnaud had sent him to Paris to fight sin, he certainly had had a spiritual workout.

CHAPTER 63

Annie walked through the Latin Quarter toward where her new job was in an office building near the Cluny museum. The company was a start-up with a new accounting software. She hated doing the tech writing on accounting software packages because she didn't understand accounting at all. On the other hand, because she didn't understand, she worked at understanding. She was less likely to overlook something which helped her set the directions out in simple terms.

Even if she didn't like it, her coffers were low. No matter that she and Roger were back together, and doing amazingly well, at least to her, she had no intention of ever being financially dependent on him. However, she had rethought her tendency to walk away whenever things didn't go her way. Sometime he might not want her back.

She came to the corner where the dig had been. Already there was equipment and she saw that a foundation had been laid over the area where they had been excavating.

"Annie Young," a voice called. She turned to see Marie-Claude Du Pont. "What are you doing here?"

"I've a consulting job. Any progress? I haven't read anything in the papers."

"Fortunately, the press has the attention span of a retarded ant. Unfortunately, I think this is one we aren't going to solve."

Annie wanted to say Crystal Martinelli, Crystal Martinelli, but Marie-Claude continued. "I know you think the wife did it, but she was too far away. I did check out any unusual activity in her bank accounts in case she might have paid someone else, but there was nothing out of the ordinary. Have you heard from any of the others on the dig?"

"I guess they went back to school, except for Philippe of course. I haven't seen him. I do so many projects that people come and go in my life."

"I better not keep you." Marie-Claude shook Annie's hand and started to walk away.

"Marie-Claude," Annie called after her. "How many murders in Paris?"

The police woman turned. "This year we're getting about two a week. Better than ten years ago when it was about four a week."

"Are any of them former lovers of Luca?" Annie asked.

"It couldn't be the wife. I keep telling you."

They said their good-byes with the traditional cheek kisses. Marie-Claude dug her keys out of her pocket and headed toward her car.

Annie watched her go. She would love to have proved that Crystal had done it, but there was no way she could. She'd seen the hatred in Crystal's eyes at the funeral. She'd heard the phone calls she'd made to Luca bordering on madness. Knowing in her heart of hearts that Crystal had killed Amelie and Luca meant nothing.

Suddenly, she turned and ran after Marie-Claude. "Wait, I've an idea."

CHAPTER 64

Paris, France, 1307

Madeleine's body swelled. As her time grew closer, she could no longer put on her shoes. Her hands looked deformed, but her father gave her no leeway when it came to her chores. "What good is she?" he'd mutter.

"Go easy on her," more than one customer would say, but the tavern owner would tell the person to mind their own business.

De Beaune told Jacques more than once how sorry he felt for Madeleine. "If she had been born to my friends, think how different her life would be."

Jacques imagined Madeleine dressed in nice clothes and living in one of the houses where he sometimes dined with de Beaune. "We are who we are because of where we are born." He did not share the story of his father promising him to God as his mother struggled to give birth to him. Would he have joined the Cistercians if his father hadn't made that promise?

Maybe.

Maybe not. He couldn't imagine himself in the wool business. Being a scholar and priest suited him, except for his body, which betrayed him too many times.

These thoughts circled in his mind as he fell asleep only to be woken just as the cock crowed with Madeleine's screaming. When de Beaune and Jacques returned that night, the screams continued into the next night. By now, though, the screams were hoarse.

"Losing business," Madeleine's father was complaining to his one customer. "No one wants to listen to that." He jerked his thumb to the ceiling.

"If you hadn't sold her, she wouldn't be pregnant," de Beaune said. Jacques kept his silence. Timewise there was a good chance the baby was his. He had yet to confess his sin, and when he did he could add the sin of lying by omission.

Although he tried to sleep, Madeleine's screams kept him awake. They were softer and melted into moans. If he were back in Fontfroide, he wouldn't have to face problems like this.

De Beaune knocked on his door. "I'm going for a midwife. I'll pay for it. We can't let her go on suffering like this." He returned within the hour with a young woman, also pregnant. She had deep circles under her eyes, and the apron over her clothes was bloodstained. "The third delivery today," she said as she disappeared into the room.

De Beaune and Jacques made their way downstairs where the moans were muffled. They pushed a bench against the stone wall and leaned against it with their eyes closed. Neither said anything.

The midwife walked down the stairs. "She says you are priests. She wants your prayers."

Both men stood up, but the midwife pointed to Jacques. "Just you. She doesn't have long."

The bedroom looked as if a battle had taken place or at least an animal had been slaughtered: there was so much blood. Madeleine lay on a straw mattress. Jacques had never seen anyone that white. Her face was wet, either from sweat or water the midwife might have used to clean her.

He touched her hand. It was as if he had thrust his fingers into a fire.

"Jacques?" Her voice was more of a croak.

He was afraid she would give away his secret. He felt guilty that as she was dying he was thinking of himself first, but not so guilty that he could change his priorities. He cursed himself that he wasn't making her more comfortable in her final moments, but he didn't know what to do. In the abbey, he never had to deal with the dying priests. When he looked up, the midwife had picked up the pan and said she was going for more water.

"I'm here." He made the sign of the cross on her forehead.

"Give my baby to the nuns. Let them raise her."

He looked across the room where the baby lay on the table. There was no movement at all.

"I will."

"Promise."

"I promise."

"I love ya . . . you and maybe . . . Jean were . . . the only . . . the only . . ."

Jacques thought she'd gone but she hadn't. ". . . the only people . . . ever . . . nice to me."

As Jacques prayed for her soul, she slipped away. He went to the baby, and wondered if this was his daughter. The midwife came back with a dish of water. Jacques used it to baptize the baby, although he wasn't sure that his prayers were good enough to make the water holy. The midwife used the rest to clean Madeleine's body.

Jacques wanted to take the baby to a convent for burial, but Madeleine's father refused. He told Jacques and de Beaune he wanted them out.

De Beaune found them lodgings in the house of one of his father's friends. After the discomfort of the inn, a room with a fireplace, a comfortable bed and plenty of candles was a luxury. Having a maid take care of his clothes and good meals served only to increase his guilt, but not enough to refuse to live there until he finished his studies and returned to Fontfroide.

CHAPTER 65

Crystal walked in the Crédit Agricole bank where she'd worked part-time after the birth of her second son. A few leaves from the tree to the left of the door chased her in, propelled by a gust of October wind. Next month she would be full-time, a schedule she had not held since before the birth of Noëllo, but without Luca's salary, she needed more money. Granted she had the life insurance, but that would be invested for the future. She headed to her small office where she acted as a loan officer.

As the widow of a murdered man, she had warranted much consideration the first few weeks after she'd used up all her holiday and compassionate-leave time. Now, her colleagues had stopped their *oohs* and *ahhs* of sympathy and were once again treating her as an associate. They were glad to have her back for their branch was a busy one, and none of them liked overload.

She poured herself a cup of coffee and placed it on her desk where several folders awaited her decisions. Things were getting back to normal, not just here, but at home.

Her younger son was no longer having nightmares. Her older son seemed to have settled into the school year. He was her studious one, and in that, he took after his father.

She had arranged for both boys to have counseling. As they grew into teenagers, a woman alone didn't need traumatized children.

CHAPTER 66

"I look ridiculous. All this *froufrou*." Annie's hands flapped at the lace and ruffles on the wedding dress. Three other discarded white gowns were piled on the chair next to the one on which Rima sat. "One could get snow blindness with all this white. Why can't I just wear here-we-go red?"

Rima let out a long sigh. "I wonder what I ever did to Roger that he asked me to go with you for this . . . this . . . torture."

Annie hiked the dress up higher on her chest. "I bet he thinks that if I see a beautiful wedding gown it will help me decide to set a date. Do you think I could wear white jeans?"

The saleslady, a woman in her mid-fifties with a measuring tape around her neck and a pin cushion worn as a bracelet, cocked her head. Rima and Annie had been speaking in English. The woman understood enough to frown as if trying to make sure she had heard correctly. "If we just nip it in here, it will fit perfectly."

"*Je ne pense pas. Un autre jour.*" Annie turned around to let the woman unzip the dress and went back into the dressing room. When she reemerged she wore her jeans, sweater and leather jacket. A scarf was looped around her neck.

"I'm out of time. I need to meet Crystal," Annie said.

Rima gathered up her own jacket and pocketbook. "Are you sure that it is a good idea?"

"Not really, but she did agree: only because I said I had some things of Luca's I thought her boys might like."

Rima shrugged. "I think you're crazy."

"Probably, but at least we'll be in a crowded place."

CHAPTER 67

Jérôme seated Annie toward the back of the small restaurant. It was too windy and cold for the outdoor tables. This was the only table left. "Have you heard from the others?" He handed her two menus.

"No. We weren't together on the dig long enough to form friendships."

"Poor Amelie. Poor Luca." He let out a long sigh. "Can I get you anything while you wait for your friend?"

Annie didn't have time to say anything. When she looked up to answer him, she saw that Crystal had spied her. The woman looked like she'd stepped out of a fashion magazine as she slipped into the seat that had its back to the original stone wall. She took off her coat, leaving it draped over the chair.

She hadn't bothered with the traditional two-cheek kisses, but Annie hadn't really expected them.

Crystal glanced at her watch. "I need to be back by fourteen hours at the latest. Now what was it you wanted to give me?"

Annie wanted to say, "Your due." Instead, she would be prudent. "Like I said on the phone, Luca left some things at Rima's and I thought your boys would like to have them. How are they doing?"

"Better, although it was hard at first. The younger one still hopes his father will come back. The older one doesn't seem as angry."

"They are wonderful-looking boys. I imagine it is difficult for you dealing with it all."

Jérôme came up with his pad and pencil. Crystal took time to glance at the menu and ordered salmon, which was the *menu du jour,* and a glass of white wine.

"*Moi aussi.*" Annie would have ordered anything Crystal had ordered, in the hope that it would break down even the tiniest of psychological barriers.

"It must have been hard being married to Luca. So handsome, but . . . but . . ."

Crystal's eyes narrowed.

"Remember I dated him. I never knew who else he might have been sleeping with. I'd hoped that when he found a wife like you, he would change." Annie reached out and touched Crystal's hand. She started to pull back, then left it under Annie's. "Was he ever faithful?"

Crystal said nothing.

"I suppose you don't want to talk about it, but sometimes it helps, especially with someone who understands." Crystal's eyes scanned the restaurant.

"There's no reason for us not to be friends, Crystal."

The woman said nothing.

"I dated him for a short time years before he met you. I won't say I totally understand what you went through with Luca, but I have an inkling of an idea."

Jérôme put the first course, two goat-cheese-and-nut salads, in front of the women.

"After Luca, I've had other boyfriends who've lied to me about other women. And it would have been worse if we'd been married." Annie picked up her fork. "You know what I don't understand?"

"What?"

"You're beautiful, Crystal. You're smart. You're a wonderful mother, according to him." She deliberately did not use Luca's name. "He said you were a great cook, a good lover. He had to be *fou,* crazy to look outside the marriage."

Luca had said none of these things, but Annie was trying everything possible to convince Crystal to talk to her.

Now was the time for silence. She picked up her fork and cut into the hot goat cheese, mixed it with a piece of the lettuce and put it in her mouth.

Annie ate some bread.

She took a sip of wine.

She waited and waited as Crystal looked at her plate without touching anything.

"The first time he cheated on me was six weeks after we'd been married and I was newly pregnant. I cried. He promised to never do it again."

"And how long before . . . ?" Annie let her voice trail off.

"*Never again* lasted three months."

"You poor thing."

Crystal let out a long sigh. "Anyone looking at us would think what an ideal couple we were. He helped around the house, he brought me flowers."

"And I know you shared many interests: movies, books, antiques. He told me how great it was that you two read to each other." Annie hoped Luca had said that.

Crystal's eyes were moist. "He made me laugh. Other wives held Luca up as an example to their husbands of how they should act. If they only knew, but I didn't want to tell them the truth."

"It would have been humiliating: I understand, because he humiliated me too, although not as much. A short-term girlfriend against a wife and mother of his children."

Crystal nodded. "I kept weighing the advantages of being married to him with his cheating versus throwing him out. 'I always come home to you and I always will,' he'd tell me each time I'd catch him."

"Do you have any good memories?" Annie stabbed at her salad. She wanted to shake the truth out of Crystal, but told herself to be patient. Take it slowly.

"Then there was a period of almost three years that I thought he'd stopped sleeping with other women. His whereabouts were an open book as they say, making it next to impossible for him to slip into an open bed, couch or closet. Those were the happiest days of my marriage. Weekends with the boys were a joy."

"Luca told me how you'd escape to your caravan parked in the Fontainebleau forest." Annie had to be careful not to make Crystal think that she'd spent too much time with Luca, but needed to prime her into memories that might get her to reveal more.

"Depending on the season, we'd picked flowers or mushrooms, wade in a nearby stream, play ball games or just relax. When Pablo slept, Luca, Noëllo and I would stretch out on lounge chairs in the sun and read."

"I don't want to be nosy," Annie said, knowing she did want to be nosy, "but when did it change?"

"Last February. I had a terrible crotch itch. At first I thought vaginitis because I'd been on antibiotics for a sore throat, but the itch was as much outside as in."

Crabs, Annie thought.

"Crabs."

"*Pauvre, toi.* I'd have wanted to kill him." Annie clapped her hand to her mouth. "I'm sorry, I'm sorry."

It was Crystal's turn to reach out for Annie's free hand. "Can you imagine he said, 'Only once in three years'?"

Annie shook her head. "I know I shouldn't speak ill of the dead . . ."

"I hated him. I still do for what he did to me. I'm glad he's dead."

Jérôme took away the salad plate and returned with the salmon in a tarragon sauce, green beans, and potatoes au gratin. He then brought two glasses of white wine. Annie could have cursed him for the interruption, but Crystal didn't seem to notice. She used the time to get a tissue from her pocketbook, dab at her eyes and blow her nose.

When they were alone again, Annie wondered how to phrase the next question. She looked around the restaurant: no one was paying any attention. Their table was slightly separated from the others. Go for it, she thought. "How did you kill him, Crystal? I promise I won't tell anyone, but I would so like to know he got what he deserved." She debated adding, "As a victory for all women who are deceived"—but decided that would be over the top.

Crystal picked up her fork and cut into the salmon. "Why do you think I killed him?"

"Because I would have in your place."

Crystal smirked. "No one can ever prove I killed him."

"Which, if you did, would make you one very smart woman." Annie ate two bites of salmon and one of green beans. She picked up her wineglass and held it up for a toast. "To smart women."

Crystal hesitated and picked up her glass. "To smart women."

"If you had done it, how would you have? Hypothetically."

"The first problem would have been getting a gun and, once that was out of the way, learning how to shoot."

"There are shooting ranges."

Crystal nodded. "Yes, and that would have left a trace: but if I went into the Pyrenees while on holiday and taught myself, there would be no record of me having a gun or even knowing what to do with one. Hypothetically, of course."

"Hypothetically, of course," Annie said. "And you were hours away from Paris taking care of a woman who couldn't be left alone, which would also make it impossible for you to carry it through."

Crystal concentrated on her meal until Annie wanted to scream, but then stopped eating. "Sleeping pills would be one way of keeping my mother calm."

"Paris is a long way to drive: there are cameras. One's license plate might be recorded," Annie said.

"It wouldn't be a problem if it were my mother's car. My brother has kept it as a second car. It's so old that the odometer no longer works. He wouldn't notice that the mileage had gone up. And no one would think to look for her car, if the police were considering me a suspect."

"So, if you did it, you would have used that car," Annie said.

"If I'd done it," Crystal said.

"But why would you have killed Amelie instead of Luca, assuming of course that you did kill Luca, which we know you didn't?"

"Perhaps Amelie was where Luca should have been? She was one of his lovers. Let's say opportunity, poetic justice." Annie waited for Crystal to add *hypothetically, of course*. This time she didn't.

"I read a lot of mysteries. I've even imagined writing them someday." Annie pushed a green bean around her plate. "I've always wondered how it would feel to see someone die knowing one was responsible."

Crystal shrugged. "I suspect—and I just suspect, mind you—that if it were one of the whores that the husband had cheated on her with, the wife would feel damn good. Watching her face as life disappeared. Watching blood seep out of her chest onto her T-shirt. Watching the stupid cat on the T-shirt turn red. Watching her unable to get out of her chair."

I've got her, Annie thought. That Amelie was wearing a T-shirt with a cat graphic and seated in a chair was never released. But then again, maybe she didn't have enough.

"I can imagine all that, but I've never seen anyone die. So I can't quite get my mind around the reality of what happens."

"Their eyes just glaze over."

Crystal's smile made Annie uncomfortable. "But that still doesn't get even with the cheating husband. Especially if the woman was only a fling."

Crystal leaned back in her chair. "Television sports."

"Television sports?"

"Instant replay. They are always redoing some maneuver."

"Do you mean doing the whole thing again?"

"Why not? The drugs, the drive, going to the site. Luca was always willing to talk about his boys or see them. He'd have met me anywhere for Noëllo and Pablo. That is if I had tried to meet him." Crystal's facial expression became hard. "Hiding him in the garbage, now that was poetic justice, don't you think?"

Annie nodded.

"Of course, we're speaking hypothetically," Crystal said.

"I'm not so sure," Marie-Claude Du Pont said as she stepped in behind Annie. "We've got everything you said on tape." She removed the microphone from under the table.

Crystal looked around the restaurant. All the other diners were standing up, coming over to the table.

"Crystal Martinelli, you're under arrest for the murders of Amelie LaFollette and Luca Martinelli."

Crystal threw the remains of her wine in Annie's face before one of the policemen could grab her. "You bitch!" As she struggled to prevent the *flics* from handcuffing her, she screamed, "You can't prove anything. We were talking hypotheticals."

"Except in your hypothesis, you gave many details that only the murderer would know." Marie-Claude lifted her head to indicate that the prisoner should be taken away. The restaurant cleared in moments as the other diners, all of them *flics*, headed back to 36 with the prisoner.

Marie-Claude sat down next to Annie. "I can't thank you enough."

Annie's hands were shaking. "I was never sure of which way to go. I always thought Crystal was a little unbalanced from listening to her scream at Luca, but I wasn't sure I could win her confidence enough to get her to tell all."

"You were brilliant." Marie-Claude turned to Jérôme who was standing next to the kitchen door, his mouth wide open. "The bill, please: for everyone who was in here."

When the restaurant was empty, Jérôme came over. "What happened, just now?"

"Get me a coffee, please, and I'll tell you."

While he was at the machine, Annie called Roger and briefed him.

"I'm proud of you," he said. "And the wedding dress, did you find one?"

"Not yet, *mon cher.* I'm still looking."

ABOUT THE AUTHOR

D-L Nelson lives in Switzerland and Southern France. Like Annie, she has lived outside her natal United States for so long, she is a third-culture adult kid, but unlike Annie she only speaks English and French and wishes she had other languages. For her experiences living in two countries read her blog at http://theexpatwriter.blogspot.com. She welcomes comments at donna-lane.nelson@wanadoo.fr.